THE PERDURABLES

*THE CHALAM FÆRYTALES
BOOK IV*

To my daughter, Adeline.
You taught me that færies are real
and reminded me of the magic in our own backyard.
Let's go collect some dandelions.

THE PERDURABLES (THE CHALAM FÆRYTALES, BOOK IV)

This book is a work of fiction. The characters, incidents, and dialogue are drawn from the author's imagination and are not to be construed as real. Any resemblance to actual events or persons, living or dead, is entirely coincidental.

A paperback edition of this book was published in 2020 by Minor 5 Publishing.

FIRST MINOR 5 PUBLISHING PAPERBACK EDITION PUBLISHED 2020.

Designed by Morgan G Farris.

ISBN 978-1-7331668-3-6

THE CHALAM FÆRYTALES BOOK IV

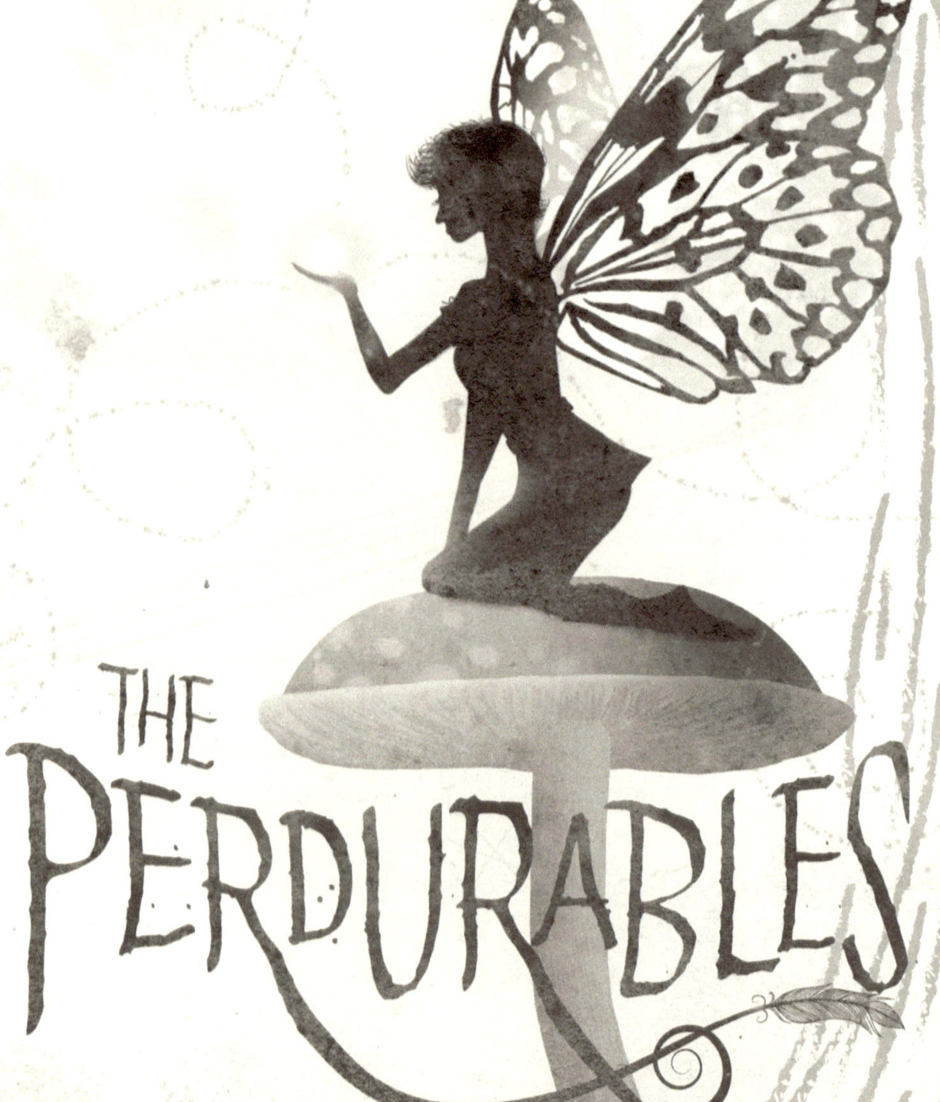

THE PERDURABLES
MORGAN G FARRIS

TABLE OF CONTENTS

Map

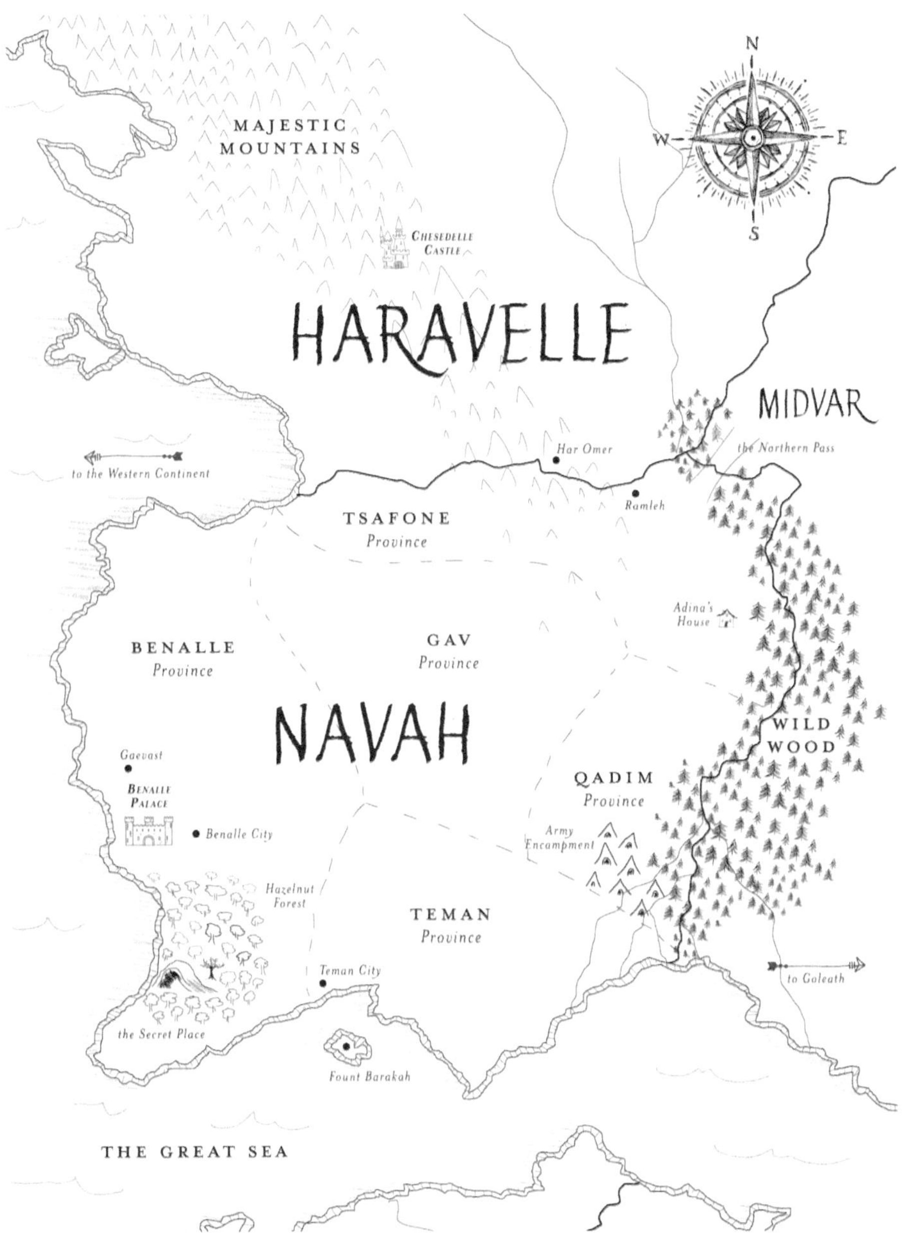

MAJESTIC
MOUNTAINS
N
W
E
S
CHESEDELLE
CASTLE
HARAVELLE
MIDVAR
to the Western Continent
Har Omer
the Northern Pass
Ramleh
TSAFONE
Province
Adina's
House
BENALLE
Province
GAV
Province
NAVAH
WILD
WOOD
Gaevast
BENALLE
PALACE
QADIM
Province
Benalle City
Army
Encampment
Hazelnut
Forest
TEMAN
Province
to Galeath
Teman City
the Secret Place
Fount Barakah
THE GREAT SEA

AUTHOR'S NOTE

My friends,

I know this is a departure. I know the moment you realize this is not a continuation of the story of Ferryl and Adelaide, that you might balk. Maybe even scoff. Slam the book shut and throw it across the room—especially after the ending of *The Parallax*.

So let me have my piece before you do.

I had no intention of writing this book. It was never in the master plan. Heck, it was never even an inkling in my mind. That is, until I wrote *The Parallax*. I realized you needed more. Not just a few little paragraphs to explain something so important, so tantamount to the story. You needed the whole story.

The story of the moths.

That's where this was birthed. Fa and Meren, they came alive in the back of my mind as I toiled over the third manuscript. So I stopped somewhere around three-quarters of the way through book three to write the story of the moths. To explain who they are and what they mean. To give you further insight into their role in Providence's world.

And to make it worse, this was originally just going to be a novella. I thought, *Give me thirty thousand words or so and I'll tell their story.*

Right.

A full novel later, I had fallen madly in love with Fa. I will say this—my art most certainly reflects my life. My characters are all people I have known or dealt with. I used to say that, of all my characters,

Titus Melamed was probably most like my husband. Until I met Fa.

Oh, Fa. How I do love you. You are your own worst enemy sometimes. A troubled soul who is, at his core, probably the best man (male) alive.

So yes, all this to say I am in love with this little book that was never meant to happen. I hope you'll forgive me for departing from our beloved prince and princess's story for just a moment. After all, you might find that this is not a departure at all (because it's not. Not really).

Yes, the moths play a huge role in the conclusion of this story. They're not just nuisance figments of Ferryl's imagination that flit about his head when he's frustrated. They are real. Very real—in my world, anyway.

This is their story.

Your slightly neurotic friend,

Morgan G Farris

EDITOR'S NOTE

Dear Chalam readers,

If you *have* been hesitating over reading this book because it doesn't feature Ferryl and Adelaide, hang on just a second.

When I was editing the end of book three, where Fa and Meren are introduced to Ferryl, what impressed me most about their characters was the strong sense of *backstory* they had. They appeared in only two short scenes, but in both, they had this aura that said 'we've been here before; we've been fighting this fight too, and we *know* the pain and ache that comes with it. We understand what you're going through, and we know from experience how much easier it is when the road is shared. We're here to do exactly that: help shoulder your burden.'

As Morgan said, this is that story. The tale of how two battle-worn færies can still carry so much joy in their hearts. How two beings so scarred can still be happy to rush to the aid of a fellow monarch and warrior. And of who brought Fa and Meren through their darkness, who helped shoulder *their* burdens.

The Chalam series wouldn't be complete without this piece of the puzzle, and I'm honored to help bring it to you.

Morgan's not-at-all-opinionated editor,

Arielle Bailey

Chapter I

The attacks always happened in the open air—the wind in her face, the skies clear and cool, and she a target, a beacon. A fool. She banked left hard, dodging a branch as she made for the cover under the canopy.

She flew as hard as her wings could carry her, not daring to risk the time it might cost her just to look over her shoulder, to see how close they were. The forest stretched before her—a maze of shadow and moonlight, flora and rot. She could not fly hard enough, her breath shards of ice in her lungs.

She didn't need to look to know how close they were. She could practically taste the foul air around them, feel the ancient blackness curling around her as she sped through the night, cutting through the air and around trees like a human weapon—a blade, honed for killing. Four. There were four of them this time!

Maybe they were the murderers, but she was no blade. And she was certainly no human.

But tonight…maybe tonight she was a shooting star, outflying the darkness.

The darkness that had chased her for as long as she could remember.

She picked up speed, a streak of lightning through the damning darkness.

~

"Holy Eloah, Meren, you look like shit!"

"Thanks, Ash," she said flatly, brushing past her friend. She plopped down on her dandelion fluff cushion, helping herself to a huge cup of water before taking a full breath.

Asher stood in the doorway with his arms crossed, furrowing his brow. No, not furrowing his brow. His brow was in a *constant* state of furrowed. Asher was always miffed with her for one reason or another. Like the brother she never had. Or wanted. She rolled her eyes, keeping her attention on her glorious cup of water, kissed with just the perfect amount of honeysuckle nectar, ignoring the ache in her back.

She'd had to fly fast this time. Too fast. Her wings seemed to scream in protest.

She picked broken leaves from her thatch of curly hair, a cerulean strand falling messily across her brow. She pushed it away absently, lost in the knowledge that one of these days, those bastards were going to catch up with her.

"What happened?" Asher scowled, his legs spread shoulder-width apart, his face set in menacing determination.

"You know what happened, Ash," she said, not bothering to look at him. But that midnight hair of his, his skin so rich and dark, the thick arms peeking out from under his sleeveless oak-leaf tunic—he was hard to ignore for long. There weren't any of the legendary Warrior færies left; all of them had been either murdered or tortured decades ago. But Asher—with the human-like weapons he had fashioned himself out of bone and stone, with his short temper and feral need to prove himself—he was as close as it came. One of those weapons, a bone blade so jagged she doubted it left much that was recognizable when he was done with it, hung ominously from his belt.

"You disobeyed my orders," he said, glaring at her from across the oddly shaped room, carved from the center of the chalam tree.

"Your orders?" She balked, still not bothering to meet his pointed stare, instead picking at the vines growing around her cushion, silently reminding herself to prune soon lest her little nook in the tree become overrun with the nuisance growth. She was absolutely uninterested in another one of his fatherly, suffocating lectures. When he let the silence grow long between them, she finally sighed through her nose, taking another long drink before she said, "I don't know how they always find me."

"I do."

"Here it comes," she said, but he ignored her, pushing off of the doorjamb.

"You're too brazen, Meren. You take too many risks." He crossed the room one step at a time. Asher always opted to walk instead of fly when he was frustrated. It drove her to madness the way he refused to use his wings when he was in a foul mood. Which was often. She lifted her gaze to his, but showed no remorse, no apology. No way would she apologize to Asher.

"It's not safe for you out there," he warned.

Her temper flared like a willow branch straining against its trunk in a violent wind. "We can't hole ourselves up in this coven forever, Asher. Jotham is wrong. We can't keep pretending that nothing is going on. There are more of us, I know it." She spoke curtly, her words swift and hot.

"We're not pretending like nothing is going on," Asher argued, his tone disapproving. He took another step. Another. Closing the gap between them. Towering over her like he was…

"Stop acting like my father," she spat.

Oh, he didn't like that comment one bit. Not one tiny bit. Asher knelt before her, gripping her chin a little too firmly, his face, his entire countenance shifting to something… Something she wasn't sure she liked.

"I'm not your father," he said, his tone a low warning. "But you'll forgive me if you scare the shit out of me too often. I forbid you to go out again."

"You know I won't listen," she said, jerking her chin from his grip. A cool sting lingered on her skin in the wake of his grip.

She could feel his gaze on her for an uncomfortable moment before he finally sighed, pushing on his knees as he stood again.

"You can't keep hoping you'll be fast enough to outfly them, Mer," he said, moving to her hearth, ripping away a few vines that had grown over the opening before working to bring a flame to life. It had always marveled her, the way the færies lit fires in the heart of trees without thought. As if one mistake wouldn't reduce their entire home to ashes. But that had never happened. In fact, there were only legends of such things, and certainly nothing from recent history. Meren had always chalked it up to the magic they used to light those flames, the same magic Asher now used, tossing a ball of færy light from his tan palm. The only magic left in the færies anymore. Light. Useful for little more than a few bobbling flames that lit their homes and warmed their hearths. No wonder most færies had gone into hiding. Their magic was nearly indistinguishable from a human these days—a far cry from the days of yore. The times her parents so often spoke or sang of. When færies were the wielders of the Light—the messengers of Eloah himself.

Those days were long gone, along with any semblance of peace. Just as the færy Light had diminished to little more than utility, so had the lore of the færies in the consciousness of most of the world. Useless. The lot of them.

Asher's flame flared to life in a flash of blue, then settled into an easy, crackling golden fire in her hearth.

"I've outflown them every time so far," she said, unable to resist arguing with him as she watched him pick up a loaf of bread that was probably too hard to eat.

His back was still to her as he said, "That is beside the point."

There was truth in that. She knew it. But it didn't matter to her. Not really. The Dark Færies were growing. Spreading. While the Light of Eloah was all but useless in the Light Færies anymore, the opposite could be said for the Darkness that was spreading across their lands. And the knowledge of that gnawed at her day and night like a wolf at a kill. It went against her nature entirely to just stand by and watch her world be devoured by the Darkness. So she argued with her friend despite the fact that she suspected he was right.

"I'm faster than you, Asher. And I'm faster than they are. They're not going to catch me."

He turned to face her, the knife in his hand like an extension of his arm. "And what happens when they do?"

It was the concern in his eyes—sincere and suffocating—that kept her from exploding into a fit of frustration. It was that genuine concern that usually kept her from killing him, despite him infuriating her on a daily basis.

She stood and padded across the shiny wooden floor, putting a hand on his shoulder. "I'll be all right, Ash," she said as warmly as she could.

To her surprise, he seized the moment to close the remaining distance between them, setting down the knife he was using to slice the stony loaf and putting his warm hands on either side of her face. "I worry about you, Mer."

"I know," she said, brushing him off. "It's annoying."

He breathed a laugh through his nose, the small gesture softening his whole demeanor. His shoulders relaxed, but his wings remained ramrod straight behind him. Not flapping lazily like a cat's tail, but rigid—as rigid as his concern for her. "When are you going to let me take care of you?"

She nodded to the loaf of bread behind him. "What do you call that?"

"Sustenance," he said. "You seem incapable of so much as boiling water."

"I am not," she protested.

He laughed and wrapped his arms around her, pulling her into a bone-crushing hug. His fiery wings at last flickered softly, as if he were calmed by her nearness. She wondered what it said about her that the thought made her uncomfortable.

She absently watched those wings over his shoulder before she pushed out of his arms, pressing a smacking kiss to his cheek and then treading to her bed, plopping down on the fluffy, feathered mattress.

He turned back to the bread and set about buttering a slice.

"I'll be much more impressed when you learn to make me toad-stool soup," she quipped.

He kept his back to her. "That will never happen."

"Why?"

He looked over his shoulder, a sly grin on his mouth. "Because it's disgusting."

"It is not!" she barked, incensed. It was, in fact, her favorite. And had been since she was a youngling.

"You have terrible taste, Mer," he said, buttering more slices of bread. She stuck out her tongue at his back and those formidable amber wings of his, lined black and patterned with gold and crimson.

By no means a cook, Asher was, at least, constantly aware of her needs. She was starving. Which was why, she supposed, she let him come in here, let him act like this was his home, his things. Let him feed her like she was a helpless færyling.

Not that he needed permission to do that. He had been treating her as a helpless færyling from the moment he had found her all those years ago.

She rolled her eyes and flopped onto her belly, turning the giant page of a book she had found on one of her ventures—a mortal story. Of wars and kings, and prophets and dragons.

Bound by the sea
For all eternity

Leviathan awaits her destiny.
By fire and flame
She sets the world ablaze
For the coming of the new age.

"I still can't believe you made me lug that stupid thing in here," he said over his shoulder, as if he knew exactly what book she'd turn to first. She bit the inside of her lip to keep from chuckling. The book had become her favorite from the moment she had found it.

The book was not færy-sized. No, it was a human-sized book she had found and then sweet-talked Asher into helping her heave it up the side of the tree and into her little home. Which, consequently, was hardly large enough for the book. She had turned it into a platform, a dais of sorts, on which she sat as she read it. Asher had suggested she throw a cushion on top and call it a bed. She had merely rolled her eyes and set about reading it.

And it had fascinated her. Page by page, she hadn't been able to put it down, stopping only to hover above and turn the page or adjust to uncover a paragraph she sat on. She had read it like that in a matter of days. Now she kept it open all the time—like a witch might reference a spellbook.

"Why do the humans call these stories færytales?" she asked absently as Asher drizzled honey from the comb onto a slice of the crusty bread. "They don't even believe in færies anymore. They think we're butterflies or moths or something."

"Eloah knows," he said. "Humans are strange."

Strange, perhaps. But intriguing. And as Meren read more of her book, she couldn't help but wonder what it would be like to meet a human. To help them as the færies once had.

To be a true færy of the Light.

Asher turned to face her at last, bringing her a slice of honeyed bread and biting into one of his own. "Jotham wants us to meet tomorrow," he said around the unnecessarily large bite in his mouth.

She ignored the sight of him chewing the food and took a bite of her own. The bread was tough. Asher hadn't been wrong—she was terrible about keeping decent food in her cupboards. She swallowed the hardly-chewed piece before she said, "Why? So that he can tell us to keep hiding? Keep pretending like they won't find us as long as we stick together?" She savagely ripped off another bite, frustration mounting as she chewed on the stony bread. The butter and honey did little to hide the fact that it was barely edible.

"It's a good plan, Mer."

"It's a coward's plan," she quipped.

"I suppose you have a better one," he said, but she didn't answer. "That's why you went out there tonight, isn't it?" When she still didn't answer, he sighed. "Meren, what is it that you think you're going to find?"

"More of us, Ash. I know there are more of us."

"There aren't," he said, standing. "They're all dead. Just like you will be if you keep going out there."

"So this is it?" she snapped, standing to her feet. "This is our life forever? Hiding here, hoping we won't be found?"

"It's better than dying!" he yelled.

"Hardly!"

"Meren—"

"Ash, I'm tired of this! I'm tired of hiding away like a coward. I'm going to do something. I *have* to do something!"

He crossed the space between them, gripping her shoulders in his calloused hands. "You are one færy, Meren. One. What exactly do you think you can do?"

"Whatever it takes," she said, and pushed out of his grip.

Chapter II

otham stood at the end of the table, his wings flaring slightly in the bobbing færy lights. Behind him, a fellow færy carried books and ledgers in his hands, a sign of respect for Jotham.

Carrying the king's burden.

It was an ancient gesture—one from bygone days when tradition and lore ruled in Færydom. To carry the king's burden was a sign of fealty to the one being served.

But for Meir, the færy carrying Jotham's books and ledgers, it was as much a sign of loyalty as it was a declaration: Jotham was the færy they all served. Not the dark male who currently sat on the færy throne. Jotham was their king in practice, if not in name. Even if he only had eleven subjects.

Not quite as exquisitely colorful as they had once been, Jotham's wings flashed in vibrant shades of gold and crimson, ochre and mustard, still glorious despite their fading hues.

Time had robbed him of so much of that former glory, that color and vibrancy that had marked the Light færies for as long as time had existed. Today…today the Light færies were few and far between… and fading.

"Is everyone here?" the formidable coven leader asked. Meren looked around the table at her friends—all eleven of them. Only eleven. When once the Light færies had flourished on the earth.

But ever since the Darkness had overcome the Light…

Ever since the war that had robbed the færies of their true king, killed him and all of his heirs, there were no other Light færies left to be found. All of them had been either killed or exiled…

Or worse…enslaved.

Her friends nodded in unison to Jotham—a signal for the meeting to start, as if he were the færy king instead of just a self-proclaimed coven leader, intent on protecting them, holing them away from the world. Meir set Jotham's things beside him on the table and flew the short distance down the table to his seat.

"It has come to my attention that Meren encountered more Dark færies last night," Jotham said without preamble.

Meren glared at Asher across the table, who glared right back, not an ounce of apology in his eyes. *Tattle-tale.* She rolled her eyes and retuned her attention to their leader.

"They are growing in numbers, aren't they?" asked Athaliah, eyeing Meir—her newly-minted mate—with a healthy portion of worry. He eyed her with equal concern, taking hold of her hand and resting it on his thigh.

"I believe they are growing in strength," said Jotham. "Which is a far more worrisome prospect."

"How is that possible?" asked Meir, gripping Athaliah's hand firmly in his own as if it were his salvation. The rest of the færies around the table seemed to be asking the same question.

"I don't know," Jotham admitted, and unease ran through every-one at his admission.

So Meren spoke up. "I do," she said as all eyes shot to her. Across the table, Asher's wings flared, even as his eyes bored into her.

Jotham turned his attention to her, nodding for her to go on. His own wings, the colors of an autumn sunset, hung motionless behind him.

"The darkness—it's growing," she said somberly.

"Meren," Asher said, sighing in protest as he pushed a hand through his chocolate locks. "You—"

"It *is*, Asher. It's growing across the land. I've seen it."

Asher leaned forward in his chair. "Meren, this is not the time—"

"What have you seen?" Jotham asked, cutting off Asher, his eyes intent on Meren.

But she did not cower under that gaze meant to intimidate. "Win-ter," she said. "It has settled on the mortal lands."

"That's hardly anything remarkable, Meren. It's almost time for winter," said Asher.

"Exactly. *Almost,*" said Meren, and Asher rolled his eyes, settling back into his chair with crossed arms. "Winter never comes this early. Never. Especially not this far south."

"C'mon, Meren," said Shira. Perfect, perfect Shira. Her wings were tucked neatly behind her, the iridescent membrane shimmering softly in the færy lights that kissed the ceiling, her golden hair spilling down her shoulders and back like a river of sunshine. "You're being a little dramatic."

From the corner of her eye, she saw Asher's brow rise in humor. It only fueled her ire. "Am I? Funny, I thought the *drama* was the fact that I got snitched on for looking for help!" she barked, gripping the edge of the rough table.

"We don't need help," said Athaliah. "We need to be safe!"

"We are not safe. We will *never* be safe," she protested, her own breaths turning shallow. "We cannot keep pretending like hiding is our only option. It's a fool's option, not ours!"

Jotham, to his credit, did not flinch at her rather contemptuous assessment of his leadership decisions over the last few decades. Instead, he remained cool and quiet at the end of the table. King or not, he was a leader. Patient. Collected. Wise.

The only problem was that Meren inherently disagreed with almost every decision he made.

But she had seen it yesterday—she had seen the unearthly winter that had settled over the mortal lands. She had flown far from the forest, far from her home, almost all the way to the human castle that hugged the edge of the sea, its white stone which usually shone bright in the blistering sun now a haunting, muted gray. The towering cliffs on which it sat overlooked a darker ocean, its waves crashing like storms onto the black sands. And she had felt it. The thick gray clouds bringing the growing winter chill. The humans had seemed oblivious to it. Or at least not nearly as concerned about it as they should have been. Bothered, maybe. But not concerned.

But she was. She had taken one look at that settling winter and knew...

The Darkness was settling in.

Permanently.

Not the darkness of night—of moonlight and stars. Nor the darkness of a winter morn clouded in gray, a parading of the change of season. No, this was a different kind of darkness—present and heavy and bone-chilling.

This was a færy-borne Darkness, swelling with magic.

Something like righteous indignation had welled in her tiny færy heart at the sight of that encroaching winter. Those plump gray clouds, swirling with an otherworldly pattern, and that icy breath of wintry wind had awoken a determination in her that she had never known before.

Because it was time. Five decades was long enough. It was time for the Light færies to take a stand again—however many of them were left. In the name of Eloah. In the name of his magic. In the name of the Light that was slowly trickling away, away, away from this world.

She could not stomach the idea of letting her parents' sacrifice be in vain. She could not fathom letting their deaths mean nothing.

They had believed.

They had believed in something so much bigger than themselves.

And then they had died for it.

She would not let their deaths be in vain. Too much was at stake. Their way of life. The world. Magic itself.

She could not let it end for nothing.

Jotham folded his hands neatly before him, his broad shoulders set squarely, his jaw tight. "What exactly do you propose we do about it, Meren?" he asked.

She looked around the table at her friends, the færies who had taken her in when she had no one. Thirty years old—she'd been little more than a youngling when her parents were murdered, slaughtered by the Dark færies who had forged a path of blood all the way to the throne that was not theirs. And if it hadn't been for the table of færies around her—these færies who had made her one of their own... She couldn't even imagine what would have happened to her.

This coven of færies had all lost something—lost too much—in that war that ravaged all of Færydom. She looked at each one of them, these friends who had given her a second chance at life, before she said, "It's time that we look for help."

A sigh came from Asher, one that she ignored. "It's time we look for the rest of the Light færies," she said, to the raised brows of her friends.

"How do you even know there are more?" Meir pointed out unhelpfully.

She didn't. Not really. But if there were...if there was even a chance that there were more of them somewhere, then maybe, just maybe...

"We'll never know until we look, will we?" she asked, and then she turned her attention back to Jotham. "Don't you see it? They're coming. They're getting stronger. You said so yourself. We can't pretend like hiding here is going to keep us safe from the Dark færies forever. We have to fight, Jotham! We have to at least try!"

To her eternal shock, Jotham didn't protest. Instead, he too looked around the table—looked to these færies whom he had so fiercely protected for nearly fifty summers. These færies he had given everything to look after, to keep alive. Maybe he wasn't a færy king, but he was respected as one. At least around this table.

And then he spoke. "There is someone who might help us."

Asher darted his eyes to their leader, his brows raised in shock. Meren's own heart beat a little faster.

"Who?" Athaliah asked, her mate beside her looking as if he'd give his very breath to protect her.

"He is called the Gibhor. The mighty one," said Jotham. And it was actually Asher who mouthed absently, *Warrior færy.*

Warrior færy. Did such a thing still exist? Her parents had always told her of that ancient line of færies, the famed ones who fought and defended with valor and honor. But they said that the warrior færies had been eliminated—slaughtered by the Darkness a long time ago. That none of them had survived. Not one.

Their own king—the true king of the færies—had been one. A Warrior færy. He and his seven sons. And they had been slaughtered. Every single one of them. That had been the start of the Færy War. When Asa and his dark-winged sons had murdered a king and his family—destroyed life as they knew it just for the sake of their own greed—and then begun the work of spreading their Darkness across the lands. The Darkness that was now reaching the mortals.

Meren looked around the table again at the færies she called her friends, at the fading colors that had once adorned their wings. Not black like the Dark færies. Not by any means.

But by no means colorful and vivid like the true færies of the Light. Like her parents' wings had been before they were slaughtered. She looked at their faces, at the grim hope that faded a little more with each passing day, with each new report of the Darkness spreading like a disease, with each new rumor of murder, of violence against anyone who protested King Asa and his ravenous ilk. Her friends looked like they didn't know what to believe anymore.

And she asked herself the question she had asked a thousand times before: were Dark færies born?

Or were they made?

"How can he help us?" Zane asked from the opposite end of the table. Usually quiet and without much to contribute, it surprised Meren that he had spoken at all.

"It is said that his strength is unmatched. That he knows the old ways," said Jotham. "Perhaps he can help us devise a strategy against the Dark færies."

The old ways. There were so few færies who even spoke of the old ways anymore. But just the mention of them brought a flood of memories of her parents aching through her. Of their zealous ways. Of their insistence on teaching her the history of Færydom. And what they had shown her of the magic of Eloah—the magic so few færies knew, much less practiced anymore.

She had learned so little from them before they were stolen from her.

"Where is this Gibhor?" Asher asked, leaning forward in his chair. Meren looked at him, waiting for him to turn to her, to speak to her with his silent glares, his quiet disdain. But he did no such thing, instead keeping his attention rapt on Jotham. So Meren decided to do the same.

"I don't know for certain," Jotham admitted.

"There are rumors," Shira said, her eyes alight as if she were keen to share some secret. "Seven days flying north. The Gibhor waits to come forth."

Seven days. A seven-day flight would put them in the heart of the hills in the northern lands of Færydom. Meren immediately began making plans, calculating just how much food…

"They say he lives alone," Jotham went on. "That he is hard to find and even harder to speak to but—"

"Why have you never spoken of him before?" Asher asked, as if he could see the thoughts already churning in Meren's mind. Thoughts he had every intention of shutting down immediately.

"I have only recently learned of him," said Jotham calmly, coolly, even as his gaze landed briefly on Shira. But she made no move, completely unfazed by the buzz that was forming around the table.

"How?" Meir asked.

"Meren is not the only one who has been looking for answers," Jotham said, to the shock of the other færies in the room. Asher swore silently under his breath. Meren couldn't help the smirk that curled her mouth.

"I will go find him," she said, ignoring the pointed stare from Asher. And Athaliah. "I will ask him to help us."

Shira's eyes landed on Meren and lingered.

"Meren, you—"

Jotham cut Asher off. "Why am I not surprised that you would volunteer yourself for this?"

She sat up more fully in her chair. "Please, Jotham. Let me go. Let me do this."

Jotham steepled his fingers in front of his mouth as if in prayer, eyeing her thoughtfully before he said, "You may go." Asher sucked in a breath to protest before Jotham went on, "And you will take Asher with you."

That protest died on his lips as Asher slid a triumphant gaze to Meren. She glared at her friend before turning her attention to her leader.

"Thank you, Jotham," she said through her teeth. He was letting her go, at least. But the fact that Asher had been tasked as her watch-dog… She bit down on the barrage of protests she wanted to utter and simply said, "I won't let you down."

Chapter III

"I suppose you've come here to gloat," Meren said, packing a satchel with a few belongings.

Asher stood resolute in her doorway, the moonlight glowing about him, casting him in silhouette.

"I've come to ask you to change your mind," he said.

"Of course you have," she said, her back to him as she slid a cloak into the small bag. A ring—her mother's—caught on the fabric of the satchel, nearly ripping the delicate weaving of the dandelion fluff. She pulled her hand out, turning the ring on her finger, an ache for her parents tearing at her heart. The engraving around its circumference glinted in the pale light, the scrolling letters of the ancient tongue a work of art unto themselves.

N'shl hevv vah shlurn.

I am my beloved's and she is mine.

She smiled at the memory of her parents as her finger trailed along the indentations.

A picture of her parents danced in her mind: her father's hand at the small of her mother's back. Her mother's head resting on her father's chest as he hummed a soft tune and twirled her gently on the air, closing his eyes and resting his head on hers as he sang. Her færyling memories were full of pictures like that—flying into a room to find her parents holding hands as they spoke in soft tones. Finding them in a long embrace. Dancing on the wind to a song of their own making, just because they could, their affection as much a part of their day as flying. Or talking. Or breathing.

"You miss them," Asher said softly. She hadn't even realized he had come so close to her side.

She nodded silently as she toyed with the delicate band. A gift from her father to her mother upon their mating. It had been a fierce love they shared. A deep love. Rare. Something pure and simple and yet profound in ways that defied words or logic. It had been that love that had impacted Meren most of all.

Asher put his hand on her arm, squeezing gently. Still wrapped in the memory of her parents like a blanket, she absently pulled her arm from his touch and continued packing.

"Meren," he said softly.

"Please don't, Ash," she said, turning her back to him. She did not want to talk about them. Not right now—the sting of their absence lingered in her throat like a rock. By way of distraction, she set about pruning the vines that had grown into her home in the trunk of the chalam tree. They were too thick. She was a terrible housekeeper. And if she was going to be gone for a few weeks, she needed to get them under control before she left.

He knelt on the ground beside her and began helping her prune. "You don't have to do this, you know," he said.

She snapped a particularly thick and stubborn vine, throwing it to the side, onto her growing pile. "Yes, I do. This house will be nothing but leaves if I don't."

"You know what I mean," he said, stopping to face her.

Yes, she did. She held a vine in her hands, stopping to face him too. "Ash, we have to do something before the Dark færies destroy everything we love." Losing her parents to them had been enough. She did not know if she could bear to lose anything or anyone else.

"Why is it your responsibility to fix the whole damned world?" he asked. And despite his harsh tone, there was such worry in his eyes that she put her hand on his arm.

"I'm not helpless, Ash."

He put his own hand over hers. "You're not invincible, either."

An incredulous look was her response. "I don't pretend to be. I never have."

He raised a chocolate brow. "Right. Because traipsing about at night alone is completely sane and wise."

"Ash," she said flatly, trimming the vines again, unwilling to indulge the impatience that was threatening to overwhelm any semblance of grief. Or sense.

"Meren, let's talk to Jotham. Maybe he'll go instead," Asher tried.

"And who will lead the coven while he's gone?" She inched away from him, working on the vines that had grown around her sitting cushions in the middle of the room.

"Why don't you?" he asked, obviously desperate for ideas.

The very idea of her leading the coven was so ridiculous that she snorted a laugh. "I'm no leader. I'm more of a nuisance. Which is why this mission is perfect for me. Gets me out of everyone's hair."

"Mer," he said, stopping his work again.

She kept on snapping vines. "Truly, Ash. Why don't you stay home, too? It's obvious I annoy the Sheol out of you. I can do this. I'll be fine."

"Meren."

She kept her back to him as he worked. "I'll be fine on my own, Asher. Why don't you just let me go and—"

His hand, strong and heavy, clasped her shoulder, turning her to face him fully. "I'm going with you." His words were so final, almost desperate, that she stopped for a moment, frozen in place by the adamance glittering in his dark eyes.

"Then stop trying to convince me not to go. I'm not your daughter; you don't need to protect me."

He sat back on his feet, his legs folded beneath him as he crossed his arms. "Stop saying that," he said, a hint of frustration mixed with disappointment in his words.

"Saying what?"

"That I treat you like a daughter."

She raised a brow, a smirk threatening her mouth. "Don't you, though?"

He inched to her, the itch to take her hand written all over him, especially in the way he raised a hand as if he would and then dropped it suddenly. His wings hung uncharacteristically limp from his shoulders. "I do not treat you like a daughter," he protested weakly.

"Oh really?" she asked, crossing her arms.

"Caring about you and looking after you is not the same as fathering you."

"You're older than I am, aren't you?"

A flat look. "By twenty summers, Mer." He moved closer a fraction. "Hardly enough to be your father."

True. Færies didn't usually sire younglings until sometime after their sixtieth summer. And even though Asher was nearing the end of his first century, he was considered young by færy standards. Still…

Her smirk was no longer just a hint around her mouth. She couldn't help but tease him just a little, knowing how it got under his skin. It had always been that way between them. He would say something ridiculous, and then she would chide him ceaselessly for it. It was the balance between them that had always worked.

For some reason, it didn't seem to be working today.

She punched his arm in an attempt to lighten the mood. But he did not retaliate as he usually would have. He did not rumple her hair or throw a rogue vine. Instead, he crossed his arms and merely glared at her, an animalistic glow to his eyes.

She cocked her head to the side. "You're no fun anymore, Ash. Old age has gotten to you."

His eyes narrowed but he said nothing, his wings flickering with annoyance. She huffed a laugh and leaned to press a kiss to his cheek. He smelled of sweat and sun and autumn leaves. "Stop being such a stick in the mud and help me prune before this whole place gets devoured by these vines."

Asher grabbed her wrist, trapping her in his vice grip as he bored holes into her with his eyes. She found she did not know where to look. Not when he was looking at her like *that*.

But strangely, he said nothing else. Not a single word as he turned and quietly continued pruning the outrageous vines in her home.

Her hands trembled as she worked in silence beside him.

~

"Thank you for your help," she said, standing to her feet, brushing off the rogue leaves clinging to her knees. Asher stood as well, a pile of vines in his arms that he took to her door. He flew out, returning a moment later with empty arms, landing with fluid grace at her door. He braced his hands on the rough-hewn jamb, but he did not enter.

"What?" she asked as he watched her gather the last of the vines. She crossed the room, handing them to him. But he did not move to discard this pile. No, he stood before her, holding her eyes with his own.

"You want to leave tomorrow?" he asked.

She nodded, swallowing, uncomfortable with his sudden intensity. "You sure you can stand me alone for a few weeks?" she teased.

A wicked smile finally gleamed in his eyes, the tension vanishing with it. "I'm sure I'll manage somehow. I've put up with you this long, haven't I?"

She rolled her eyes, turning her back at the sound of him flying off with the last of the vines. She turned to finish tidying up her home, surprised when she felt his warm body close behind her a moment later.

She kept her back to him as she busied herself with picking up fallen leaves. "You're acting weird, Ash. What's wrong with you?" she asked as nonchalantly as she could. But when she turned to face him, he was wearing *that* look again. The one she didn't know how to define. It was too new, too different. Too…much.

"Ash?" she tried again. "What is it?"

He pursed his lips, glancing at hers for a moment before he said, "Nothing. See you in the morning."

And he turned and flew off into the darkness.

Chapter IV

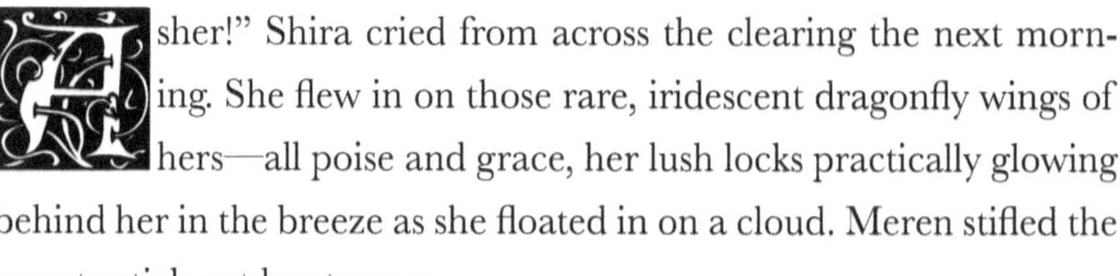sher!" Shira cried from across the clearing the next morning. She flew in on those rare, iridescent dragonfly wings of hers—all poise and grace, her lush locks practically glowing behind her in the breeze as she floated in on a cloud. Meren stifled the urge to stick out her tongue.

She had slept fitfully most of the night, unable to shake the oddness between her and Asher last night. Unable to stop wondering what had gotten into him and why he had been looking at her so intently. The sight of perfect, primped Shira first thing this morning did nothing to brighten her mood.

Shira was nothing but sunshine and brightness and glossy curls and lips that were a perfect shade of spring rose without the barest help from any sort of berry juice or petal paste. In other words, she was the complete opposite of Meren with her choppy opaline curls, splattered like paint with all shades of cerulean and lavender and copper, refusing to cooperate into any semblance of style. She had kept her hair chopped off just to keep the obnoxious curls out of her face. Not to mention her utterly plain white wings, with no hint of color. Which she supposed was fitting, pairing well with her patent disregard for all things female and delicate. It's not that she didn't like her femininity—it was more like she had better things to think about than her hair. Or dab berry juice on her lips every morning. Or take more than a half of a moment to consider what she would wear for the day, much less *how* she would wear it. A tunic made of leaves, tights that fit close to her skinny legs, and supple leather boots were about as fashionable as she ever bothered with.

Shira landed in the clearing beneath the chalam tree with a fluidity that mimicked mist rolling across a stream. Meren rolled her eyes at the perfect female and her graceful landing before Asher.

Asher seemed all but indifferent to Shira's presence.

"Asher." Shira tried again.

Asher turned to face her, tilting his head to the side.

Shira fiddled with her fingers, toeing a pebble as if she couldn't meet his eyes. Meren rolled her eyes and set about securing her satchel.

"Everything all right, Shira?" Asher asked.

It was as if the sound of her name on his lips was nearly Shira's undoing, for she raised her eyes to him, smiling so vibrantly the sun itself paled in comparison.

"I just…" She fussed with those delicate fingers some more. "I bid you a safe journey."

"Oh," he said stupidly, and Meren kept her snicker to herself. "Well, thank you." He nodded once, turning his attention to Meren, who shrugged and turned back to her satchel, checking once more to make sure it was securely closed.

It was to her eternal shock that she felt a small hand on her shoulder and turned to find Shira before her, a strange sort of glow to her eyes. Meren flicked her eyes across the way to Asher, but he was oblivious, busy in a conversation with Jotham.

Meren looked back at Shira.

"He will say yes, Meren. But he will not mean it."

"What?" Meren asked, her brows narrowing.

Shira went on. "He will not mean it, Meren. Do not forget that, and your sacrifice will not be in vain."

"My sacrifice? Shira, what are you talking about?"

But Shira said nothing more, merely kissing Meren's cheek before she flew away. Meren looked around, hoping to find someone who might understand what had just happened. But Athaliah was clueless to the transaction, too wrapped up in Meir at the moment. Asher was no help either.

"There is a grove of chalam trees," she heard Jotham say, and she turned to see him standing behind her, his arms crossed, his face serious. "North of the conifer forests, near the cliff's edge. It's at least seven days from here. He is rumored to be there."

"That's it?" Asher balked, crossing his arms. "That's all you know of his whereabouts? Is he even real, this mythical Gibhor?"

"He is real," Jotham said, unfazed by Asher's arrogance. He turned his unreadable eyes to Meren. "And if it is in your destiny that you should find him, then you will."

Meren caught her breath, wondering if she had indeed been destined to help find the legendary Gibhor. To bring him here. To find a way to stop the Darkness from spreading once and for all.

Asher nodded once, as if determined to get this whole ordeal over with. "We won't let you down."

"Do not be surprised," Jotham continued, his searing gaze still on

Meren, "if he is difficult to find. He has been in hiding for decades."

"I'll find him," she promised, clenching her hands at her side, her wings flickering eagerly. "And I'll convince him."

Jotham merely nodded, but whether or not he believed her, his face did not betray his thoughts. "Safe journey," he said, clasping Asher's arms. Asher nodded.

Jotham stepped to Meren, taking her hands in his—a firm grasp, nothing gentle or affectionate in his touch. "Be safe, Meren. And listen to Asher for once in your life."

She nodded, refusing to look at Asher or acknowledge the throaty little chuckle she heard from him. Instead, she took flight with a quick flick of her wings. Asher was close behind.

~

"Remind me again why we're doing this," Asher grumbled for the fifth time in two hours.

Meren dodged a branch, flying between two leaves, intentionally letting one of them slap Asher in the face as he passed, taking a small amount of satisfaction from the throaty bark he made upon impact. She pursed a smirk. "I'm not flying in open air, Ash. We've been through this."

"Meren, your theory is ridiculous," he said, bursting through a particularly thick tuft of leaves. She pursed a snicker at the remaining leaf bits in his chocolate hair. "We could get there much faster if we could just fly above the canopy."

"Tired of my company already then?" she purred, raising an eyebrow at him.

He rolled his eyes, his amber-and-onyx wings a blur above him as he flew with predatory grace. Asher was a fast flyer.

But she was faster.

She raced ahead, relishing the briny wind on her face, the smell of the ocean in the not too far distance. The humans called this cliffside land Navah, if she remembered correctly from her lessons growing up. But to her, to her friends, it had always just been Færydom. Creation. The place that Eloah had once forged from Light, from magic. The place he had given to the færies to tend, to steward his magic.

Oh, how far away from that they had drifted.

So much of that old magic forgotten, so much of that legacy lost with the centuries.

Now the færies wandered in secret, running from the Darkness, the blight that threatened to consume them all.

As if following her thoughts, Asher's eyes were locked on the cerulean skies, keen to find any lingering predators, færy or otherwise, his wicked bone blades glistening at his belt and his back, polished and sharpened and at the ready.

And not for the first time, Meren wondered who was the real predator in these skies.

His wings were not dark—not in the way that the Dark færies were—but they were by no means bright and luminous like the Light færies she remembered from her childhood. And the violent orange and red shades of his wings had grown dimmer, duller over the years, as if the Darkness crept slowly through his veins.

But Asher had saved her, protected her from King Asa and his wicked sons all those years ago. When the king was intent on killing any who challenged his stolen reign, it was her parents in the line of fire. And while the king had been successful in destroying *them*, had it not been for Asher, she would have known the same fate. He had found her, smuggled her through the night, through the thick hazelnut forests on the cliff's edge until he had brought her to the safety of Jotham's coven. And she had been forever grateful for it, for his kindness. Her parents had been slaughtered before her eyes, their shimmering blood still splattered all over her, caking her hair, when he had found her. But he hadn't balked. He hadn't hesitated a moment when he had scooped her up—she a young færyling and he barely a grown male—and taken her to safety.

But despite that kindness, despite the light that she knew dwelled within him, she had often wondered over the years, often questioned if there wasn't a darkness in Asher. If that same Darkness that had plagued the wicked King Asa and his ilk had somehow penetrated Asher's very soul, too.

Asher flew higher, his eyes steadfast on the sky, his hand instinctively resting on the hilt of that wicked bone blade at his side. Chills spider-walked down her spine. She knew that look, that predatory intent that gleamed in his eyes. And she did not like what it meant.

But she kept low, her wings brushing blades of grass as she passed, kept out of sight—little more than a blur of glowing blue færy light to any above passersby.

Hopefully.

Asher's faint orange glow descended again, but he said nothing, his eyes darting around them.

"See anything?" she almost whispered.

He did not look at her as he flew. "No," was all he said.

But the way he said it… "What is it, Ash?"

Those keen eyes of his found hers. "We're being followed."

~

"We'll sleep here for the night," he said, flying up the side of a knotted trunk, at last disappearing behind a thick branch.

"I'd rather we slept down there." She pointed to the ground, following him.

"I'm not sleeping on the ground like an insect, Meren. Neither are you," he called, flitting about the giant tree, searching for any signs of danger.

"There are plenty of insects in the trees, Ash," she pointed out, following in the wake of his faint glow as he wound round the tree.

He peeked his head around the trunk. "We're sleeping up here," he said, gesturing to a hollow at the base of a thick branch.

She floated before the hole to which he was pointing, crossing her arms. "So you'd rather be owl dinner?"

He rolled his eyes, flying toward the darkness. "It's hardly big enough for owls, Mer."

He flew inside, the faint glow of his magic illuminating the little place that would be their home for the night. No owls, thank Eloah. But…

"Don't you think this is a little cramped?" she asked, raising a brow.

"Need a luxury suite, Your Highness?" he purred, picking up an acorn husk and throwing it out.

Indeed, the nook in the tree trunk was small. Even for færy standards. Too small. They would not exactly have room to sleep anywhere but very close…

Asher was already pulling out the dandelion fluff blankets from their packs, laying them out on the ground of the cramped space.

Uninterested in thinking of just how closely she would be sleeping next to Asher, she turned and flew out of the nook again, calling over her shoulder that she was off to find dinner.

~

Honestly, she had been surprised when Asher let her set out on her own to find sustenance for the two of them. That is until she realized he hadn't but had followed her the whole way through the grove until she found a patch of berries and a toadstool. She had brought her bounty up to the nook, only to find Asher gone. She set down their dinner and turned to look for him, her heart pounding at the thought of making the rest of this trek without him…only to realize he was behind her, arms crossed.

"You're not very observant, Mer," he said, shouldering past her.

"You were following me?" She frowned, crossing her arms as she watched him slice a berry with deadly precision.

"I told Jotham I would protect you," was his only response, his attention fixed on the juicy berry.

"By hovering over my every move?" she sneered.

He looked up, the weapon in his hand such a natural extension.

And the way the juices dripped thick and red down the white blade…

"You're not exactly careful, Mer. I was behind you the whole time, and you had no idea."

"I knew you were there," she lied.

He snorted a laugh and started cutting the mushroom next.

"When are you going to admit that you need me, Mer?"

It was the way he asked it… There was something about it she didn't like. How it sounded not like brotherly concern, but more like… possession.

So she changed the subject.

"When are you going to put on your big boy pants and do something about Shira?" she drawled, not bothering to hide the smirk that slowly curled her mouth. She leaned against the opening of the nook as he worked, the cool outside breezes kissing her wings—a welcome, relaxing touch after a long day of flying.

He slowly looked up from his work. "I don't know what you're talking about."

"Right." She laughed. "Because she was practically dropping her pretty little underthings for you this morning."

"Excuse me?" he asked incredulously before returning his now searing attention to the mushroom.

"Don't act like you didn't notice," she said, relishing the way she had so easily gotten under his skin. It was such a rare treat that she pushed off the opening and took the single step across the space between them, crouching down and popping one of the diced pieces of toadstool into her mouth.

The bite burst with flavor on her tongue, and she immediately grabbed three more pieces, rolling them in her hand, marveling at the way the serrations along his blade had left trenches in the fleshy fungus. Pondering what a blade like that could do to another færy…

"Shira and I are friends," he said, cleaning his blade on his pant leg.

"Well, I can say with absolute certainty that she wants to be more. Much more," she added with a wiggle of her eyebrows.

He rolled his eyes and sat back against the wall, extending his legs before him as he popped a berry piece in his mouth.

"It's not going to happen."

"Why not?" she asked, relaxing too, folding her knees against her chest.

"Because we're friends," he said curtly, taking another piece of berry, conspicuously avoiding the mushrooms. He had always hated them.

"What's wrong with being friends with your lover?" she asked casually, regretting the question the moment his eyes flew to hers… and lingered.

She hated the heat that she knew was kissing her cheeks, hated the fact that all she could think about was how strangely he had acted the night before—the way he had looked at her like…

…like he had wanted her, that's what.

Shit.

"Ash…"

"Just drop it, all right, Mer? We need to get some rest." And with that, he turned his back to her, preparing their makeshift bed for the night.

Their much-too-small-for-two-færies makeshift bed.

She swallowed the last bite of mushroom, the flavor suddenly ash in her mouth.

There was nothing wrong with being friends with your lover, of course.

Except when you didn't want that lover to stop being your friend.

Chapter V

sher, mercifully, hadn't said another word on the subject of Shira. Or Meren, thank Eloah. And he had slept a respectable distance from her that night and every night for the six days they had been flying north. They'd had a relatively uneventful journey, dodging a few birds here and there, but with no sign of the Dark færies. Meren would take a bird of prey over them any day.

Whatever it was that Asher had discovered following them on that first day hadn't appeared again, either.

They had been following a mighty river as it slithered along the landscape, the gray skies that reflected off of its placid waters giving it the impression of a giant silver snake curling and sliding along the hills and valleys. The hills to the north grew larger with each passing day—the hills that somewhere held a færy, a legend, who might help them. She watched their reflections in the water: hers a blur of blue light, vivid and radiant as it refracted along the waters, Asher's a blur of orange and crimson, like a streak of autumnal fire blazing down the river.

But it was a third reflection that caught her eye on the silver waters—a shadow of mighty wings high above them, floating as if on a fell wind.

Eagle.

Terror coursed down her spine, even as Asher sidled in closer to her. He had seen those wings. Of course he had. And here on this open, wide river, the two of them might as well have been a pealing dinner bell to the giant bird.

How she hated eagles. And hawks. And owls. Any birds of prey, really.

Hated them for their abiding love for færy meat.

"Stay close to the bank," Asher breathed, and for once, she obeyed his orders without protest, completely uninterested in becoming dinner.

"She's the one that's been following us," she said, understanding dawning as she watched Asher survey the skies with those sharp eyes of his.

He only nodded.

"Where are you going?" she asked as Asher banked right, nearly disappearing into the grasses.

"Just stay close to the bank. I'll be right back."

"Where are you going?" she tried again, the panic in her voice more apparent.

"To scout," was all he said before he disappeared, leaving her alone along the river, her only companion the hum of her wings and the shadow of the eagle above.

She swallowed back her fear, swallowed her pride at the realization that she did not want to journey even a moment without Asher.

Silently, she prayed to Eloah that he would not be gone long.

The wind picked up, icy and remorseless, chilling her to her bones as she flew as fast as she could, the eagle mercifully staying high above.

It was then that she noticed the river beneath her. The way the wake of her wings carved through the waters in a perfect slice—a trench. As if she were the wind and the water her plaything. She reached out, running her fingers along the tip of the perfectly-curling wave beneath her, the water arching up at her touch—like a cat waiting to be scratched.

"Hello, beautiful," she heard, whipping her head toward the black face that was somehow right beside her.

Her eyes grew wide at the sight of him—his pointed teeth, his leathery skin, his eyes as black as his wings.

A Dark færy. A black moth. A kiss of death.

It was on instinct that she banked left, careening a white-hot ball of færy light toward the wicked creature.

He dodged it with ease.

"You'll have to do better than that, darling," he purred, his voice a caress, ancient and young at the same time, slithering along her spine.

He flew alongside her again, but did not touch her.

"I've been looking for you," he said. And at his words, at the way he said them…

She looked the Dark færy in the eyes, the river a blur of silver beneath them as they sped along its banks.

Where was Asher?

The færy smiled, a serpent admiring its prey, his wicked teeth perfectly sharpened for devouring…

Without thought, she hurled another ball of light toward the færy, and this time, he hissed as it grazed his black cheek. His laugh sent a wave of gooseflesh along her skin.

"What do you want with me?" She heard herself breathe, wondering why she bothered to speak to the fell beast.

"It's not me, love," he purred. "My father, he has been looking for you."

Her breaths shortened, her heart a pounding drum in her throat. His *father?*

The river turned west, a hard bank to the left as she followed along the edge. The Dark færy followed with ease, running his gnarled finger along her arm as he did. She snatched her arm away, hissing at the burn from his touch.

And with that swift movement, the river itself seemed to answer, a sudden wave of briny water careening toward the Dark færy with deadly accuracy.

The færy barely dodged the swift water.

"Who is your father?" she asked.

He only smiled, if you could call it a smile.

And then he lunged.

She screamed as he grabbed her, his hands a brand everywhere he touched, as if her very being repelled him. She gathered her magic within her, a raging storm of Light poised to devour him whole. The only magic she knew, the only magic she had ever attempted. The magic her parents had taught her—the magic of the Light.

But he snatched her into his arms, surging with shocking speed into the open skies.

Right towards the eagle.

She struggled against him, his arms shackles around her as she fought to free herself. But he was strong—too strong. And if she were to worm her way out of his arms, then those talons along his fingers would surely shred her wings…

A sharp cry tore through the skies, the eagle just above them. And for a brief moment, she could have sworn terror shone in the Dark færy's eyes.

Then again, she knew it was shining in hers. And she was not sure which was worse: to be taken by a Dark færy or eaten by an eagle.

Where in Sheol was Asher?

As if he'd heard her thoughts, he appeared before her, a bone weapon in each hand, his eyes alight with rage and death. Predator, indeed.

Asher flung a ball of orange light toward her captor, who banked to dodge it, the sensation a sickening drop to her stomach. Above them, the eagle's wings flapped, a kiss of fell wind rustling her hair. Her captor laughed, wicked and cruel as he said, "Well, hello, Asher. It's been such a long time!"

The eagle swooped past them, flipping on her back below them with wicked grace as she extended her deadly talons and grabbed Meren and the Dark færy in her clutches.

Asher cried out, his voice a growl in the wind as he flung his blade through the sky, wrapped in a ball of fiery orange light, landing with impossible precision right into the eagle's claw.

She shrieked, dropping Meren and the Dark færy, the momentary free fall a shock to them both.

But the Dark færy soon righted himself, swooping fast and capturing Meren in his grip once more.

So she grabbed his face, searing him, branding him with her

Light magic, savoring his shrieks as his very skin burned and smoked beneath her hands. Let the bastard burn. Let all the Darkness burn.

The eagle swooped again, snapping her sharp beak mere inches from Meren, who used the Dark færy's distraction to burn him once more with her Light.

His shrill cry pierced the sky, but was soon cut off by a bone blade sinking into his throat. Meren gagged at the sound of blade slicing flesh.

His grip slackened, and he free-fell as Asher swooped in, grabbing Meren in his arms and banking hard away from the fray.

He landed on the branch of a sycamore tree a heartbeat later, still holding her close to his chest as he rushed to hide her in a nook of the tree much too small for an eagle to reach.

She collapsed on the bark with a sigh that was almost a cry. Asher collapsed on his knees before her, taking her face in his hands.

"Eloah, Meren. Are you all right?" he gasped, his breaths as labored as her own.

"It's fine, Ash. I'm fine," she said. But it wasn't fine. Not really. What had that færy meant? That his father was looking for her? Who was his father? And what did he want with her?

"Mer," Asher said. His jagged breaths were warm on her face, his eyes heavy with remorse.

"It's all right. Really," she lied.

"I failed you," he protested, shaking his head. "I couldn't focus on anything but that eagle, and I didn't see him coming. I didn't even see that bastard before it was too late and—"

"Ash, neither of us did," she pointed out. But it did little to assuage his remorse.

He shook his head, disgusted in himself. "I'm sorry, Mer. I'm so sorry."

"Ash, it's fine," she said, failing to stifle the tremble working its way to the tips of her fingers, the ends of her toes.

Asher kissed her brow, and she wasn't sure if it was her own trembling or his that she felt.

But that night, after settling down enough to eat a bite or two of some nuts they found in the forest, Asher did not keep a respectable distance between them as they slept—his arms tight around her middle, his breaths warm and steady against her hair.

~

Her own cry woke her, her eyes adjusting to the darkness around them. It was a dream—it had only been a dream.

But the bloodied faces of her mother and father still loomed before her as if they were alive.

As if they blamed her for it all.

You should have saved us, her father said, his silver eyes haunting in the moonlight, her mother on his arm, a look of disappointment on her beautiful, young face. *You should have found a way to stop them.*

"I know," Meren breathed into the still night, a nearby cricket stopping her midnight song at the sound.

"Mer?"

She turned her gaze from the ghostly visages of her dead parents to see Asher beside her, sitting up and adjusting his blanket at his waist.

"What's wrong?" he asked.

And maybe it had been that Dark færy, the hatred in his eyes; maybe it had been those talons clutched tightly around her as the eagle went to tear them away, but she could not shake the tremors that had settled in, just as she could not shake the image of her murdered parents from her mind, her dreams.

The Darkness, it was spreading.

"It's nothing, Ash. I'm fine. Just go back to sleep," she said, hugging her knees to her chest.

"You dreamt of your parents again, didn't you?" And even though he was right beside her, she knew no comfort from his nearness, his warmth slowly ebbing away, the icy coolness of the night spreading over her like hoarfrost.

"I'm fine, Ash."

"Your problem is that you think about it too much, Meren. You've got to stop blaming yourself for—"

"I don't need you to fix it for me." She looked over her shoulder at him, his animalistic eyes glowing in the silvery light, the tips of his pointed ears touched by moonlight.

Those eyes narrowed. "No, you don't, do you? You never need me for anything."

"Ash—" she tried, but he had already laid down again, turning his back to her.

She did not sleep for the rest of the night.

Chapter VI

What do you suppose it is we're looking for, exactly?" Meren asked, peering around a particularly fat trunk.

Asher all but ignored her, flying determinedly through the loamy forest in search of their target. In fact, he hadn't spoken to her all day. Not a single word.

"A nook? A hole in the ground? A cave?" she asked, ignoring his scowl as she flew. "If you were a legendary Warrior færy, where would you live?"

Asher picked up a rock, peering into the hole behind it. But the hole must have been empty, because he soon dropped the rock and resumed his silent, brooding search.

"So are you ever going to speak to me again or what?" she asked, crossing her arms as she hovered behind him, waiting for him to face her.

"What do you want me to say, Meren?" he sneered, still with his back to her as he flew. His glow was a little more red than orange today. Ass.

She huffed a breath. "You know, this is your problem, Ash. I never know where I stand with you! One minute you're brooding like a færyling and the next minute you're looking at me like…" Like *what*, she wondered, even as Asher whirled to face her, his eyes keen on her, eager for her to finish that damning sentence.

What did he look at her like?

Even as she asked herself the question, she didn't want to answer it. Didn't want to, because then it would be real. And then she would have to face it.

"Ash—" But her words were cut off by a pulling. No, a yanking, really. On her very soul.

A pulling she could not ignore.

She looked around, at the skies, at the surrounding trees, but there was nothing—no sign of where that pull had come from.

Or what that pull had been.

"What is wrong with you?" Asher demanded.

She faced him again. "Did you feel that?"

He obviously had not, because he crossed his arms, that ever-present scowl on his face as he barked, "This is so typical of you, Meren. You never want to talk about anyth—"

"Shhhh," she chastised, the pull—that *yank*—calling her again. She ran her eyes over the trees around her, scouring for any sign of what had caused it, ignoring Asher's searing gaze.

I'm here. I'm here. I'm here, it said. Over and again. Calling. Beckoning.

You know who I am.

But she did not. Not really. She did not know who called to her. Who beckoned her very soul.

"Get off my land," a voice growled. She and Asher whirled to face it, and even from the corner of her eye, she did not miss the bone blade Asher was already palming.

Or the growl curling his lips.

The wind picked up, warm and menacing, swirling around the one who had spoken. The male before her was…he was…she didn't know *what* he was.

"Who are you?" she asked, but the færy did not look at her, did not acknowledge she even existed, his menacing glare fixated solely on Asher. She could have sworn the wind gathered around him—a snake coiling around its prey. The færy growled.

But that growl was by no means the most terrifying thing about him. He stood on the ground, his feet shoulder-width apart, his thick arms folded across his broad chest. He wore no weapons—at least none that were visible. But he didn't need to. *He* was the weapon, for his eyes, his very demeanor reeked of the promise of violence.

He was tall, even for a færy, his hair an unruly swath of silver atop his head with a single shock of black streaking from his brow. His skin was a golden tan, flecked with scars—the perfect contrast to his hair. Silver and gold. Gold and silver. His eyes shone bright in the evening sun—a black so deep, so true, it might have held the entirety of the firmament, kissed with a thousand upon a thousand stars, swirling with galaxies and worlds beyond.

But it wasn't his eyes that held her gaze. No, it was his wings, hanging from his formidable shoulders in indescribable shades of gray and white. Not silver. Not iridescent either. Pearlescent. Radiant. Like ash kissed with morning dew. Like a river of quicksilver. A breath of wind touched them, and that's when she realized…his wings were in tatters.

Shredded. Destroyed.

The færy could not fly. Not with that sort of devastation to his wings.

A Warrior færy, indeed.

A legend made flesh.

"I will say this only once more," the warrior growled. "Get. Off. My. Land." The wind seemed to echo his warning, gathering, coalescing—as if it were poising itself to wipe them off the face of the earth.

Asher took hold of her arm, his grip so tight she sucked in a breath.

"Ash," she said through her teeth. He all but ignored her, glaring at the warrior before them with predatory intent.

"Please," Meren said, stepping forward. "Are you the one they call the Gibhor?"

Ash's grip on her arm became excruciating.

The warrior at last turned his attention to her, raking his eyes over her from the ground up, his unashamed appraisal kissing her cheeks with heat.

But when he met her eyes, he froze as still as death, his nostrils flaring once, his head tilting to the side—a caracal measuring his prey. "What do you want?" he growled under his breath.

Heart. Pounding. She almost couldn't breathe through the pounding of her heart. But she did not cower. She would not cower under this monster's gaze.

"Please," she said, hating the word on her tongue. "We need your help."

The warrior said nothing, *showed* nothing on his face but the remnants of a snarl. She pressed on anyway. "The Darkness; it is spreading, and we must stop it. We have come to ask for your help."

"I do not help," he said.

"Come, Meren. We are leaving," Asher said, pulling her away.

She held her ground. "No," she said. "Come on, Ash. We have to at least try."

"He is not going to help us," Asher practically growled, pulling so hard on her arm that her eyes began to water.

"Asher, stop," she said, but he did not let go.

"I would suggest you let her go," the warrior growled, the wind tightening around her, around Asher. Suffocating. At the warrior's words, Asher glared at him once more.

And the way they looked at each other… "Do you…do you know each other?"

Neither of them answered, locked in a death-stare, Asher twirling the wicked bone blade in his free hand.

"Please, Gibhor. We need your help," Meren went on, ignoring their silent battle.

"You've come to the wrong place," the Gibhor said.

"No!" Meren cried, the panic stealing over her. "Please. You must help us before there are none of us left! The Darkness—they are growing in numbers, killing any dissenters. My own parents were murdered before my eyes nearly fifty winters ago. We cannot just stand by and let them destroy all that is good. We must stop them. And you must help us!"

The warrior's black eyes found hers, appraising her once more. "You speak of ideals, young one. The Darkness," he said, turning his attention to Asher once more, "cannot be stopped."

Asher merely glared, baring his teeth.

"Of course it can!" she protested, knowing how desperate she sounded. "There is still Light. And while there is Light, there is hope!"

"Take your ideals somewhere else," he said, turning his back to them both. The wind picked up behind him, swirling leaves and pine needles in his wake like the waves curling around a rock.

But she would not have it. She moved to step forward again, nearly crying out at the death grip Asher kept on her arm. She would bruise from it, no doubt.

"If you will not help your fellow færies, will you at least help the mortals?"

The warrior turned slowly to face her again, and she rushed on. "Surely you've seen it—the winter encroaches upon us all. Soon both mortal and immortal alike will be plunged into the Darkness if we do not do something to stop it. If you won't help us, at least help the humans!"

"The humans, young one," said the warrior, "have made their choice. They have forgotten the Light. They cannot be helped. As I said, take your ideals—"

"So you would rather stay hidden away here like a coward?"

She regretted the words immediately at the look on his face. He stepped towards her—only one step—before he breathed, "Do not mistake my presence here for cowardice. Get off of my land and find someone who gives a damn."

And with that, the warrior turned on his heel and walked— walked, not flew—away.

~

"Come on," Asher said, his grip tightening even more on her arm.

"Ow!" she cried as he yanked her into the air.

"We're going home," was all he said.

Anger seethed within her. The Gibhor—oh he was definitely a legend, a warrior, perhaps the only surviving one—but he was no hero.

"Thanks for all your help," Meren sneered.

"He was not going to help us," Asher said as they broke above the first level of trees.

"Not with the way you were acting," she spat.

Asher ignored her, pulling her ever higher toward the skies. The sun was almost set now, the last rays of the day clinging to the skies in violent shades of crimson and lavender. It was only then that she realized that storm clouds hovered not far off, closing in on them.

"We're not flying up there," she protested, pulling back. Still, his hand remained on her like a death grip.

"Yes. We are," he said. "We're getting as far away from here as quickly as we can."

"Do you know him?"

Asher said nothing as they at last broke through the canopy, the sky vast and breathtaking before them, above them, behind them.

"Ash, do you know him?" she tried to ask again, her tone more insistent.

"Everyone knows him, Meren," he said condescendingly.

"Well, I don't."

A clap of thunder rumbled in the distance, lightning flaring before them.

"We shouldn't be up here, Asher," she said.

"We're staying up here as long as we can. Besides, we'll have to stop flying soon. It's almost night—"

Asher's words were cut off, a sudden, deadly silence prickling her skin, a ripple of darkness careening toward them, sending Asher tumbling away from her.

"Asher!" she cried, but it was too late, for his limp body disappeared into the canopy below, his own light guttering from the dark ripple that had assaulted him.

Panic stole over her as she frantically searched the darkening sky for the source of that ripple.

Not from the thunderstorm rapidly approaching.

From Dark Magic.

From a Dark færy.

The eerie stillness, the deafening silence was nearly her undoing as she searched the skies. But there was nothing.

"Asher?" she called again, knowing herself to be a fool for making her location so obvious. But she could not see him, could not see where he had fallen. Finding him would be—

Another ripple of darkness, this one accompanied by a wicked laugh. She flung herself below, dodging the blackness by little more than a hairsbreadth.

Bursting through the canopy, she careened down into the forest, scouring for any sign of Asher.

"Ash! Please! Where are you?"

He did not answer.

Thunder rumbled again, the black-bellied clouds closing out the last vestiges of sunlight. Fat, errant drops began to fall around her, and she flew maniacally to dodge them.

"Asher!"

The rain grew heavier with each breath, her own panic welling with every second that she did not find her friend.

But she did not get to look for him anymore before Darkness—not the kind borne from a thunderstorm—swallowed her whole.

# Chapter VII

he awoke to the awareness of two things: blinding pain in her wing and…

…and the smell of something delectable.

She moved to sit up from the warm place in which she lay but cried out in protest at the pain that lanced down her back.

"You need to keep still," someone said across from her.

She opened her eyes, wincing as she adjusted to the light, lulled into near intoxication by the smell of—

Another flash of pain struck, like lightning careening down her back, her shoulder, and the edge of her wing.

"Where am I?" she asked, her voice weak and gravelly.

"If you want to fly again, you are going to need to listen to me," said the voice again, vaguely familiar. But from her position on what she now realized was a bed, she could not see from whom the voice came.

Still, that smell…

Visions danced in her mind of flying through spring grasses and over ponds so clear as to be a looking glass. Her father's radiant smile. Her mother's infectious laugh.

Was this heaven? Was she dead?

"Where am I?"

"Just rest, Meren. You'll need to if you want to heal."

"What happened to me?" she asked, ignoring the warnings of the voice across the room. A male. Why was he so familiar?

Here. Here. Here.

The words echoed in her soul, a reminder of something, some pull…

"Your wing is broken," the male said, at last stepping into her line of vision. He held a bowl of something steaming—the source of that delicious smell. She nearly moaned as she said, "Toadstool soup."

The dandelion fluff mattress shifted as he sat beside her, gingerly placing the bowl on a nearby table. But it wasn't until he turned to help prop her up that she realized who he was.

"You!" she growled, sitting up. But her seething anger was soon replaced with a yelp as agonizing pain consumed her once more.

"You need to listen to me, Meren," said the Gibhor. "If you ever want to fly again," he added darkly.

She did want to fly again. But her betraying eyes instinctively shot to the shreds of wings hanging from his shoulders, and she couldn't help but wonder if perhaps he knew a thing or two about what she should be doing to heal—things he possibly *didn't* do.

"Where am I?" she asked, but he paid her no heed, effortlessly lifting her so that he might set her upright. Then he gathered the steaming bowl into his lap, spooning out its contents. Eloah above, was he going to feed her?

"I can do that myself," she said, sucking in a shuddering breath as she tried—and failed—to snatch the spoon from his hands.

The pain—it was too much.

"I'm sure you can. But the question is whether you should," he said.

His black eyes were boundless. Like midnight and firmament. Like the hour just before the sun makes her morning appearance. They betrayed nothing of what he might have been thinking as he fed her the first spoonful.

An embarrassing moan escaped her at the taste of the soup. Her favorite.

The male's angular face was hard. Expressionless. And then it occurred to her…

She attempted to shift away from him, frightened at what he might really be feeding her.

"Try not to move. Just eat. You need your rest if you want to heal properly." He scooped up another bite, resting the spoon on her lips, waiting for her to sip.

"What happened to me?" she asked after she swallowed. Eloah, this soup was good. Better than her mother's. Not that she would tell him that. If she was being poisoned, Eloah help her, it was a delightful way to die.

"I don't know," he said. "I found you like this."

"The storm. Is it over then?" she asked, remembering the rain that had begun to fall before…

"The storm?" he asked. "It passed days ago."

"Days?" She breathed deeply, closing her eyes against the tears that were threatening to fall. Not tears of sadness. No, tears of pain.

"You've been asleep for two days, Meren," the Gibhor said, spooning another bite. She sipped it willingly, embracing the soothing warmth of the soup.

Two days? She had been asleep for *two days*? Well, that would explain the ravaging hunger.

And the soreness. At least partly.

He spooned another bite. "Why are you helping me?" she asked. It didn't come out as icily as she had hoped, but he got the point nonetheless.

"Would you rather I left you to die at the hands of those monsters?" He lifted a silver brow in incredulity. There was something distinctly different about him now. Gone was that tense, seething hatred with which he had greeted them in the forest. That temper as sharp as the edge of a blade.

Now he was relaxed. His shoulders soft. His eyes calm. Black and menacing but calm. And then she realized…

"Is this…your home?" she asked, looking around. It was obviously the inside of a tree, its corner-less walls and barky interior a telltale sign. But it was unlike any færy home she had ever seen.

Its walls towered, exposing several levels, most above her, one below. She realized she was not on the lowest level, for there was a level below her that looked something like a living space and hearth. But above her…

Above her was a level of nothing but books. Books of all sizes and shapes and colors. Some færy-sized, some human-sized. They climbed above them some thirty or forty stacks high. She only wondered for a moment how a færy with no flight could reach such heights, for there, carved into nearly every spare space of the walls, were little holes— climbing holes—perfect for færy hands and feet.

Losing his wings had not stopped him. The Gibhor had just found a way to adapt.

He fed her until the bowl was empty. "Want some more?" he asked, and though it was faint, she could have sworn she detected a hint of pleasure at her approval of the fare.

When she nodded, he set the spoon down on the table beside her and gathered the bowl.

But he did not climb down the holes carved for his hands and feet.

No, the Gibhor jumped.

More like soared, really. For it was not gravity that eased him to the ground, but some sort of *wind*.

Magic Wind.

She watched him on the level below as he spooned another bowlful for her, realizing that he had an amply stocked kitchen—spoons and knives and bowls and pots, herbs and spices and fruits and vegetables.

The Gibhor liked to cook.

That magic Wind carried him back to her level again. He was not flying so much as he was leaping, but it was mesmerizing to watch. Never had she seen such a thing in all her life. Hauntingly beautiful. Devastatingly impossible.

"Who are you?" she asked, when he at last landed gracefully beside her again.

He picked up the spoon without a word and set about feeding her once more, the warmth so inviting, so delicious that she sighed.

Three spoonfuls later, when he still did not answer, she asked, "Will you at least tell me your name?"

He held her gaze then, as if asking himself a question.

That voice, it called to her soul again.

You know him, it sang.

And she wondered why she felt as if she did.

"My name is Fa," he said at last. "That is all you need to know."

"Fa," she parroted, the name an anthem, a song. "An ancient name," she said.

He nodded once, feeding her again. She could feel the effects of the soup warming her whole body, taking the edge off the pain.

"Garlic," he said. "And turmeric. You will sleep well tonight, Tipharah."

Tipharah?

"Thank you," she said, clumsily adding, "Fa" to the end.

And indeed, she finished the soup and fell into a deep slumber once more.

Chapter VIII

innamon. Berries. Some sort of concoction of earthy herbs she didn't recognize wafted through the air, coaxing her to wake. She sat up, wincing at the pain, though her wing was somehow a little less painful than it had been yesterday.

That is, if she hadn't been asleep for days again.

"Hungry?" she heard somewhere below. It wasn't exactly a cheery morning salutation, but she supposed it was kind enough, considering the source.

"Yes," she said, attempting to stand up.

"Just stay there, Meren," Fa said. "There is no need to rush things."

Her broken wing seemed to agree with the idea, for it protested every movement, sending shards of blinding pain down her back and legs every time she stirred.

Fa leapt to her level with predatory ease, his broad shoulders stretching his green tunic taut. His wings floated on a phantom breeze behind him as he leapt—a devastating sort of beauty that evoked both pity and wonder.

He held a clamshell platter, filled to the brim with… "What are those?" she asked, trying not to look too thrilled at the prospect of another delectable meal. Maybe her captor was an ass, but he certainly made a mouthwatering toadstool soup. If this breakfast was anything like that...

"Hand pies," he said, offering her one. She eyed it skeptically, marveling at the warmth of the little pastry in her hand.

She slid her eyes to him, raising a brow. "Are you slowly poisoning me? Is that what all this is about?"

He tilted his head to the side, a look of annoyance on his face. "Why would I bother with all that when I could have just left you to die in the forest?"

She held the hand pie before her, still not daring to take a bite. But the smell...Eloah above, the smell would be her downfall. She had no self control whatsoever...at least when it came to this færy's cooking.

"I am not your enemy, Meren," he said when she still hadn't taken a bite.

"You certainly seemed like it the other day."

He appraised her for a moment before taking a seat in a chair beside the bed. "Fair enough. But you'll forgive me if I found your traveling companion less than agreeable."

"You know each other, don't you." It wasn't a question.

He held her eyes for only a moment before he chose a pie from the platter and took a bite. He chewed and swallowed before he said another word.

"We have met before, yes."

She watched him take another bite, his movements precise and graceful—a skilled, seasoned warrior, comfortable in his own skin.

"When?" she asked, daring to bite into her own pie.

Eloah above, it was good.

"Long before you were born, I would hazard," was all he said.

"Why do you hate each other?" she asked, losing any trepidation she had about being poisoned as the bites melted with buttery goodness in her mouth. Glorious way to die, indeed.

She got another appraising look from the warrior before he said, "That is a story for another time, Tipharah."

"Then at least tell me this," she spat. "Why do you refuse to help?"

"Because there is no point," he answered matter-of-factly.

"Have you lost all faith that you hold no hope for færykind?"

He appraised her with his black eyes, searching for a moment before he simply said, "It is not færykind I have lost hope in."

"Then what?"

But Fa did not answer, his attention on the small pie in his hand.

"What a pathetic existence," she hissed.

"That is why you came to me," he said, tilting his head to the side. "Because you hold out hope."

"Unlike you, I am not so jaded by this world to believe such nonsense that there is no hope," she said, chewing another bite.

He contemplated her words for a long moment, letting the silence yawn between them. But then he said, "Hope died a long time ago, Tipharah. Along with everything else that matters."

"I don't believe that."

He stood, setting the platter on the table beside her. "Then you are as naïve as you are young."

"I'm not that young," she said, but he had already turned his back to her, leaping off the platform.

~

"Where are you going?" she asked, watching him on the level below as he packed a satchel with a few things: a small blade, some nuts and dried berries, a warm cloak.

"I'll be back later," he said.

She sat up quickly, wincing at the pain. He looked her over carefully, but he made no move toward her, simply saying, "Rest, Meren. And try not to move." He flung his satchel over his shoulder.

"But where are you going?"

"To scout," he said, donning the cloak. He pulled up the hood, its shadows menacing across his face. A faint glow of silvery light shone around him, giving the shadows even more depth. "There are plenty of pies left, should you get hungry."

"You're going to leave me here alone?" she asked.

His laugh was humorless. "I have every day since you arrived."

"What are you scouting for?" she asked.

"What do you think?" he asked with a raised brow.

His hand was on the door handle when she said hastily, "But if there are Dark færies about, should you really leave me here?"

He turned to face her again, and even from the level below, his eyes seemed to pierce right through her. "This tree is well warded, Meren. No one will find you here."

"But *I* found you!" she protested, knowing she sounded desperate.

He held her gaze for a long moment, something she couldn't read in his eyes. "And that is a mystery I'm trying to solve," he said, and then he was gone.

~

The day was long. And boring. When the sun had risen halfway across the sky and Fa still hadn't come back, she grudgingly grabbed another pie and ate. She was already tired of being cooped up in this bed all the time. The monotonous silence didn't help, either. Nor did the library towering above her—the one she didn't dare touch for fear of whatever retribution he might exact when he found her perusing his personal things. So when it was nearly nightfall and he still hadn't returned, she was ready to come out of her skin.

At last, when the sun had only a single paltry ray shining through the window, Fa returned, quiet and contemplative.

"What happened?" she asked, when he walked in.

He looked up at her from the level below. "I thought you'd be asleep."

"I'm tired of sleeping. I'm tired of resting," she snapped.

He huffed a dark laugh. "Then come down." He set about putting away his things, meticulous and neat—there was a place for everything. So very different from the haphazard mess she called home.

"In case you've forgotten, I can't fly." The moment she said it, she regretted it, knowing how callous, how petulant she sounded. His tattered wings fluttered behind him. "Sorry," she muttered from the bed. "I just—"

"It's fine," he said, leaping to her platform. He took hold of her hand, and when she realized it was to help her stand up, she let him. As soon as she was on her feet, he inched around her, inspecting her wing thoroughly before saying, "You're healing nicely. Slowly. But nicely."

She looked over her shoulder at him, uneasy with how close to her he hovered. "Do you…do you think I'll fly again?" she asked.

He gave her a nod, his scent invading her senses—amber and sunlight and salt-kissed wind. "If you listen to me and don't get any wild ideas, then yes," he said, and she could have sworn there was a hint of humor in his voice.

"Why would you think I would get wild ideas?" she snapped, furrowing her brow.

The lone silvery brow he raised was his only reply, and at it, she chuckled.

To her surprise, he chuckled too, the small smile enough to light up his whole face.

"Come on," he said, extending his hand. "I'll make you some tea."

She eyed the little handholds along the wall warily. "I'm not a very good climber."

"You've stayed in this bed all day?" he asked incredulously.

"What else was I supposed to do?" She huffed, crossing her arms. He, however, kept his hand extended to her.

"You didn't think to read, perhaps?"

"You would let me?" she asked, not bothering to hide the eagerness in her words. The thought of getting her hands on all those books…

"I am not your enemy, Meren," he said, crossing his arms over his broad chest.

"I just…" She felt foolish. "I didn't know how you would feel about it."

He uncrossed his arms, extending his hand to her once more.

"Read all you like."

"Thank you," she said, heat rising to her cheeks. She looked down, fiddling with her fingers.

"Are you coming down or not?" he asked.

When she looked up, she couldn't help but fixate on his extended hand—the callouses, the strength, the sheer size of it. His hand would surely swallow hers whole.

"I can't climb that well," she said.

"Good thing you don't need to," he said, and this time, she was certain that a wicked grin threatened his mouth.

Reluctantly, she put her hand in his. His skin was rough like hide but gentle, somehow. Indeed, his hand was at least twice the size of hers. But he held it carefully, as if her hand were a hummingbird egg. He guided her to the edge of the platform. Warmth surrounded them. Wind, soft like a lover's breath. The fine hairs on her arms and neck rose at the sensation. She caught only a glimpse of a gleam in his eye before he leapt.

She let out a little yelp at the sensation, expecting to free-fall. But they did not free-fall.

They glided.

And it was gloriously smooth. Like a soft spring breeze rustling a patch of hydrangeas. Like a gentle rain misting the skies. They just… floated down to the first level of Fa's home.

"May I ask you a personal question?" she asked, nearly breathless as they landed.

He let go of her hand and turned to face her, cocking his head to one side.

"Do you…" she started, fiddling with her mother's ring. "Do you even need to fly?"

"That is an interesting question, Meren."

She looked up, meeting his eyes. "Why?"

"Does anyone really *need* to?"

"I…you know what I mean," she said. But just standing again felt good, blood rushing back into her limbs, her wings.

"Indeed, but I wonder if you do," he said. He turned, walking with fluid grace to his hearth. He stoked the fire back to life, the flames roaring merrily within no time. Then he hung a kettle on the hook and pushed it over the flames.

"What do you mean?" she asked as she watched him work.

"We færies forget. We take the skies for granted," he said. "In some ways, I think we lust for them. And that lust blinds us to what else is out there."

With his back to her, he moved toward a mortar and pestle, grinding dried petals and leaves of varying colors together. His wings—so glorious, even in their devastation—hung limply from his shoulders, swaying and bobbing softly with every movement he made. Lifeless, dead. And yet beautiful. Magnificent in their own right. A haunting testament to the wonder he must have once been.

"Losing my wings, Meren, taught me many things. And perhaps they were lessons I might not have willingly learned otherwise."

He turned to face her at last, leaning against his gnarled wooden counter, crossing his arms across his chest.

"What?" she asked curiously. "What did you learn?"

"To catch the Wind," was all he said.

"What does that mean? To catch the Wind?" She took a step towards him, tentative and yet awed. The Gibhor, this warrior—he was a legend incarnate.

"Would you like to learn?"

A nod.

"Then I will show you," he said.

"How old are you?" she blurted, wondering if it was an insulting question.

He merely chuckled. "How old do you think I am?"

She didn't know. Not really. He didn't look old—his skin was still taut and youthful, his hair thick and glossy. Not the cottony gray of an aging færy, but thick, luxurious silver locks, painted with a shock of black at his brow. But despite his skin and his unusual hair, he seemed old. Wise. Otherworldly.

As if he had been born of another time or place.

Perhaps he had been.

"I don't know, honestly," she admitted. "Sometimes I think we are close in age."

"And other times?" he asked—and it was genuine curiosity she saw in his eyes.

"And other times I think you might be ancient."

He barked a laugh as the kettle began to softly whistle over the flames. He ignored it as he asked, "How old are you?"

"Next year will be my eightieth summer," she answered.

"And you are not paired?" he asked.

"What?" she asked, blinking at him. "Why are you asking me that?"

He shrugged. "You seemed keen the other day to point out that

Asher was not your lover. I simply wondered why."

She sighed, plopping into the nearest chair, running her nails along the shallow grains of the wooden table before her. "You're not the only one who wonders that," she said, defeated.

He turned to the kettle, which had begun to whistle more angrily, and pulled it from the fire with a thick cloth. He poured the steaming water into two cups as he spoke. "Are you aware that he is in love with you?"

She sucked in a breath to protest, stopping herself when she realized there was no point. "Yes," she sighed, chastising herself. Yes, she knew. Perhaps she hadn't wanted to know. But she had known of Asher's feelings nonetheless.

"But you are not in love with him," he said.

"I've tried to be, but it's not working," she admitted.

He turned to face her, handing her a cup before taking a seat across from her. "I don't think that's how it works, Meren."

"I don't think I *know* how it works," she said, sipping from her cup, marveling at the riot of flavors—vanilla and cinnamon, berry and— "What is this?" she asked, lifting her cup.

"Hibiscus," he said.

"It's glorious," she said, sipping again.

He merely raised his cup before drinking from it.

"And I don't think you're exactly one to be taking advice from, considering you hate Asher," she added with a snarl.

He raised a brow as he drank wordlessly from his cup. There was nothing delicate about this male before her. He was a weapon honed for battle, a stark contrast to the male who woke her with handmade pies and tea. Who took painstaking measures to keep her comfortable.

Who opened his home for her that she might heal.

Who was this Gibhor, and what did he want with her?

"I don't even know if he's alive," she finally said after a pregnant pause. "He fell, same as I did. What if he's out there, hurt?"

"He's not," Fa said flatly.

She set down her cup. "How do you know?"

"Because I've been looking for him," he said without meeting her eyes.

"You've been what?" she asked incredulously.

"He is not in the forest. And there are no tracks to indicate that he was injured...or dragged away," Fa said, setting down his cup. He finally met Meren's eyes. "I have been searching for him for three days. I have every reason to believe that he flew away."

Her heart pounded wildly. "But...the Darkness, it came for us. It hit us both."

"You were attacked, yes. But not to be killed, Meren."

"How do you know that?"

"The Dark færies have no interest in killing us. They want us alive. As slaves."

"What if they took Asher?" she said, standing to her feet. She winced as her wing screamed in pain, but marched to the door nonetheless.

"I don't believe they did," said Fa, his voice calm, careful. He put a hand on her shoulder, and at his touch, she slowed, turning to face him. She hadn't even heard him follow her.

"How do you know that?"

"There would be signs," he said, almost apologetically.

"What signs?" she asked.

It was definitely apology in his eyes now as he said, "They would have taken his wings."

Blood, he meant. There would be blood. Everywhere. She looked at the sliver of tattered wing visible behind his broad form—the jagged cuts across his wings, so gnarled and ugly. Whoever had done that to him had been thorough. Merciless.

She met his eyes again, his hand still on her shoulder.

"We have every reason to believe that he escaped unharmed," he added.

It was a tear that fell down her cheek as she looked down again, fiddling with her mother's ring.

"I know you are frightened, Meren. But I will keep you safe until you are well enough—"

"Why?" she asked, looking up again. "Why did you look for him if you hate him?"

He took a moment to answer, his eyes fixated on her shoulder. But then he said, "Because I can see how much he means to you." He squeezed her shoulder gently, a small smile ghosting his mouth before he added, "And I have no desire to incur the wrath of Meren should she wake to find out that no one had been looking for someone she cares about."

She breathed a laugh, another tear escaping. "Thank you," she managed.

Fa only nodded.

Chapter IX

everal days passed in much the same manner: a glorious breakfast, and then a whole day of nothing to do while Fa scouted for Dark færies. On the fourth morning, she finally mustered the courage to brave the little climbing holes so that she could explore the third level—the vast library of færy and human books just beckoning to her.

Fa must have been an avid reader, for upon reaching the level, she realized that there were even more books than she could see from the bed below. History books. Books on magic. Politics. Legends. Færy-tales. Books small enough to fit in the palm of her hand, and books so large she couldn't have lifted them if her life depended on it. She wondered how he had gotten them up here, especially considering he couldn't fly.

Catch the Wind, he had told her. She wondered what he meant. Fa had learned to adapt to a world without the one thing every færy took for granted—wings. He had created for himself his own little world—a haven of the things he enjoyed. And that haven was in stark contrast to the warrior she had met that first day—the male who seethed with hatred. Seemed to thrive on it.

Maybe Fa bore no hope for færy or humankind. But Fa was not a hopeless male. Reclusive, perhaps. But not hopeless. If anything, judging by the wealth of books around her, by the little trinkets and tokens carefully placed around his home, a hoard of a thousand treasures of creation, it was apparent that Fa cared deeply for many things, especially for the Light of Eloah. For the magic that connected all of creation.

Perhaps Fa hadn't lost faith in færies and humans.

Perhaps Fa had only lost faith in himself.

~

She had been there about a week, she figured, what with the days a little mixed up, having slept through the first few. Regardless, one thing was certain: she needed to get healed and get home. Surely Asher was worried sick about her by now.

But Fa had been gone all day and had not returned as he usually did at dusk. The sky was inky black as she looked out of the windows, hunting for any sign of him. It was only after a moment that she realized she shouldn't be scouring the skies. He wouldn't be there. He would be walking. On the ground. Because he could not fly.

It was easy to forget that about him with how easily he moved about his home. The Wind he spoke of—he wielded it effortlessly to glide about from level to level. But flying? She doubted that same Wind could carry him across open skies. She opened the door, peering down the fat trunk of the tree in which Fa lived, hoping to see him climbing up the side.

But he was not.

And several hours later, he still wasn't back.

"Fa!" she called from the door for what felt like the hundredth time in a few hours. But he did not answer, did not manifest; there was no sign of his silvery glow in the darkness.

Worry gnawed away at her, a caracal gnawing away at the bones of her—

She sucked in a sharp breath, pain lancing down her arm and her back. She cried out, whirling to face whatever had hurt her.

But there was nothing there. No intruder, no sign of anyone or anything but the glow of the dying fire in the hearth.

Pain struck again, and she grabbed her arm, squeezing as if she could stop the pain that way. Pain like—like a dagger wound.

What in the world?

Fa landed on the threshold of his doorway, but it was not with the grace to which she had grown accustomed when watching him glide through the air.

"Fa!" she cried, darting to his side at the sight of the shimmering blood that stained his clothes and dripped from his arm.

Blood from a dagger wound.

"Eloah, Fa! What happened to you?"

"I'm fine," he said, wincing. He was winded and cold, his hair sticking up on the ends, also coated in blood. *His* blood, from the looks of it.

She took hold of his good arm, bracing him on the back so she could usher him to a chair. But he sucked in a breath at her touch, and she quickly let go. Blood coated the hand that had touched his back—

he was apparently wounded there, too. And the blood…coating her hands…

Visions of her parents, dead and prone before her, robbed her of her breath, her hands shaking violently before her.

"Meren?" Fa asked.

She looked at him, but she could only see her father, tears streaming down his face.

Run, Meren. Run and never look back.

But she hadn't run. And the blood dripping down her hand…

"Meren," Fa tried again, taking her face in his hands.

"I'm sorry," she said, trembling as she focused on him at last. "I'm sorry," she said again.

"What happened?" he asked as if his own wounds were nothing.

"Let's get you inside. You need to sit down."

He held her gaze a bit longer, his countenance shifting when he realized she was not ready to speak of the sudden vision of her dead father. "It's fine," he said, shuffling into his sitting room. "I'm fine."

"Forgive me," she said, "but it's obvious that you are not."

Fa shuffled his way across the main floor, plopping down onto a cushion as he held the wound on his arm together with his other hand.

"Fa, what happened?" she asked, following him into the room. She did not sit down with him, however, making her way to a small basin of water in his kitchen. She found a rag and wetted it, filling a bowl with water before returning to him, towel and bowl in hand.

She sat down before him and started cleaning the wound on his arm.

He sucked in a breath at her touch but did not stop her. The wound was deep. Too deep.

"Was it a Dark færy?" she asked.

He merely met her eyes, his face betraying nothing of his thoughts. She carefully washed the blood from his arm, his hands. It was only when she started wiping the blood from his face that he spoke at last.

"You don't have to help me," he said. There was almost an apology in his words.

So she said, "You didn't have to help me either."

He watched her intently as she cleaned his wounds. She averted her eyes, inspecting him for any more wounds. When she found none, she said, "Turn around." And to her surprise, he obeyed.

His tunic was ripped just below his shoulder blade, the tatters of his wings hiding the gnarly wound beneath. Carefully—so carefully—she helped him remove the blood-soaked tunic. His blood oozed thick and glistening down his back, the wound deep and angry. It would scar, no doubt. A scar to match the many that marred his taut golden skin.

"This has happened to you before," she said.

He merely nodded as she worked, his muscles tensing with every touch. It was obvious he was in a good deal of pain, despite the fact that he spoke nothing of it. These wounds—they had been meant to kill.

"Why did this happen, Fa? I thought you said they don't want to kill us."

"I am not one of the ones they want alive," he said.

She pressed the rag into his wound, putting pressure on it to staunch the bleeding. He did not balk, did not protest, despite the tension mounting in his shoulders.

"Why do they want to kill you?" she asked softly.

"Because I wasn't supposed to live," was his only reply.

Disgust burned in the back of her throat. Disgust and seething rage. "I am…I am glad they didn't succeed," she said.

"Don't be so sure," he said.

"Why?"

He looked over his shoulder but did not meet her eyes. "Because I did not let him live to tell the tale." There was a menacing darkness in his words—hearkening back to the first time they had met. The beast within him seemed to roar.

"Good," was all she said as she continued to clean the blood from his back.

"Good?" he objected. "I tell you that I murdered a færy, and you respond with *good?*"

"He deserved to die."

"I am surprised that you have such a calloused indifference to the sanctity of life."

"There is no sanctity to the life of a Dark færy," she practically growled, gritting her teeth. The blood had soaked the rag completely, so she dropped it into the bowl, rinsed it, and wrung it out again before continuing.

"You speak as if all færies fall into one category or the other," Fa said.

"Do they not?"

He moved to look over his shoulder again, this time meeting her eyes. "What would you say that I am, Meren?"

She looked at him for a moment, looked long at the ashen wings that hung from his shoulders. They were not bright, as vivid as she imagined all færies of the Light to be. But they were not dark either.

They were just…dead.

"We all have the Light in us, Meren," Fa went on when she did not answer. "And we all have the Darkness. It is what we choose to be that defines us."

"And what have you chosen to be?" she asked before she could think about it.

He sighed, taking a moment before he answered. "There was a time when I would have said unequivocally that I was a færy of the Light."

"And now?" she asked, inching back around to face him, having finished cleaning his back.

He met her eyes, surprising her with the sorrow that remained there—the regret that lined them. "And now I know that I have given in to the Darkness too often for the Light to ever claim me again."

She looked long into his eyes, black and boundless—an ocean of secrets and stories told long before she was born. But despite that shadow, despite that mystery, she could see the Light behind them. It shone through, flickering and hopeful. A candle in the darkness.

So she was not afraid.

"How did you kill him?" she asked. "You carry no weapons beyond what might slice an apple."

He practically snarled. "Weapons are for the cowards who do not know how to wield the gifts we were given at creation."

She thought of Asher—of his bone blades, hanging from the scabbards strapped across his body. Was he a coward? She had never thought of him in that way. No, to her, Asher had always been the hero who had rescued her from the hands of the Dark færies who had killed her parents.

"You killed him with magic?" she asked, the answer dawning on her.

A nod was Fa's only answer.

"I want you to show me," she said.

"What?"

"I want you to show me how you do it. The old ways. I want you to teach me the magic we have forgotten."

He shook his head, looking down to the now clean wound on his arm. She stood so that she might retrieve some clean rags.

"I don't think I've ever met anyone like you, Tipharah," he said as she walked back toward him.

"What is that supposed to mean?" she asked, a smirk ghosting her mouth.

"You are brave," he said. "Much braver than you think you are."

She squatted before him again, tearing a rag into strips and laying them across her knee.

"Here," he said, reaching into his satchel. He handed her a small tin.

"What is this?" she asked, her senses coming alive as she opened it and smelled the earthy, herbal scent.

"A healing balm," he said. "It also eases the pain a bit."

The scent hit her—a familiar scent, but one she couldn't quite place. It took over her senses, her own wing seeming to sing in response, as if longing for the balm's soothing kiss.

He looked at her, holding her gaze with his own. But he said nothing.

She scooped out a healthy amount of the balm, gently smoothing it over his arm before tying the wound with a strip of cloth. Next, she did the same with his back. It was only once she had finished dressing and tying the wounds that he spoke again.

"Thank you, Meren." He covered her hand with his, swallowing it whole with the sheer breadth of it, flecked with scars and glowing softly with his magic. Her own hand flared at his touch, and it struck her how beautifully her magic mingled with his—silver and blue, swirling and toying in whorls and curls between them. Melody and harmony. Question and answer.

When she looked at him again, his eyes were haunted, but his smile was genuine.

So was hers.

Chapter X

"Who are you really, Fa? And what are you doing hiding here?"

Fa had finished cleaning up the last of their dinner, his back to her as he washed the last pot. She watched his devastated wings bob and fleck as he moved with expert grace. His wounds were healing nicely. In fact, in three days, they were nearly gone. The magic within him must have been strong that such wounds should heal so quickly.

As for Meren's wing…it would be a while yet before she could fly. Delicate wings would take a lot longer to heal than flesh and bone. But the longing to feel the wind on her face had begun to take its toll. She was on edge, grumpy, which was why she supposed she had found the gumption to bark such an abrupt question.

"Are you avoiding the question?" she prodded as he kept his back to her, working diligently on a pot that was more than sufficiently cleaned. She thumbed through one of the many books from his library that she had been reading. This one was a book of the mortal prophecies.

A queen in the shadows
Who will bring forth the light
A king's song sung through the night
On the wings of eagles they would fly
That the way for the promised one *would be made.*

A queen in the shadows…weren't they all living in the shadows these days?

"You ask a loaded question, Tipharah," Fa said, interrupting her thoughts.

She closed the ancient book in her hands. "I was told you are the Gibhor—a legend. A Warrior færy. But I was under the impression that the warriors had died out with the last of the true king's sons."

Fa's back tightened, his shoulders stiff as he paused his work. He dumped the last of the boiled water over the pot and set it back on the hook over the fire to dry before he responded. "You are not wrong about that. The king's line was the last of the Warriors."

"Why did my coven leader think you would help us, then?"

"I don't know," he admitted, at last turning to face her. He came to sit by her on the cushions in his sitting area. "Perhaps he was mistaken."

"He was not mistaken. He was certain of who you were and how you could help us. I think the only mistake he made was underestimating your stubbornness."

To that, Fa laughed. "Perhaps, Tipharah."

"Tell me your story, then," she said. And she meant it genuinely—she simply wanted to know more about him.

Perhaps Fa sensed that, for to her surprise, he said, "Well, what do you want to know?"

"Do you have parents?"

"No," he said, looking down, fiddling with a thread on his pants. "They are dead."

It wasn't just ache she saw in him, in the slump of his shoulders. It was something else. Something that looked a lot like rage. She wondered if it was wise to keep asking questions. For some reason, she did. "What happened to them?"

"My father was murdered. Mother…" He stopped fiddling with the thread long enough to look up at her. He searched her face for a moment before he turned his attention elsewhere, looking at nothing in particular. "My mother died of a broken heart."

"Who broke her heart?" she asked.

"My father."

"Did he not love her?"

"Did your parents love each other?" he asked sardonically. "Do færies ever love each other for any amount of time?"

"My parents loved each other very much. To the day they died, they were in love," Meren said, a need to defend them rising in her like the tide coming in to the sea.

Fa's eyes were sad. Achingly haunted. She wanted to reach out, to touch him, to comfort him. But she kept her hands to herself.

"Then your parents were the exception," he said. "My father was a whoremonger, among many other things. Murderer. Liar. He kept my mother in a gilded cage, just close enough that she could never leave him and just far enough away that he could dabble about with whatever harlot he wanted without complaint. He was a bastard if ever there was one."

"What happened to him?" Meren asked, surprised at the ache she felt when she saw the deep sorrow in Fa's eyes.

"He got what was coming to him. We all did."

Meren glanced at Fa's wings, her cheeks heating instantly when she realized he had seen her. She looked down, fiddling with her fingers as he went on.

"There are a great many things I regret in my life. Thinking for one moment that I should hope to be anything like my father tops the list."

"Do you have any other family?"

"Not blood, no. I had six younger brothers—half brothers, the lot of them—sons of my father's whores. They were all killed too. I am the only one who survived."

I am not one of the ones they want alive. His words echoed in her mind. Who were *they*? And why didn't they want him alive?

"Survived what?" she asked.

He met her eyes. And it felt like an eternity before he finally said, "The Dark færies, Meren."

"That is why you hunt them."

"That is why I scout to keep them at bay. If they come anywhere near this place, their life is forfeit."

"Good," she said.

"You keep saying that. As if murder is ever justified."

"The Darkness; it is spreading, Fa. Anything to stop it is justified in my book."

"Then your book is as noble as it is naïve."

"Is that why you won't help me? Why you hole yourself up in here like a mole?"

"You don't know what they're capable of," Fa muttered.

"Don't I?" she shouted. "I watched my own parents' slaughter before my very eyes. I have been haunted by their dying pleas all of my life. I, for one, am keenly aware of what the Dark færies are capable of, Fa. But unlike you, I don't want to keep hiding away, hoping they'll disappear. I want to stop them. I came to you hoping you'd want to help me. But perhaps Asher was right. Perhaps you won't help me after all."

She stood, storming off to the footholds at the edge of the room. Footholds that led her to the bed at the next level. Fa did not stop her.

~

The next morning, she did not wake to the familiar smells of breakfast nor the bustle of her companion. She woke to silence. She sat up in the bed, too soft for its own good, wincing at the pain that lanced her wing. She rubbed her shoulder for good measure as she looked around Fa's home. He was nowhere to be found.

Fine.

Coward.

She spotted a note at the table below. So she climbed down the footholds and marched across the space, snapping up the small parchment.

There is some bread in the cupboard.

That was it. That was his note. She tore it up and flung it on the floor, huffing and pacing about, completely uninterested in the bread. Or water. Or anything else.

He wouldn't help her. He was a bitter old bastard who would rather hide away like everyone else than help her. For a moment—for a brief moment, she had thought he might. When she saw those wounds on his back and arms, when she realized his strength and the determination with which he had fought. She had thought that maybe he would help her after all. Come back with her. Help her coven find a way to stop the Darkness from spreading.

But she had been terribly wrong.

Fa was gone all day.

~

It was not until after dusk that he returned, and while he was a little worse for wear, he bore no visible wounds. So she ignored him as he shuffled about his home, though it was soon clear that he was busy making dinner, the smells taking over the place.

She huffed in frustration, unwilling to allow herself to be lured once more by his stupid talent in the kitchen. So she marched herself outside and perched on the branch that jutted from his doorway.

She had been there for the better part of an hour before he bothered to check on her. The fireflies danced lazily in the darkness of the forest, crickets singing their nighttime sonnets when she felt him sit down beside her.

And then she smelled it.

Her eyes fastened on the source of the smell—the steaming bowl he was extending to her. Toadstool soup.

A peace offering.

"You seemed to like it when I first gave it to you," he said. She did not take the bowl even though he continued to hold it out to her. "So I thought I would make you some more."

She crossed her arms and turned away, hating how tempted she was by how good it smelled.

Fine. She was being petulant. And ridiculous. But one bowl of soup didn't change the fact that he was being just as petulant and ridiculous.

"I'm sorry I upset you, Meren," Fa tried. And in his words, his voice, she could tell he genuinely meant it. "I know you know what they're capable of. And it was stupid of me to suggest otherwise."

She uncrossed her arms, but she still did not look at him. The night wind caressed her face, tossing an unruly curl into her eyes. She brushed it away with a huff.

She heard him puff a breath.

"Are you laughing at me?" she nearly barked, finally turning to face him.

"You just might be as stubborn as you are determined, Meren. I find it charming."

He was still extending the bowl to her. And it felt impertinent not to take it. So she did. And nearly moaned when she sipped the first spoonful.

"You like toadstool soup," he said, sipping from his own spoon.

"My mother used to make it for me all the time. It was always my favorite."

"I'll have to remember that," he said, his eyes fixed on the forest around them as he ate.

She watched him for a moment. He was at home perched in this tree. Comfortable. At ease. Beautiful in his own way. Yes, he was as beautiful as he was stubborn.

Her eyes fell back to her bowl when he turned to look at her.

They ate in silence on the branch of the tree.

Chapter XI

She woke the next morning to the sounds of breakfast being prepared below—the steady *chop chop chop* of a knife, the clank of a spoon against a cauldron.

"What are you making?" she asked, braving the little footholds that she might come down from the platform on her own.

Fa turned to face her, dashing across the room in a streak of silver light, offering her his hand as she made her way down.

"I would have brought you down, Tipharah," he said.

"I'm not helpless, you know." She huffed.

He cocked his head to one side. "Why would you assume I think you're helpless simply because I offered to help you down?"

She paused, looking him over. There was no mockery, no ulterior motive in his words. Just a simple observation to which she had no answer.

"Come," he said, ignoring the puzzled look on her face. "You need to eat."

"Why?" she asked, following him across the room, the delectable smells of breakfast luring her like a moth to a flame. A spread of breads, fruits, nuts, and honey with the comb lay before them on the table.

"Because we're going to fly today."

We. Not she. *We.*

When she narrowed her eyes, he wiggled his silver-white brows and sat down.

She sat down across from him and asked, "Do you always eat like this?"

"Like what?" he asked, offering her a piece of buttered bread.

She gestured to the spread in front of them before accepting the bread. "Like a king." She smirked.

He met her eyes, gobbling up the joke with a searing gaze that went on for far too long before he relaxed his shoulders and simply said, "How would you suggest I eat, pray tell?"

She stifled the urge to moan at the floral sweetness of the honey. "Don't you ever just find something in the forest and call it a meal?"

"I have been known to do so on occasion," he said, a smile ghosting over his mouth. "But I find it rather boring as a habit."

She took a bite of fruit, sipping on her tea and observing him the way he ate—meticulously. Brutally methodical. Every bite precise, every movement refined. As if summers and summers of training had honed him into a masterpiece.

A real, bonafide Warrior færy.

"How exactly are we going to fly?" she asked, avoiding his eyes. She didn't dare finish that question—what would she have said? *With my broken wings and your tatters.* No, she wouldn't say that aloud.

"I told you, Tipharah. We're going to catch the Wind." He took a bite of bread, and she could have sworn she saw savage amusement dance in his eyes.

~

"This is your idea of flying?" She balked, crossing her arms. "Jumping off of a limb?" The breeze tossed a curl across her brow, kissing her face and her wings with the promise of winter. She brushed the curl away with a huff.

Fa only chuckled. "Don't tell me you're scared, Tipharah."

"Why do you keep calling me that?" she barked.

"Because it suits you," was his only response as he observed the drop below them, seeming to measure the wind, his keen eyes scouring the trees—likely for any signs of Dark færies roaming about.

"It's the old language, isn't it?" she asked, softening at the mesmerizing way he observed the world around them. *Fascinating* was the only word she could find to describe him. Plain and simple, he was fascinating.

He turned to face her. "You know the language?"

"I recognize it." She shrugged, turning toward the forest around them, taking in the view of the shimmering leaves, the streaming sunlight as it poured like a golden river from the canopy. The air was crisp today. Brisk. A premature winter kissed the wind, sending a rush of shivers down her spine that had nothing to do with the cold.

With the early winter came the Darkness.

"Yes, it's the old language," he said, though she could still feel his eyes all over her. "Do you speak it?"

She shook her head. "Not really. There are few who do, Fa." She faced him again before she said, "I take it you do."

He gave her a single nod, his eyes fixed on her. Sometimes it seemed as if he could see right through her. Straight to her very soul.

Perhaps he could.

"Are you going to tell me what it means?" she asked, ignoring that strange voice that spoke to her sometimes when he was near.

He only smiled. And Eloah help her if it wasn't beautiful, this enigma before her. This scarred warrior who woke her with a fresh meal every morning. Who killed without qualms and yet helped her as if it were his responsibility. Yes, his smile was beautiful. A work of art unto itself.

So she smiled back.

He only extended his hand and said, "Not today. Today, Tipharah, you're going to learn to catch the Wind."

She eyed his extended hand reluctantly. "How exactly am I going to do that?"

He did not move his hand, though she had not taken it. "You're going to jump. And I'm going to jump with you."

"Is this that flying thing you do?"

He nodded. "It is not flying, not really."

"So does that mean we can fall?"

Another nod. "If we fell from high enough, we wouldn't be able to stop. Not without wings."

She peered over the edge of the fat branch on which they stood. "And… are we high enough?"

His savage grin was answer enough.

"Have you lost your mind?" she spat.

"A long time ago," he said, taking hold of her hand despite her not reaching out. His grip was firm. Confident.

At least one of them was.

She swallowed and peered over the edge again. "How do I do this, exactly?"

"Feel it within you, Meren."

She shut her eyes, concentrating, the ice-kissed wind tossing her choppy locks. She brushed that nuisance curl from her brow once more.

"You're not concentrating," Fa said. "Let the Wind speak to you."

"Speak to me?" she protested, her eyes still closed. "What exactly does it have to say? 'Nice to meet you?'"

He squeezed her hand in reprimand, and while he did not chuckle, she could hear a smile in his words as he said, "Focus, Meren."

So she did. Or tried, anyway, though whatever it was she was supposed to be listening for did not caress her ears. She squinted her eyes shut, pushing out any thoughts that might distract. But still, she heard nothing but the breeze and an errant bird chirping in the morning light.

"Do you feel it?" he asked.

She glanced at him, shaking her head.

"Try again."

"What exactly am I listening for?" She huffed.

"I cannot tell you that, Meren. It is different for each of us—our giftings from Eloah never manifest the same way. But you will know it when you hear it."

She wondered then if that voice that spoke to her whenever he was around—was that the same voice she was listening for in the wind?

If it was, that voice was silent.

He squeezed her hand again. "Focus," he commanded.

She huffed a sigh, squeezing her eyes shut again, listening…listening…

"I don't hear anything."

"You're not listening, Meren."

"I *am,*" she snapped, her eyes still closed tightly.

"Listen harder."

"What does that even mean?"

"The Light—it is bright within you, Meren. I have felt it. Listen for it. Learn its voice."

"I can wield a few balls of færy light, Fa. That's about it. I don't—"

"Færy light?" he asked. "You can wield the Flame?"

She opened her eyes, sliding them to him. "Is that so strange?"

But Fa's thoughts were somewhere else, his eyes fixated on nothing and yet everything.

"Fa?" she tried again. "What's so strange about færy light?"

"Nothing," he said, shaking his head once, his eyes focusing once more.

"But why did you—"

"You're stalling, Meren. *Listen.*"

"I don't even know what—"

But before she could finish that thought, she found herself free-falling off of the side of the branch. No, not falling. She had been *pulled* off. By Fa.

"What in all of Sheol is wrong with you?" she yelled as they careened down the side of the towering tree. Instinctively, she reached for his other hand, grabbing it as if it would help. The bark of the tree was little more than a blur of brown and green as they sped toward the ground.

"Catch the Wind, Meren," he simply said, holding her hands securely in his.

"I can't!" she panted over the ferocious wind whipping past them. "Have you lost your mind?"

"Like I said, a long time ago."

The air tore past their bodies, whipping his silver-and-black hair wildly about his brow, his tattered wings flapping with unearthly beauty behind him, impossible shades of silver and opal shimmering in the sunlight. Her own hair flapped uselessly into her eyes as they fell, her heart having found a new home in her throat.

"Is this your way of killing me off?"

"Do you enjoy small talk while free-falling to your death, Meren?"

She stuck out her tongue before she closed her eyes tightly, listening desperately for any sound, any whisper of the *Wind* Fa spoke of. Her heart pounded mercilessly, a death drum signaling the end of her useless life.

But then…

It was gentle. Subtle at first, but even as the ground swelled dangerously closer, she felt it. Calling to her. Caressing her soul in a lover's touch. A caress of magic and Light. Fa…he was…

"Open your eyes, Tipharah."

Reluctantly, slowly, she opened her eyes, only to realize—

"Are you doing this?" she breathed, in awe.

He only shook his head, a smile hovering on his mouth.

They weren't flying. In fact, they were still falling. Just at a *much* reduced speed. Like an autumn leaf might fall to the ground. Albeit a *heavy* leaf. "We're still going to die, aren't we?" she asked.

But Fa only chuckled, and that's when she felt it—his magic kissing her own. Mingling. Melding. Forging.

And then they were flying. No, not flying. Because they couldn't fly. But…they could soar. An eagle floating on a phantom wind. The earth suddenly fell away from them again, the branch from which they had jumped growing closer and closer…

"How are you doing that?" she asked, unabashed by the wonder in her voice.

"I'm not, Meren. *We* are." She could have sworn there was a little wonder in his voice, too.

"Did you…did you know we could do this?"

He only shook his head, his eyes finding her own again. They soared higher and higher until at last they reached the branch, landing with fluid grace on the rough bark.

She looked at him for a moment. Just looked. In awe as much by what had just happened as she was by the look on his face: wonder mingled with something else. Something that looked a lot like approval.

"Does magic work like that?" she asked. "Does it always work *together* like that?" Not once had her magic ever *spoken* to Asher's the way it had to Fa's…

He shook his head, but that was his only reply as his gaze remained steadfastly on her.

So she pushed him. Hard. The bastard deserved it for taking such a risk. For not telling her what he knew…and what he *didn't* know. For tricking her.

She had not meant to push him off the branch. She really hadn't. But she did.

And unadulterated terror coursed through her very soul as she watched him fall from this height so high that his Wind alone could not save him.

She jumped without hesitation, careening herself with as much speed as she could muster, the forest surging past her in a blur of autumnal fauna, until she was face to face with him, body to body. She wrapped her arms around him, calling on that Wind, beckoning it.

But this time, she did not feel it.

"Do not let fear defeat you, Tipharah," he said calmly. As if death did not scare him.

But still, the Wind did not answer her. And fear choked her, slowly and surely.

"Fa, help me!" she cried desperately, undeterred by how tightly she clung to him.

But that's when she realized—he *was* helping her. He was already using his Wind. They weren't falling as quickly.

But they were still falling. And if she didn't figure out—

Fa's arms came around her, and her eyes flew open, taken aback at just how close he was—his breath mingling with her own, his eyes locked on her. She could feel it, his Wind. It called to her. Spoke to her.

Yes, it seemed to say. *Yes.*

And her Wind—it answered. Instinctively, it answered him. Gracefully, effortlessly, they landed on their feet on the loamy forest floor.

"I'm sorry," she began, pushing out of his arms the moment they landed. "I'm so sorry, Fa. I didn't mean to—"

"Tipharah," he said, stepping towards her. "You did it."

It was the pride, pure and unabashed in his voice, that caught her attention. He wasn't angry at her, he was…he was proud of her!

"I could have killed you!" she protested.

A smile slowly curled his mouth even as he reached between them and took her hand in his. Not with a firm grip this time but a gentle touch. "This coming from the female who even a few days ago would have been glad to see me die." He chuckled.

"You're a terrible teacher," she fumed. He only laughed more, a sparkle in his black eyes that seemed to come from somewhere deep within.

"You're a quick learner. It takes most færies years to master that."

"You could have died! *I* could have died!" she cried, wondering why in the world he had risked his life—and her own—in such a flippant way.

"I will not let you die, Tipharah," he said. And the sincerity, the finality with which he said it…

She met his eyes again, suddenly flustered at his hand still wrapped around hers, at the way he was looking at her.

She dropped his hand and turned away, pushing a shaky hand through her wind-tossed hair. She took a deep breath. Another. Near death was… Well, it was…

"Don't tell me you've lost your gumption, Meren," he said from behind her.

She turned slowly on her heel, narrowing her eyes on him. "You're insane."

He only wiggled his brows.

"I fail to understand your obsession with tempting death," she growled, turning away from him. She crossed her arms over her chest, exhaling a frustrated breath.

She didn't hear him step up to her, didn't even realize he had moved from his spot until she felt his hand on her arm. "I know I scared you," he said. She cut her eyes over her shoulder at the apology in his tone. "But death will not come courteously; she will not come with a smile on her face. The Dark færies—"

"I know about the Dark færies," she said, cutting him off.

He searched her for a moment. "I know you do."

And the way he said it… She believed him. She believed that he thought her brave. That this little experiment with the Wind hadn't been for the sole purpose of scaring her.

It had been to prepare her. Not to run from the Darkness.

But to face it.

"Let's go again," she said at last, turning to face him fully.

His smile was broad and wickedly delighted.

Chapter XII

They soared and glided endlessly for three days. Through the forest, threading through the branches like needles, through open fields of wheat bowing low in the autumn winds as if worshipping Eloah himself. They stopped only to eat and sleep, and then every morning just as the sun began her march across the skies, they were back out again, gliding and soaring and experimenting with the magic that apparently flowed wild and free through her veins.

In a word, it was glorious. The freedom, the thought that for once she was actually doing something, learning something useful, not hiding—it was intoxicating.

She caught a glimpse of her reflection in the water below them—a small pool nestled deep in the forest. The wind had made her curls particularly unruly, and she rolled her eyes at her unkempt reflection, at just how utterly plain she was. Nothing like Shira—Shira with her perfectly sunshine-gold locks, Shira with her smile that could light up the whole coven.

The thought of her coven sent a pang of worry down her gut. Were they all right? Had what attacked her and Asher found the coven? And what of Asher? Had he indeed made it home? Was he alive?

And if he was, would he be looking for her?

The pool over which they glided wasn't terribly large. But it was much wider than any attempt they had yet made to catch the Wind in such a way. They had leapt laps over the placid pool for the better part of the day, one after the other, testing and training, really. Durability. It would be key in any fight she might face against the Dark færies. So she did not balk. She did not protest as Fa insisted they go again and again. But she was getting tired, her wings instinctively trying to keep her aloft where her magic wavered.

"You all right?" Fa asked, gliding alongside her, focusing his attention on her at the wince that had inadvertently come out of her mouth.

"Sorry. Yes. My wing, it just—"

"Here," he said, grabbing her hand, guiding her on the Wind to the sandy bank. She landed with an unbecoming plop, her wing aching with pain and fatigue.

He knelt beside her, his keen eyes scouring her wing, his deft hands gentle explorers of the delicate membrane. She shut her eyes at the sensation, at the care with which he attended her.

"Maybe we should call it a day," Fa offered.

"Have I made it worse?" she asked.

"Not that I can see. But why don't we take—"

"I don't want to take a break," she said, abruptly standing and jumping into the air again, sending her body soaring over the water once more. The Darkness would not take a break. Why should she?

Fa did not argue as she had expected him to, did not soar alongside her with a barrage of retorts. Instead, he just joined her in the misty air above the forest pool and resumed their relentless exploration of the possibilities of their combined Wind magic. Flying. Without wings. Well, not really flying. But gliding for long periods of time, anyway. It was exhausting. But a useful tool, to be sure.

But then… "What is that?" he asked.

"What do you mean?"

"That. The water," Fa said, pointing below her.

Sure enough, the water parted beneath her, a perfectly curled wave in the wake of her flight.

"I don't know," she said, shrugging. "Is that strange? Does the water not react to you?"

But she looked beneath him and realized…the water below him was smooth, as placid as a looking glass.

He gave her an incredulous look. "My magic is the Wind. So is yours. All færies have magic, but it manifests in one of the elements—Wind, Water, or Flame. The Dark færies—most of them have the magic of Flame. They revere the fire as if it is superior. They are drawn to each other—moths to that Flame, if you will. But the færies of the Light—most have forgotten the magic within them. And so the Wind and the Waters have been forgotten. Left up to Eloah to manage."

The elements. The magic gifted to the færies from Eloah. Forgotten, save for a few.

And for the Darkness.

"I've never heard of a færy having more than one element," Fa went on. "Much less all three."

"All three! I do not have all three!" she said incredulously. She did *not* have the magic of the Dark færies, thank you very much!

"You said you could make a ball of færy light, didn't you?"

Yes. Yes, she had. So could most of her coven. But…they were *good* færies.

"Fret not, Tipharah," Fa said, a smile ghosting his mouth. "It is not the Flame that is corrupted, but the wielders of it."

Oh.

Yes, of course. But still…all three? The færies had elemental magic?

And she had all *three*?

Perhaps her Flame—perhaps that had drawn those Dark færies to her…

"That was the purpose for the færies," Fa went on, ignoring her shock. "That was the reason we were made—to call upon the very elements of the Light of Eloah. His magic. The mortals call it weather. The seasons. Storms. But it is the magic of Eloah. And it is the job of the færies to carry it.

"Or it *was*, anyway," he said. "Before we forgot who we are. Before we forgot everything. But each of us, we have been gifted with one of the elements of Light: the Wind, the Water, or the Flame. And each færy has a certain proclivity for one. But not three. Never all three."

"Never?" she asked.

"I've never heard of anyone with all three, Tipharah."

"And you think that's what I have?"

"It's in you, yes. Whether you know it or not. The Light shines brightly within you."

She hadn't even realized that she had landed on the opposite shore of the pool until her feet hit the soft sand. She stared blankly before her, taking in all that Fa was saying.

All three elements. Wind. Water. Flame.

She had all three within her.

Fa put his hand on her shoulder, and when at last she met his eyes, she did not see fear there. Nor did she see worry. She only saw the kindness of a friend and the hint of a smile. "Let's get you home, Tipharah. You've done enough today."

Home. Yes.

Home. She wondered why she hadn't missed the coven more. Had it ever really been home for her?

He took her by the hand, and they walked—walked, not glided— the whole way back to his house in the tree.

~

She couldn't sleep. It was ridiculous—as tired as she was, as full as her belly was from the meal Fa had insisted on making her even though it was obvious he was as tired as she was, she couldn't fall asleep. Her wing ached in protest, stealing any chance she might have had of sleeping soundly. So she tossed and turned, trying to find new positions that wouldn't agitate the wing. But none of them worked for very long.

Somewhere in the darkness of his home, Fa surely slept soundly, his body cooperating after such a taxing day. But not her. Of course. Not her.

She was startled then, when she sensed the presence of someone behind her. She rolled over quickly, her heart pounding, only to find Fa sitting down on the edge of her bed, a tin in his hand.

"Can't sleep?" he asked.

"My wing, it—"

"I know," he said, and even in the darkness, she could see the understanding lingering in his eyes. She stole a glance at his tattered wings before he said, "Roll over."

She warily eyed the tin in his hand but obeyed nonetheless, breathing deeply of the sudden scent of herbs kissing her nose.

Balm. It was the same balm she had used on his arm and back only a few days ago. The herbs pungent and earthy, but refreshing and crisp and familiar… She sucked in a breath at the cool sensation on her wing, turning slightly to watch him.

"You've used this before," she said.

Fa said nothing, continuing his wordless application of the silky balm.

"You've used this on me every night, haven't you." It was not a question. Not really. "While I'm asleep."

He huffed a small laugh, and she could have sworn there was a hint of red crawling up his cheeks. "Well, you were *only* asleep when I first brought you here. And then when you woke and decided that I was probably poisoning you, I didn't figure you'd trust me with herbs."

"So you waited every night until I was asleep to apply a healing balm to my wing?"

He shrugged, as if it were nothing. "I know how painful that kind of wound can be," he said, finishing the sentence softly.

She took hold of his hand on her wing, grasping his fingers. "Fa," she breathed. "Thank you."

He merely shook his head, removing his fingers from hers after a moment so that he might continue kneading, working the balm over her weary wing, her aching shoulders.

And it hit her. Shame colored her cheeks that she hadn't realized this before, had been too selfish to even think of it. "Is this your bed?" she asked, looking—finally—around the little nook in which her bed was situated. The shelves peppering the walls, covered in books and tchotchkes, personal effects. This was…this was Fa's bedroom.

"Where are you sleeping, Fa?" she protested, exasperated, appalled at herself for not having thought of it before now. He had given up his room. He had given up his own bed for her.

"Down there." He gestured with his head, even as he continued to apply the balm.

"Down there? On the cushions?"

"They're quite comfortable, Tipharah." He chuckled.

"Fa," she said, moving to sit up. "You cannot give up your bed!"

He gently tried to guide her back down. "You need to rest, Meren."

"But your bed, Fa! I cannot ask you to give it up!"

"It is yours, Meren. For as long as you need it."

But she ignored his attempts to convince her to lie back down and instead sat up fully, taking the tin from his hands and setting it aside. She took hold of his hands in her own, looking down at them as she said, "I don't know why you've been so kind to me." She looked back up, meeting his eyes. "I don't know what I've done to deserve it."

But Fa said nothing, too distracted by their joined hands, his thumbs tentatively brushing over the backs of hers. So she leaned forward, toward him. And when his eyes locked on hers, she decided to press a simple kiss to his lips. A thank you.

Magic flared between them, bright and true. *Home,* the familiar voice said, the world clanging through her even as her lips left his.

Home.

She held his gaze, his eyes conveying nothing even though her heart thundered wildly in her chest. Surely he could hear it.

Home.

Fa said nothing before he stood, turned on his heel, and disappeared into the darkness below.

Chapter XIII

It was that damned curl.

That's what he told himself as he walked briskly through the forest, the leaves already turning colors and falling with the premature winter settling in. He wrapped his mouse-hide fur more tightly around his shoulders and walked on, gliding here and there over little ponds and crags. Thanks to Meren, he had gotten much better at it, what with her insistence on practicing all hours of every day.

Eloah, that female.

For what felt like the thousandth time, Fa wondered why in the world he had brought her into his home to begin with, much less why he hadn't kicked her out yet.

And for the love of Eloah, he had no idea why he had let her kiss him last night.

She shouldn't have. He damn well shouldn't have let her.

But she had. And Eloah damn him…

It was probably that ridiculous curl. The way it refused to fall anywhere but across her brow—the one place that drove her insane.

He had found himself transfixed by that copper-and-cobalt curl every time he looked at it.

Fa growled, a short, miffed sort of sound as he made his way through the forest. Far away from her.

~

"Aha!" said a familiar voice as he emerged into the underground cave. Illuminated with nothing more than færy lights, the place had always had a certain eeriness to it. But that eeriness was nothing compared to its occupant.

"Melekfa! How I have missed you, my old friend," said the færy, his watery gaze no less formidable with age.

The legends spoke of færy perdurability. But so few had ever lived long enough to find out if they were true, the war claiming too many long before their time and the Darkness claiming the rest. But if Nabi was any indication, then perhaps the immortality of færykind was no myth. Aging, however, was another story.

The ancient færy flew with a frailty that betrayed his age, his thin wings seemingly incapable of keeping him aloft. But they did. And Nabi landed with preternatural grace before Fa, a smile on his frail mouth. He clasped a heavy hand on the younger færy's shoulder. "How are you, Melekfa?"

Melekfa. No one called him that anymore. Not since his father had died. It was a name Fa had no intention of living up to. A name he had abandoned, along with everything else in his life.

"I am well, Nabi," said Fa, kissing the old male on both cheeks.

A greeting typically reserved for family. Fitting, perhaps, considering Nabi was the only person Fa had ever really considered family.

Except for his mother.

"What brings you here?" Nabi asked, turning back toward the ornate seat on the edge of the room. A single seat, expertly carved from the roots that grew deep into the ground here. Nabi insisted it was not a throne, despite the fact that it bore a striking resemblance to one. It had always made Fa laugh—the presumption to sit in such a seat, when the king of the færies was such a far cry from this man before him.

Nabi sat down, his hands shaking, age having robbed him of his former glory but not his fearsomeness. Not his formidableness.

Nabi should have been a king.

"I'm surprised you're even asking me that question," Fa said, standing before his old friend. Nabi always seemed to know exactly when Fa would come. And why. It was part of his gifts.

A mischievous smirk curled the old male's mouth. "I ask for the simple reason that I want to know why *you* think you're here."

"Why do *you* think I'm here?" Fa asked, crossing his arms.

"It is written all over you, my son," said Nabi.

"Is that so?" Fa smirked, knowing Nabi was baiting him.

"Indeed," said the old male, undaunted. "You want to know if it's true."

"Well," Fa said. "Is it?"

Nabi cocked his head to the side, the ornate cuffs of metal running along his pointed ears catching the light. "What do you think?"

Fa already knew the answer. Deep down, he knew it well. But he had come here today to see if Nabi did too. Judging by the look on his face—that smug smirk he always got when he knew his predictions had been correct—he knew. *Damn him.*

"I can't do this, Nabi."

"Why?"

"Because…" Because she was better than this, that's what. Nabi had told him a thousand times this day would come. And Fa hadn't really believed him. But the moment he had met her, the moment he had seen her standing there in the forest, looking for all the world like she would tear him into ribbons, he had known.

In his gut, he had known the truth.

And it had scared the shit out of him then just as it scared the shit out of him now.

"Tell me, Melekfa. What would your mother think?"

His mother.

He had done everything within his power not to think of her, not to remember her. The last time he had seen her—

But there she was, standing before him as if she were a ghost. Her smile lazy and mischievous, her silver hair falling in polished curls around her shoulders, a sparkle in her gold eyes to match the sparkle of the ornate cuffs that decorated her delicately pointed ears. His mother and Nabi had been the only two people in the world who didn't look at him like a mistake. Like a waste of breath.

Until now.

He knew exactly what his mother would think. And that scared the shit out of him too.

"I can't do this, Nabi," Fa said, turning his back on his friend and pacing the vast room.

"You seem to be under the impression you have a choice."

"Maybe I don't. But she does. And—"

"As in all things, Melekfa, it is both a choice and a compulsion. We are led to places we are meant to go, but it is still our choice whether we put one foot in front of the other. That is the enigma of Eloah."

"You're making no sense."

"The truth, Melekfa, is never a choice. It is always truth whether we like it or not. The only part that is a choice is whether we will believe or not believe."

"She is…she is too good. For all of this."

"She wants to fight. Is that not why she sought you out?"

How Nabi knew that…how he knew *any* of it… It shouldn't surprise him, not anymore.

But it still did.

Fa whirled to face Nabi again. "This is not her war to fight. She… she's too good, too pure for this mess."

A chuckle. "Were you hoping your B'sheirt would be less?"

Fa froze like a stag on alert. *B'sheirt.* He had known it, but hearing it, hearing the word…

Something tugged on his soul at the sound of it.

No, not something, *someone.* Someone close by.

Fa turned to face the entrance of the vast cave, breaking into a sprint.

B'sheirt.

After all this time, all these years, all those mistakes and lies, murders…

B'sheirt.

The word was a gong ringing loud and clear, singing through his bones.

He could not run fast enough.

<h1 style="text-align:center">Chapter XIV</h1>

He was angry with her.

He had to be.

It was the only explanation for why he was all but silent at breakfast, why he suddenly said he 'had somewhere to go' as soon as they finished eating, why he disappeared without another word.

He was angry with her for that kiss.

She hadn't meant anything by it. Truly. It had been offered in gratitude, nothing more.

But it had become more.

She had felt magic strong and pure between them. And she wondered what it meant. Wondered what he had been thinking when he just…stood. Stood and went to bed without a word.

Oddly enough, even though he had been gone for more than an hour, she had still sensed him. Sensed his presence nearby. He hadn't gone far, that much was apparent. Until now.

Now…now she could not sense him, could not feel his constant presence nearby—the thrum of his heart, the steady cadence of his soul whispering, pulling at her soul.

She could not feel him anymore.

And it was eating her alive.

She had first thought she would ignore it. That it probably meant he had just gone far enough that she could no longer sense his nearness.

But he had left her many mornings before—to scout for Dark færies, even to look for Asher. And no doubt he had gone quite far on those excursions. Surely he had not stayed so close to his home all this time.

So why could she no longer feel him now?

Then again, why could she feel his presence at all? And why now that it was gone, did she feel an aching void she could hardly bear?

She had no idea where she was going. She had no idea why she was going at all.

But as Meren called on the Wind, as she let it guide her down the side of his tree, she knew she had to find Fa, broken wing be damned.

~

It was like a thread. That was the only way she could describe it. She was being drawn through the forest like her soul had been tied to a thread. Where she was going, she couldn't say. The terrain was as unfamiliar as it was unforgiving. But just like the very first day she had met Fa, something deep and unreachable pulled her, drew her. For reasons she didn't understand, Meren followed that pulling through increasingly denser brambles, occasionally calling on the Wind to carry her over dangerous roots and crags, toying with the water in pools and streams, making little droplets converge into spheres large enough to do some harm. But never—never touching the magic of Flame within her.

And all the while, she wondered where in the world she was going.

~

It was a cave. Or at least something like a cave. Deep within the forest, the brush so dense the sunlight did not penetrate, Meren found herself staring down the mouth of a cave. Magic—it *buzzed* here. Not just the thread she followed, but…more. Older magic.

Deeper.

Like a fool, she stuck her head into the cave.

"Hello?" she called, but the only answer was the echo of her voice.

So she went inside.

The cave was small—only large enough for a field mouse or perhaps small rabbits. But it was not overgrown or riddled with spiderwebs, which was either a good sign or a bad one—she couldn't decide. Bobbing blue færy lights kissed the ceiling of the cave every now and then, giving off just enough light to show the next few steps, but little more.

She walked gingerly over the soft dirt, looking for any sign of whatever it was she thought she would find down here. What was she looking for? She was following nothing more than instinct, a gut feeling.

Ridiculous, really. What with all the Dark færies that lurked about these woods, she could be walking right into a trap.

Maybe she was.

But she could feel *him* again. She could feel Fa. Intermingled with that old magic, she could feel her friend—his simmering power, warm like a summer evening, kissed with a hint of irony and a healthy dose of tenacity that she had grown to both admire and despise.

It was with a grin curling her mouth that she walked on. Determined to find him, to apologize for the mess she had made. Resolved to set things right with this male who had taken her in, who had shown her a kindness she had not deserved.

The cave was eerily silent—no sounds of scurrying creatures, no hint of any family of rodents that might call this cave home. Nothing. Nothing but…

Was that mumbling?

Down and down, further into the cave, she could have sworn she heard the distant sounds of a conversation.

She walked a little faster, her heart thrumming in time with the pace she kept, wondering what she was hearing. Wondering if she had lost her mind.

Perhaps Fa had rubbed off on her after spending so many days around him.

The thought curled the grin on her mouth into a full-fledged smile.

And then the cave tunnel rounded a bend and…

Lights. Thousands of lights. Færy lights. Flame so hot it was blue, converging, pointing to an opening on the other side. This place—it was unlike anything she had ever seen.

And the magic here was unstoppable.

She ran through the corridor of lights, in awe at the preternatural glow, the ancient magic that thrummed here like blood through veins.

She ran and ran until she smacked into…

"Fa!" she exclaimed, trying to right herself. The collision had almost knocked her over.

Fa caught her before she toppled like a stalk of snapped wheat, his large hands wrapped around her arms, steadying her.

"Sorry, I—"

"Meren. What are you doing here?" Fa asked, a mixture of wonder and horror in his eyes.

"Fa, I came to apologize. I never meant to—"

"Apologize? For what?"

"For last night." His eyes narrowed, but she swallowed and pressed on, determined to say what she had come to say, no matter how awkward. "I never meant to—I mean, if I offended you in any way…"

"Tipharah," he said, his countenance softening. His hands still warm around her arms, he squeezed them gently. "You don't owe me an apology."

"I do," she protested. "I didn't mean—I mean, I never meant—it meant nothing!" she stammered. "Truly, I—I meant nothing by that kiss; it was just—it was nothing."

"Nothing," Fa echoed in agreement. "Of course. Yes." He let go of her arms, stepping back a fraction. "Nothing. Of course, I—yes, of course."

"Fa," she tried, her voice small, her thoughts scrambled.

"It was nothing, Meren," he interjected. "Think nothing of it."

He turned away from her, looking above them, a small, bobbing færy light catching his attention. They floated above his head in a steady pulse—a dance, a rhythm that seemed to match the heartbeat of this place.

"Where are we?" she asked, looking around, taking in the giant roots that plunged deep into the earth on either side of them, the færy lights illuminating shimmering, muddy walls, the air rife with the competing smells of flora and rot.

He at last turned to face her again, a sort of resolution to his eyes that hadn't been there a moment before.

"Come," he said, but he did not extend his hand. "There's someone I want you to meet."

~

It did not take long to venture deeper into the cave, the earthen walls growing narrower around them until at last they spilled into a giant room—if it could be called a room.

A sanctuary was more like it.

Shimmering pools of what looked like liquid starlight spread along the ground, reflecting and refracting the bobbing blue færy lights in a mesmerizing display. Roots as thick as tree trunks dug deeply into the earth in a tangled web, encircling the vast space on all sides. In the far corner, a waterfall careened down a particularly wide patch of roots, spilling into a glittering pool that fed a small stream.

And magic. Ancient and mysterious magic. In every corner, every step, every breath.

This place was unlike anywhere she had ever been.

And there, sitting on a throne at the end of the room, was perhaps the oldest færy she had ever seen.

"Ah," said the ancient færy. "Malkah Neharah. We have been

waiting a long time for you, dear one."

She turned to Fa, whose eyes had gone as wide as harvest moons as he observed the ancient færy.

"Malkah?" she whispered to Fa with a grin threatening her mouth. She elbowed his side, wondering if it was some nickname he hated. But Fa said nothing, made no indication that he had even heard her question.

"What's wrong, Melekfa?" the old færy asked with his own grin.

"*Nabi,*" Fa said through his teeth, warning shining in his black eyes. His tattered wings fluttered on a phantom wind behind him. Meren did everything within her power to keep from giggling. Whatever this færy wanted to tell her, Fa didn't want her to hear it. So of course she would make sure she did hear it.

"So, Malkah," the old færy said, turning his attention back to Meren. "What brought you here?"

She flashed her attention back to Fa upon the realization that the nickname was meant for *her,* not Fa. Fa only shrugged as he shook his head and rolled his eyes. "He's a seer, Tipharah," he said. "And a mouthy one at that."

The old færy merely chuckled. "They call me Nabi," he said. "I am glad of your presence here, Meren of the Light. But you have not answered my question."

Perhaps it was strange that a tiny færy should feel any smaller, but in that moment she felt minuscule in the presence of such a being, especially considering that for the life of her, she couldn't remember his question.

And he must have known that, for Nabi chuckled again and said, "What is it that brings you here, my dear?"

"Oh, I um…" she stammered, fiddling with her fingers, heat kissing her cheeks. "I couldn't fee—" She cleared her throat. *"Find* Fa. I didn't know where he had gone, and I—"

"No, my dear. Not here. What brought you to Fa in the first place?" Nabi asked kindly, genuine curiosity dancing in his eyes.

She looked to Fa, who merely smirked as he shook his head. "In addition to being mouthy, he's a nosy seer as well."

She turned her attention back to the old male. "I was looking," she said. "Looking for someone to help. And I had heard of a great warrior. The Gibhor." From the corner of her eye, she spotted Fa looking down at his feet, toeing a small stone on the ground.

"I see," said Nabi. "And so you found your Fa."

A nod was her only reply.

"Well then, Malkah Neharah," said Nabi, standing to his frail feet. His wings spread wide behind him, a network of iridescence and radiant energy in impossible shades of cerulean and amber and pearl. He flew gracefully to Meren, landing before her and Fa.

"Do you believe you have found what you are looking for?" he asked.

"Yes," she answered softly, not daring to look at Fa directly for fear of embarrassing him more. After last night…

"Then let us speak," said Nabi, nodding to Fa.

But Fa did not seem keen on the silent dismissal. "Nabi," he warned again through his teeth. Meren observed the peculiar exchange with a furrow to her brows and a tilt to her head, that nuisance curl of hers falling across her brow and into her line of sight. She pushed it away absently.

"Bobiqshh 'l t'shh 'tizh," said Fa, that warning still shining in his black eyes. The old language. They were speaking it fluently.

Nabi held the younger færy's gaze, undeterred. "Yn meh lacheshawsh, Melekfa."

"Shewm dibr ch'wts memk." Fa smirked, to which Nabi only chuckled.

"Have I ever given you reason to doubt me?" Nabi asked.

"Yes," said Fa matter-of-factly, crossing his arms, though Meren did not miss the hint of a smile that threatened her friend's eyes. But then he turned to Meren. "It is up to you whether you stay or not, Meren. It is your choice."

"I will stay," she said, cursing herself for the eagerness in her voice. Fa observed her for a moment, holding her eyes with his. He at last nodded and turned toward the tunnel from which they had come. "If you need me, I shall be outside."

And then he was gone.

"Stubborn, that one," Nabi said, turning away from her, flying low over the soggy ground back towards his throne. "Always has been." When he turned to face Meren again, he said, "I suppose that has always been one of my favorite qualities about him." He spoke of Fa with such an affectionate tone. Almost fatherly. And Meren couldn't help but wonder…

"How do you know Fa?" she asked, walking toward the ancient færy, missing her ability to fly for the first time in a long time. She wondered when her wing would be healed enough to try.

"Soon," Nabi said, and she looked at him quickly.

"What?" she asked, her eyes narrowed.

"You were wondering when you could fly again. Soon, I should think. Which means the time approaches."

"The time? What time?" she blurted, ignoring the fact that he had just read her thoughts.

"The time you have been waiting for. The reason you sought out Melekfa in the first place. Your time approaches, Malkah."

She did not know the protocol for this situation; she had never been around a færy as ancient as Nabi, so she did not know if it was rude to question him. But she did anyway. "Why exactly do you think I have sought out Fa?"

"To stop the Darkness."

The silence yawned between them as she understood that Fa hadn't been exaggerating—Nabi was indeed a seer. A rare færy. Thought to be extinct, like so much of the magic færykind had abandoned over the centuries.

"What do I do?" she asked, stepping closer to him. He settled back on his throne, and she couldn't help but notice the lovingly worn arms of the giant root seat—as if it had gladly conformed to the male who sat in it. Indeed, this færy was old. Ancient. As ancient as this place. Maybe older.

"That is not the question you should be asking," he said, folding his hands across his stomach.

"What should I be asking?"

"Right now, Malkah, your sole focus should be on convincing your friend to come with you."

"Come with me where?"

"He will know the way."

"The way to where?"

A soft chuckle. "One step at a time, young one. One step at a time."

"Are you being intentionally vague?" she snapped, crossing her arms.

"Indeed, you two are well-matched," Nabi said, ignoring her frustration. "You sound just like him. Though I think that mutual stubbornness will be both an asset and a nuisance."

"You are making no sense."

"Such is the plight of a seer." He chuckled again.

She sighed, exasperated. "Just tell me what I need to do to stop the Darkness."

"Do not make the mistake of thinking the task is yours alone, Malkah. There are many players in this game. And the stakes are high."

"I know that," she said, a little exasperated.

He chuckled, but it was not mocking, she realized. "You are strong, Meren. You are well-suited for your task. But do not forget, young one, that when the færies of the Light are gathered, that is when the real task begins. That is when the real war commences."

"War," she breathed.

"War," Nabi parroted. "By the end of all of this, mortal and immortal alike must face each other. The plight of Darkness and Light will be determined once and for all. Make no mistake, Malkah Neharah. Eloah will have his way. And the Demon King must fall."

"The Demon King? You mean King Asa? The King of the Færies?"

"No, Meren. Asa is no demon. Asa is merely a product of the Darkness that was introduced into this world a very long time ago. The Demon King—the mortal king of the East—will soon march. He will soon make his stand. Even now, he has already begun. He has secretly plotted to murder the king of the West."

"The king of the West?" Meren asked, her heart picking up its pace. She searched her memory, scouring her mind for the history lessons her parents had insisted upon. "King Aiken of Navah?" she finally said. "King Aiken is dead?"

"His son is now king, with the Hidden Queen beside him. The war, Malkah, has already begun. But the Perdurables cannot fight until we are united once more. We cannot help the mortal kings until we are summoned under the Light."

"Tell me, Nabi. Tell me what I must do," she begged, desperation welling in her soul. The war…the war was starting. It had already begun. She had to fight. She had to do something.

"You are on the path, child. I am telling you that your next step is to get your Fa to walk that path with you."

"He is not *my* Fa. And you yourself said it—he's stubborn. I don't think he will help. He has already made it clear that he thinks the Darkness is beyond stopping."

"Your paths have crossed for a reason. Eloah does not make mistakes. Your next step is to convince him to come with you."

"I don't even know where I'm going!" she cried in frustration.

The old færy stood, flying the short distance to her, resting his surprisingly strong hands on her shoulders when he landed before her. "You would be hard-pressed to find anyone—mortal or immortal alike—who does. Just stay the course, Malkah. The rest will sort itself out."

"Malkah, Tipharah. Why is it that you two cannot seem to call anyone by their true name?" she asked, crossing her arms.

He raised his eyebrows at her. "How do you know that we are

not?" When she had no response, he went on. "And I should think that your Fa will have another name for you soon enough, Malkah."

"Another name? How many must I decipher?"

He chuckled as he patted her cheek. "Convince him, Meren of the Light. And worry yourself not with such things as names just now."

Chapter XV

ren't you going to ask me what he said?" Meren teased, watching Fa as he bustled around his kitchen. He chopped a fingerling potato with painstaking accuracy, his back to her. He hadn't said a word on their journey back to his home, nor had he said much as he began preparing dinner. "We should eat." That's all he had said.

And the way he had looked when she told him that the kiss had meant nothing…

She wondered if it really had.

"It is not for me to ask."

"Oh, come on!" she cried, crossing her arms. "No one is that noble. Surely you're curious."

He breathed a chuckle, his broad shoulders bobbing and his tattered wings dancing with his laugh. "Of course I'm curious, Tipharah." He set down his knife and turned to face her. "But I have no doubt you will tell me whether I ask or not."

She rolled her eyes, crossing to the counter for the knife, picking up where he left off with the potatoes. "You're impossible."

He nudged her with his shoulder as he took a place beside her.

"All right, Meren. What did Nabi tell you?"

"That's none of your business," she purred, slicing carefully through the thin purple skin of the potato.

His hand tickling her waist had her dodging, turning to fully face him. But it was the mischief—mischief mixed with a healthy dose of intensity—which transfixed her. His eyes. As black as midnight and as unending, too. She had never noticed how the light danced off of them, as if the stars had been borrowed just to kiss his eyes with wonder. Those eyes of his held hers for a good moment, her heart pounding in her chest the longer he stared. It was only then she realized his hand still rested on her waist. And suddenly her every thought honed in on that hand, burning and branding with every second it lingered.

"Are you planning on impaling me with that knife?" Fa asked, one eyebrow raised, a dimple appearing at the corner of his mouth where a smile threatened.

She looked down to see that she had the knife angled right at his heart. She lowered it quickly, heat kissing her cheeks.

"Sorry," she muttered.

He laughed, taking the knife from her and setting it down on the counter beside them.

When he turned his branding gaze back to hers, she blurted, "Come with me, Fa."

"Come with you where?" he asked, his hand tightening slightly on her waist. She found the gumption to rest her hands on his arms. A silent plea.

"Come help me. Help me fight the Darkness."

He tilted his head to the side, appraising her, but said nothing.

She took a fraction of a step closer to him, leaving little more than a breath between them. "We can do this. Together. I think… I think we're supposed to."

Nabi's words became a chant, a credo in her mind. *Convince him, Meren of the Light. Convince him.*

"Please, Fa. Come back to the coven with me. Let's fight this together."

It was as if someone had shattered the moment, shards by the thousands scattering across her heart at the look on Fa's face.

His hand slackened at her waist, but he did not move away. "Meren," he said quietly.

"Please, Fa," she protested, tightening her grip on his arms. Solid. Unyielding. Strong. The Warrior was a fortress. "I know we can do this. There is magic between us. I know you have felt it." He said nothing, made no indication that he could feel her heart beating as hard as she could feel his—two drums in rhythm together, calling them to wars mortal and immortal. But she went on anyway. "I think it's a sign, Fa. Nabi said it—Eloah does not make mistakes. Maybe we met for a reason."

"Meren," he said again, pain lurking in his eyes.

"What happened to Tipharah?" she asked. "Isn't that my name?"

He looked down, breathing in deeply. So she dared touch his chin, dared lift his face to hers again. "Fa. *Melekfa,*" she tried, his eyes narrowing at her use of the name Nabi had given him. "Come with me."

"I cannot," he said at last.

"Why?"

"Because I cannot."

Her grip slackened on his arms.

"Why, Fa? Can you tell me why?"

But Fa only turned, stepping away, scrubbing his face with his hands as he crossed the room.

"Is it Asher?" she asked, the idea dawning on her. "Is he the reason you will not return with me?"

"It doesn't matter."

She walked across the room, gripping him by the shoulder, forcing him to face her. "What is between you? Why do you hate each other so?"

"It doesn't matter," he said again, that pain coloring his features more sharply.

"It does matter, Fa. It matters if it is the reason you will not return with me."

Fa tried to turn his back on her again, but she did not let him, her grip a vice.

"Tell me, Fa."

"It's in the past, Meren. It doesn't matter anymore."

"Why won't you tell me? Do you not trust me?"

He crossed the gap between them in one breath. "Of course," he said, brushing a knuckle down her cheek. "Of course I trust you, Tipharah."

She closed her eyes, held fast by the tenderness of his touch. She took hold of his hand, pressing it against her face, brushing her lips against his finger. Fa froze, as still as death before her.

"Please, Fa. Please come back with me. That's what Nabi told me. That it was my job to convince you to help me."

"He was wrong, Meren."

"I thought you said he was a seer."

"A seer. Not a prophet. He is not infallible. And his words are not canon. They are…they are…"

"Are what, Fa? You seemed to trust him. He is like a father to you, isn't he?"

It was the pain in his eyes that told her she was right. Nabi was the father to Fa that his own had never been. She took hold of his face with both of her hands, holding his eyes.

"Don't be afraid, Fa. We can do this. Together."

He looked down again, shutting his eyes. "I cannot, Meren. I am sorry."

"Cannot? Or *will* not?" she asked.

He lifted his eyes to meet hers, pain pounding through his veins. Through hers. "Both."

She dropped her hands, stepping back. One step. And then another, shaking her head.

"You would truly rather be alone? You would rather be alone than come back with…with someone who cares?"

Fa's face seemed turned to stone, his arms slack by his side when he simply said, "Yes."

Chapter XVI

eren," Fa said as she turned her back on him. Her wings shone gloriously in the afternoon sun spilling through his windows. Spread wide behind her, the injured wing had healed nicely, the white membrane as pure as freshly fallen snow, peppered with flecks of obsidian.

In a word: breathtaking.

"Please," he tried again as he watched her breast rise and fall with her labored breaths, her wings mimicking the movement with gentle flaps. "Let me explain."

Still, she kept her back to him. "There is nothing to explain," she said. "I understand perfectly."

But she didn't. Not really. Not when Fa had neglected to tell her the truth. Perhaps Nabi had been right—perhaps she deserved the truth. But Fa was not sure whether he would have been able to stand the devastation in her eyes when she learned it.

So he had kept his mouth shut.

"Meren," he tried again, crossing the gap between them. But just before he reached her, just before he could rest his hand on her slender shoulder, she whirled to face him again, meeting his eyes for a breath before ascending into the air and flying across the room. She landed gracefully at his door, putting her hand on the handle, and said over her shoulder, "Thank you, Fa. For healing me." She met his eyes and held them before she said, "For everything."

And then she disappeared.

~

He waited, pacing the room, his breath being slowly stolen from his lungs as her presence waned. She was leaving.

She had left.

He had denied her the one thing she had asked of him. And it had destroyed her. He had felt it—a crack, a tear in her heart at his words, his lie. Or maybe that tear had been in his own soul. Fa couldn't be sure.

Either way, she was gone. With every breath, her soul faded from his—the distance like a wall, a human wall of steel and stone and ad- amance. And the feeling devastated him.

For he had met her. His *B'sheirt.* He had met her now. There was no going back from it.

He wasn't sure if there would be any going forward, either.

Meren had never flown so fast in her life.

Perhaps before she had been a gust of wind through a pile of autumn leaves. But now, with the Wind magic encouraging her wings, she was lightning caressing a wide valley. She was the breath of a hurricane, devouring the land. A flicker of light over the grass and through the trees, there and then gone.

The speed felt so good.

Three days, she thought with a wrench. She had flown straight for three days without knowing fatigue or hunger. Only pain. A thrashing pain that grew with every breath. As if someone had reached into her chest and ripped out her soul, shredding it into ribbons. That's how it felt as she flew farther and farther from Fa.

Perhaps that magic between them…perhaps it was some sort of tether. A connection. Unearthly and beautiful. And now that it had been severed…

Her breath caught, a gasp escaping her lips as she sped through the canopy, the air careening past her so quickly it stole tears from her eyes. Or perhaps she was shedding those of her own accord. It was hard to say anymore.

Still she flew. And she did not look back.

~

One more day, and she was nearly home. What had taken her and Asher a little longer than a week to fly had now taken her only four days, thanks to her newfound magic. Water. And Wind.

The Flame she still avoided.

She had stopped only twice for water and a quick meal. But she hadn't slept. She hadn't allowed herself to be still long enough to think on any of it: what had happened in her time with Fa. What would never happen now that he had made himself clear.

He would rather be alone. Not with her. Not with someone who had grown to care about him. Deeply.

He would rather be alone.

And now he would.

And so would she.

~

She collapsed onto her bed, her face buried in her pillow, her wings aching with the nonstop flying. It was only as she rested that she realized she was hungry. No, not hungry. Ravenous. She felt like she could eat a meal large enough for a human.

She sat up, rolling her neck and stretching her arms before moseying to her cupboards…until she remembered that she had been gone for weeks. Nearly two months. Nothing in her cupboard would be salvageable by now.

For a heartbeat, she wondered what Fa would make her tonight. Perhaps she could talk him into making toadstool soup—

Meren slammed the cupboard door, putting her hand up to her head and massaging her temples. Fa would not make her dinner tonight. Or any night.

Fa had chosen to stay behind. He had chosen to live his life away from her.

Meren found her bed and did not rise.

<h1 style="text-align:center">CHAPTER XVII</h1>

eren was awoken by the sound of her own stomach. She looked around her home, her eyes squinting to adjust to the complete darkness, and wondered how long she had been asleep. Judging by the way her stomach protested, it was more than just a few hours. The crick in her neck suggested she had been asleep for days. Maybe longer. It didn't really matter anymore.

But she was starving, and the incessant rumblings of her stomach had her flopping out of bed and stumbling through her little home. She barked a curse when she tripped over a vine growing across her floor. The place was too dark to see a thing. She needed light.

Which required magic.

Light magic.

Flame magic.

Bile burned in her throat at the thought of using the magic that the Dark færies had bastardized. How many færy lights had she seen in her life and never thought a thing about them? But it was the very magic she loathed—that she had grown to fear—that she would need to use in order to see.

Breathing another curse, she cupped her hand before her and

willed a ball of light to her palm. Easy. It was too easy to summon the magic within her, but she cast the glowing blue light to her ceiling and formed a few more for good measure, figuring she could worry about the power in her veins another day.

With light to finally guide her way, she stumbled to the kitchen, her stomach incessantly reminding her of her lack of sustenance. Like a desperate beggar, she rummaged through her cupboards for anything suitable for consuming. She managed to find a small bowl of stale nuts, which she devoured in all of three seconds. Still hungry, she found herself some water, deciding a trek into the forest for something more substantial was inevitable.

She had brushed the nuisance curl from her brow and plopped herself down in a nearby chair, devouring her water in hasty gulps, when someone burst into the room, armed with a wicked bone knife and a look that promised a swift death to any who crossed him.

Asher.

"Meren?" he breathed, freezing in her doorway. "Meren, is that you?" he asked, panic and shock rising in his voice.

"It's me, Ash," she said, resting her brow in her hand. She was developing a pounding headache.

Within a matter of a breath, Asher had crossed the room and yanked her from her chair, crushing her in his arms. His breath was warm on her hair as he said, "Eloah, Meren. I thought you were dead!"

"I thought you were, too," she said, at which he pulled her away, gripping her upper arms and appraising her as if she were a ghost. But after a moment, he yanked her back into his arms and brushed a calloused hand down her hair.

"Oh, Mer," he said, his voice softer. Broken. "Mer, I was so worried."

"I'm sorry, Ash. Truly," she said into his chest. He smelled of sweat and fire, and she could feel his heart pounding beneath her ear. Not the way she could feel Fa's heart—not as if his heart beat within her own chest. Just the physical pulsations in Asher's body. Asher, her friend. The friend who had rescued her from the Dark færies when she was only a child. The one who had never pushed her away. Unlike…

She hugged him a little closer.

"I'm the one who should be apologizing, Meren," he said, to her shock. "I shouldn't have let you get lost in those woods. I should have protected you. You were counting on me and—"

"Lost?" she asked, pulling away from him. "I wasn't lost."

"What do you mean? Of course you were lost! How else did you wander away from me?"

She jutted her chin backward, her brows furrowed. "I didn't wander from you, Ash. I fell. We both fell, struck by the Darkness. And when I fell, I broke my wing and—"

Asher seemed uninterested in the rest of her story, whirling her around to inspect her wing. "It's not broken, Mer. You probably just—"

"It was," she said, turning to face him again. "Snapped in two. But Fa helped me and—"

"*Fa?*" Asher asked, stepping back a fraction. "The Gibhor?"

She met his eyes, searching for any clues to whatever had happened between him and Fa. "Yes, he saved me, Ash. He found me in the woods and took me to his home to heal me."

"Found you," Asher repeated, but it wasn't a question. "In that darkness? Meren, it was pitch black."

"Well, he found me nonetheless."

"Right."

"What? You don't believe me?"

"Meren, I looked for you for days. That night, it was as black as a beetle's back. No one could have found you in that storm, Meren. No one."

"What are you implying?"

"Are you really that naïve?"

She crossed her arms and waited.

"Meren, he obviously trapped you."

"Trapped me? Asher, you're being ridiculous!"

"Am I?"

"Why would he trap me just to heal me?"

"Heal you," he sneered, crossing his arms.

"Yes. He healed me," she insisted. Asher only raised a brow, incredulity stiffening his shoulders and flattening his lips.

"What?" she asked.

"Fa. Healed you."

"Yes, Ash. I know you two are mortal enemies," she said without thinking. "But yes, he healed me. Took care of me and—"

"Is that what he told you?" Asher interrupted.

"What?"

"That we are mortal enemies?"

"No," she said, at which Asher huffed and turned away from her, pacing around the cushions in the room.

"He didn't, Ash. But I'm not stupid. I figured it out on my own."

"And what is it that you figured out?" he asked, whirling to face her again.

"That you hate him. And he hates you." She crossed her arms and waited—waited for Asher's explanation.

But it did not come.

"Are you going to explain it to me, or are you going to leave me to guess, too?"

Asher's eyes shot to hers again, narrowing, appraising for a long moment. Then he said, "It doesn't matter."

"I'm really sick of hearing that," she growled.

But Asher ignored her frustration, crossing the room in three steps. "I'm sorry you were hurt. And I'm sorry I wasn't there to help you."

"It's fine, Ash. Really."

"No, it's not fine. I should have helped you. I should have found you. I was going out of my mind worrying. I looked for you. For three days, I scoured that forest for any sign of you. But…nothing. I thought I would go out of my mind worrying. But then this ancient færy was there. Out of nowhere, really. And he told me…" Asher looked down, toeing the ground as if he were embarrassed to finish the story. "He told me you were fine and I…I believed him. For some reason, I just felt like he knew. So I left.

"I don't know why. I don't know why I believed him. But I did. He just… I have never seen a færy like him. He was old. I didn't think it was possible for færies to live that long."

An ancient færy. Meren wondered if the færy Asher had encountered was the same one who had been wrong about Fa. The one who had told her that her only job was to convince Fa to help her stop the

Dark færies. The one who had been wrong. So very, very wrong.

Had Asher met Nabi?

"I had been home for three days before the inanity of it hit me," Asher went on. "That I had believed a complete stranger as to your wellbeing. That I had abandoned you.

"So I set out, searching for you. Every day for weeks, I hunted for you. Jotham told me to stop. Told me you were likely dead. But I couldn't. I didn't. I kept looking. Kept hoping. And every night I'd come back here and hope to find you asleep in your bed. Hoped I'd wake from this nightmare."

"Ash," she breathed, torn by the pain in his eyes. She touched his cheek, and the anguish that rippled off of him tore a new ache in her heart.

"Did you..." he started, the words catching in his throat. He touched her cheek as well, cupping her jaw. "Did you not worry for me, Meren? Did you not wonder where I was?"

"I did, Asher," she assured him. "But I knew you were all right."

He furrowed his dark brows. "How?"

"Fa told me. He tracked you. For my sake. He searched until he found evidence that you were alive and safe."

Asher's hand trembled on her cheek, but whether in concern or hatred, she couldn't be sure.

"He became...he became my friend, Asher. He helped me. He didn't have to, but he did, and I wish..."

Asher's hand dropped from her cheek, a muscle feathering in his jaw as he turned away from her.

"I wish you would believe me."

"Why?" he asked, turning toward her again. "Where is he now,

Meren? If he was such a good friend to you, why did you come back alone? Why did he not help us?"

She couldn't answer him, couldn't even meet his eyes, instead fiddling with her fingers and willing away the lump that was forming in her throat.

"It should have been me," he breathed, and once more, he crossed the gap between them, touching her cheek with a featherlight caress. "I should have been the one to help you. I'm sorry, Meren. I'm sorry I failed you."

His finger did not leave her cheek, the others joining it until he cupped her jaw in his calloused hand.

"We both failed, Asher," she said, an ache tearing anew at her heart for the færy who hadn't come back to help them.

"We'll find a way," Asher promised. "We'll stop this Darkness."

"I know," she said, closing her eyes. For now more than ever, she knew she had to find a way, Fa or no Fa. She had to stop the Darkness from destroying the only people she had left.

Chapter XVIII

eren began to pick through the berries and seeds she had foraged for her breakfast, the chill in the morning air seeping into her bones. She stoked her fire, hoping to warm herself a little more. But the longer the fire burned, the more she knew the truth—the chill had nothing to do with the encroaching winter and everything to do with the grating absence of one Warrior færy. Still, the dandelion tea she sipped helped a bit—a tiny kindling flame sparking to life in her soul, like a whisper on the wind.

She rummaged through a couple of pine needles, reminiscing on the way Fa had used them to flavor soups and stews, and missed him all the more. She threw the needles out her small window and huffed a sigh.

Sipping her tea again, there came a knock on her door.

"It's open," she said, not bothering to look up from her cup.

Asher emerged, an armful of breads and sweet cakes in tow. "Brought you some sustenance."

"I'm not hungry," she said, pushing around the pile of breakfast in front of her.

Asher ignored her, setting the array of baked goods on her counter. "You should eat something more than that, Meren. You've been through a lot."

She nodded absently, staring out the window, the morning sun glittering on the chalam tree's leaves, turning them to shimmering sheets of gold.

"It's a beautiful morning," Asher said, coming to her side. "The sun is deceptive though. That wind is biting."

"Since when are you one for small talk?" she asked, but Asher ignored her, placing his heavy hand on her shoulder as he too stared out the window.

"You should keep a fire going all day, Mer. It's only getting colder out there."

"I am capable of taking care of myself, Asher."

"Considering you got lost for the better part of two months, I think I am entitled to worry about you."

"I did not get lost!" she snapped. "I was rescued. Rescued and healed, in case you've already forgotten."

"Meren," Asher said, tilting his head to one side.

"Don't," she barked, standing to her feet.

"Don't what?" Asher asked.

"Don't look at me like that."

"Like what?"

"Like a færyling in need of a good lecture."

"You cannot deny that you were in great danger——"

"I *can* deny it, because I wasn't. And for the love of Eloah, I wish you would stop treating me like a færyling!"

Asher paused, obviously weighing his words. Then he said slowly, "I don't want to fight."

"Then stop picking them."

Asher's shoulders sank, and he sighed. "I worry about you, Mer. Is that so wrong?"

"Must you worry in such a smothering way? I was a child when you found me, yes. Perhaps you had a right to worry then. But I'm not a child anymore, Ash. I'm old enough to take care of myself. Old enough to Mate, for Eloah's sake!"

Asher's eyes darted to hers then, holding her gaze, his expression unreadable.

"I just mean that I don't need you to father me anymore," she said, turning away from him, unable to stand the look in his eyes.

"I'm not trying to father you, Meren," he said, his voice changing. Softening. The hair on the back of her neck stood at the shift in his tone. "I'm trying to take care of you. I'm trying… I'm trying to love you, Meren. But you won't let me."

She turned to face him again, unsure what she would say. "Asher."

"Just hear me out, Meren. That's all I ask."

He crossed the gap between them, taking her arms in his hands, holding her in place with his gripping gaze. "I am in love with you, Meren. I have been for a long time. And thinking I'd lost you, I…I don't know why I haven't told you before."

She sucked in a breath, readying herself to protest his words. But she swallowed her retort and let him go on.

"But it seems that every time I try to take care of you, try to protect you, you push me away. I don't want to upset you. I don't want to fight. I just want…" His hands, gripping her upper arms, were trembling. "I just want us to be together. As we should be. It was meant to be this way, Meren. Don't you see it? We were meant to find each other, to be together. As mates."

Mates.

The word clamored through her soul, a clap of thunder before a raging storm. And that tiny flame in her soul seemed to flare at the word.

"You…" she tried, swallowing the lump in her throat. "You want us to be mates?"

"I've wanted it for a long time," he said, stepping closer to her. She found her breath catching.

"Asher."

"Everyone agrees we're a good match. They've just been waiting for this to happen."

"What? No one has ever said anything like that to me."

He huffed a laugh. "Maybe you weren't paying attention."

"I have been, Asher. I know what you want. I've known it for a long time."

"You have?"

She sighed, shutting her eyes. "Asher, we cannot be mates."

"Why?"

"You are my friend. And I love you but…"

He took another step, his body nearly pressed against hers. "See? You just said it. You love me."

"I can love a friend. I can love a father. It's different than loving a…mate."

"I am not your father, Meren. But I am your friend. And that's as good a start as any. We *can* be mates. You need to accept that."

"Stop telling me what I need to do," she said.

"We're friends, Meren," he said and then repeated, "that's as good a start as any."

"It's more than that, Ash."

He tilted his head to the side, a pitying smile on his mouth—as if she were a child too young to understand. "You'll grow to feel more in time."

"Asher, it has been nearly fifty years. When exactly am I supposed to feel more?"

"You just haven't given it a chance, that's all. I know if you did, you'd see what I see."

"And what is that?"

"That you're meant to be mine."

"Asher, please don't do this."

"Meren," he said, wrapping his arms around her. "All I'm asking is that you give it a chance."

"Ash."

"Just give it a chance, Meren," he said softly, tilting her chin with his finger. She met his eyes, simultaneously loathing and pitying the determination she saw there. "Please."

She swallowed, wishing she had better words, wishing he hadn't put her in the position of even needing such words.

"Just tell me this," he said, his hand still cupping her chin. "Would you truly rather be alone?"

Her eyes flew open. "What did you say?"

"I care about you, Meren. I know you know that. Would you truly rather be alone than be with someone who cares about you?"

And it was his question—the way he worded it—that ripped her tattered soul into shreds. A single tear fell down her cheek, but Asher did not wipe it away as she heard herself breathe, "No."

"You don't have to answer now, Meren. Just promise me you will consider it."

She nodded, shutting her eyes as if she could shut him out too.

But she could not shut out the brush of his lips against hers—a simple kiss, a kiss that meant both nothing and everything. She could not ignore the way he held her tightly against him, possessively.

"You need to rest today, Meren," he said, relinquishing her. "I'll see you at dusk."

"Dusk?" she asked, shaking her head as if coming out of a fog. "What's at dusk?"

"A coven meeting, of course," he said, but before she could protest, before she could say another word, much less form a coherent thought, Asher disappeared through her door.

Chapter XIX

t's true," Athaliah said, crushing Meren with her slender arms. Her wings fluttered rapidly behind her shoulder. "Eloah, Meren, it's true. You're alive."

"I'm alive, Ath," Meren said, breathing a laugh into her friend's shoulder. "I'm sorry I scared you."

"Are you kidding me?" Athaliah cried, pulling Meren out of her arms. "We were worried sick about you, and you're apologizing! I can't believe Asher lost you like that!"

From the corner of her eye, Meren caught Asher glaring at Athaliah.

"He didn't lose me, Ath. I lost him," Meren clarified.

"What?" Athaliah asked, her narrow brows furrowed. "Your mate lost you?"

"My *what?*" Meren asked, nearly choking on her own words. She turned her attention to Asher, but he was engaged in a conversation on the other side of the room, and whether intentionally or not, he did not make eye contact with her.

"Asher told us the news. He's been going on about it all day. I was surprised, to be honest," Athaliah went on. "But I get it. You two have been so close for so long. Might as well mate him."

"Might as well?" Meren asked, anger boiling in her gut. "Is that all mating is? A might-as-well scenario?"

Still, Asher conveniently ignored her.

"Meren, what's wrong?" Athaliah asked.

"Let us give Meren some space," Jotham said, flying into the coven meeting room. He landed gracefully on his long legs, his height towering above anyone in the room. "I am sure she would like to answer these questions only once tonight. She has been through much."

"Jotham," Meren said, flying to him. He took her face in his hands when she landed, kissing her brow with fatherly tenderness.

"Meren," he said. "I am glad to see you alive and well. When Asher told me you had returned, I hardly believed it. Yet here you are, standing before us."

"I am sorry I could not return sooner," she said.

"Do not apologize, young one," said Jotham. "What is important is that you are alive. And if you are up for it," he continued, turning to face the rest of the coven now gathered in the cozy room carved in the top of the chalam trunk, "I would ask you to share what happened to you. It might help us to better understand what these Dark færies want."

Meren nodded, silently taking a seat at the table, Asher sitting down in his usual place across from her. She tried to catch his eye, to seethe at him. But conveniently, he never noticed her glare. The coven joined them, Athaliah snatching the seat next to Meren, and Meir sitting down on the other side of Athaliah. The way he smiled at her— he was consumed by Athaliah, body and soul. They were what mates should be. Not this…whatever was between her and Asher.

And *wasn't* between them.

But she realized all eyes were on her, so Meren sighed, knowing it was time. The coven deserved to know what had happened to her, and as exhausted as she was, she needed to tell them.

So she did.

For the better part of an hour, Meren explained every detail of what had transpired over the past weeks, with Jotham particularly interested in Fa—in everything he had done, every move he had made. And with every new question about the friend she had lost to stubborn pride, Meren wished very much that the meeting would just end so that she could go back to pretending she had never met Fa.

But she had.

And her soul ached more with every passing day away from him.

But somewhere, distantly, the kindling flame in her soul grew. A reminder. A promise. As if Fa were a part of her. Inextricable. Perdurable.

She wasn't sure she could stand the pain that came with it. Not for much longer.

Asher kept his eyes on her, assessing every word as if he would catch her in a lie. What lie, she couldn't say, but every time Jotham asked another question about Fa, Asher practically bored holes into Meren with his silent, branding gaze.

But it was when Meren spoke of Nabi that Jotham's interest was particularly piqued. "He gave you no more details than that?" Jotham asked.

All eyes were glued to Meren as she spoke of the ancient færy. "He only told me that I was on the path to stopping the Darkness. Nothing more." Her words caught in her throat at the lie, and she pursed her lips, making sure to keep her gaze anywhere but on Asher. For that wasn't true—Nabi hadn't told her she was on the course. He had told her she was on the course as long as Fa was with her.

And he was not.

But it didn't matter. She would stay the course with or without him. She had to. Somehow, she knew she could not give up. Not with war on the horizon and with the hovering darkness, the winter encroaching on them all. This blight would not be vanquished by hiding; it would have to be faced. And she would face it. Even if she had to face it alone.

Meren would find a way to stop this Darkness from destroying everything—and everyone she loved. The flame in her soul seemed to flare.

"Seers," Asher scoffed, crossing his arms and leaning back against his chair, his wings folded tightly behind him. "They are useless. Nothing more than charlatans."

"Wasn't it a seer that told you Meren was alive?" Athaliah asked, and Meren folded her smirk behind pursed lips. "Doesn't sound like a charlatan to me."

"It was a fluke that he was right. He put a spell on me or something," Asher said.

"But he was right," Jotham pointed out. "And perhaps he was right about Meren, too. If so, we must figure out what that means. For all of us."

He is not infallible. And his words are not canon. Fa's words echoed in her head, and she wondered what she was supposed to believe. Her gut? Jotham? Asher? Nabi? She wanted to help, she wanted to do whatever it took.

But Nabi had been terribly wrong about Fa. So maybe he was wrong about her, too.

A knock at the door startled the færies around the scarred table, all eyes turning toward the little hall down which lay the entrance to their coven.

"Who could be visiting us?" Asher asked, standing.

No one. No one should be visiting. Because their coven was a secret.

Or it had been.

Meren's heart pounded mercilessly in her chest. She hadn't told Fa where she lived. Even if he were angry or seeking some sort of spiteful revenge for her daring to ask him to leave his home, to upend his careful life…he could not betray her location to anyone.

Meir stood as well, giving Athaliah a worried look before saying, "I will see who it is."

The knock came again, stronger this time.

But then she felt it…a yanking. Without thinking, Meren stood, the abrupt movement scraping her chair across the floor with a jarring screech.

"Meren," Asher said. "Sit down."

She ignored him, turning her attention toward the entrance. It was too dark to see anything, to tell who might be knocking.

But that yanking…that tug on her very soul…

Meir returned after only a moment, bewildered. "Meren," he said, "there's someone here to see you."

Meren practically leapt into the air, ignoring Asher's protests behind her as she flew down the little hall.

And there, standing in the doorway, was a færy with golden skin and silver hair, the shock of black hair at his brow glistening in the bobbing færy lights overhead.

Meir eyed the guest warily for a moment, his hand curling into a fist at his side. "What do you want with Meren?" he asked.

The færy was all but indifferent to Meir's predatory glare, his eyes fixed on Meren. "Tipharah," he said, relief and apology coloring his words.

Meren flung herself into Fa's arms, caring little why he was here and caring even less what Meir thought. She breathed in his familiar scent, her nose buried in his neck, his arms solid around her as his own breaths kissed her hair with puffs of warmth.

"Tipharah," he said again. A plea. A prayer.

She had not heard Meir leave, but when she finally looked up again, he was nowhere in sight. It might as well have been just her and Fa in all the world.

"What are you doing here?" she asked him, her words breathless.

He brushed her stupid curl from her brow, and she was struck speechless by the silver she saw lining his eyes.

"I'm sorry," he said, wrapping his arms more securely around her. "I'm so sorry I hurt you, Meren. The moment you left, I knew what a fool I'd been. I never meant to hurt you. Never. But I did, and I hate myself for it."

"You're here," she breathed, tears filling her eyes too. "You're really here."

He pressed his brow to hers, drawing a deep breath. "Forgive me, Meren."

"It doesn't matter," she said, joy like a rushing wave welling in her belly, that tear in her soul where Fa's absence gnawed knitting together breath by breath, the flame in her soul a forest fire now, a raging inferno.

"It does, Tipharah. It matters. I should never have said—"

"I don't care," she interrupted, and she meant it. "You're here. That's all that matters to me. You're here."

"I'm here," he said, a sad smile on his mouth. "And I'm not leaving you."

He took her face in his hands, pressing his lips to her brow. And she could have sworn that even through her closed eyes, she saw a flash of light at his touch. But it was gone before she could open her eyes again.

He pressed his brow to hers again, and she allowed herself a moment to breathe him in, to savor his sweet scent before she said, "You must come and meet everyone."

"What, now?" he asked, still holding her close to him.

"Yes, now." She laughed. "They're just in there," she added, nodding towards the meeting room.

"In there?" he asked, taking a moment to look around. "Is this not your home?"

"No," she said. "This is where the coven meets. My home is further up the tree."

And it occurred to her then—crashed into her, really—that he had found her. Come right to her. Just as he had found her in the woods when she had fallen. Just as she had found him in Nabi's lair.

Because they were connected, she and Fa. And now that he had returned, it was as if she could breathe again, as if her soul were no longer wounded, no longer aching for the part of her she cherished most.

She embraced him fiercely again before she said, "Come and meet everyone."

He stole a wary glance down the hall, knowing who was on the other side of that light. Knowing what he faced. But he laced his hand through hers and simply said, "Lead the way, Tipharah."

The meeting room was a mixture of gaping mouths and silent stares as Meren emerged with Fa in tow. Asher's eyes went immediately to their clasped hands and did not leave, and heat kissed Meren's cheeks. But she did not drop Fa's hand. Nor did she plan on letting go of it any time soon. Fa traced idle circles on the palm of her hand with his thumb as she spoke. "Everyone, this is Fa—the friend I was just telling you about."

Jotham stood, flying across the room with liquid grace. He landed before Fa and extended his hand. Fa gripped the coven leader's hand in solidarity, and Jotham bowed his head. "We are in great debt to you, Gibhor. Welcome."

Fa, too, bowed his head to Jotham. "I did not realize I was interrupting your meeting."

Jotham smiled. "Your presence is serendipitous, my friend. We were just learning of your kindness to Meren. And Asher."

Fa turned to catch Meren's eyes, furrowing his silver brows. She only smiled and squeezed his hand, ignoring the seething rage roiling from across the room, not to mention the eyes that stared at her friend's tattered wings with gaping awe.

"To what do we owe the *pleasure* of your visit, Gibhor?" Asher drawled, standing again.

To his credit, Fa did not look bothered or even slightly intimidated as he met Asher's demanding gaze with cool eyes. He bowed his head to Asher and said, "I am come with news that will help us all."

Meren's gaze darted to Fa's face. "What news?" she asked.

Fa met her eyes. "News from a seer."

"Psh," Asher said, plopping down in his chair. "Not this nonsense again."

"Asher," Meren scolded. But he ignored her, fiddling instead with the hilt of the bone knife at his waist as if daring Fa to cross a line.

Jotham extended his hand, inviting Fa to take a seat at the table. Athaliah willingly gave up her seat next to Meren, a twinkle of mischief in her eyes as she urged Meir and the rest of the færies on her side of the table to move down. Meren ignored her friend and sat down next to Fa. Without a word, he took hold of her hand again under the table, lacing his fingers between hers without taking his eyes off of Jotham.

"Tell us your news, Gibhor," said Jotham.

"It's just Fa," he said, to which Jotham nodded. "I am come to relay information that was given to me by an ancient færy—one who has been a friend of mine my whole life."

"Yes," Jotham said. "Meren has told us about him."

Across the table, a muscle feathered in Asher's jaw as he narrowed his eyes, branding Meren with the rage in his gaze. She swallowed and did her best to listen to Fa instead.

"There might be a way," Fa said, "to summon the rest of Færies of the Light. Whoever is still alive."

"For what purpose?" Asher asked, his face stone.

"For war," Fa said, and when Meren's grip tightened on his hand, he used his thumb to stroke a soothing path down it. The fire in her soul flickered, calming in his presence.

"War?" Meir asked. "We cannot go to war with the Darkness."

"The Darkness has already gone to war with us," Fa said, his cool gaze shifting to Asher. "We just haven't admitted it."

"There cannot be many of us left," said Meir. "What good would summoning us do?"

"The Darkness," Fa said, "has waged war on all life, not just færy-kind. The mortals are in danger as well. Even now, the mortal king of the eastern lands prepares to march on the king of the west. Not to conquer. Not to vanquish. To destroy. To burn his kingdom to the ground. This war—this blight—is not a war of one ideal versus an-other. This is a war against Eloah and his ways. It is a war for our very lives."

"How do you know this? Did your *seer* tell you?" Asher snapped, crossing his arms.

"Can you not see it? Can you not feel it in the very winds?" Fa asked, looking into Asher's cold eyes. "Darkness encroaches. And Meren is right, we must do something about it." Under the table, Fa squeezed Meren's hand.

"Why the sudden change, Fa?" Asher asked, mocking in his tone. "You left her to return home alone, didn't you? To journey here by her-self, knowing the dangers the Dark Færies pose. And now you would return? Now you would swoop in and be the hero to us all. Why?"

"I was wrong to not return with Meren."

"Ah, I see. So we're all supposed to grovel at your feet now, is it?" Asher growled.

"Ash," Meren said. "Stop."

"No, I will not stop, Meren. I want to know how we are supposed to trust a male who would abandon you in your time of need."

"He did not abandon me—"

"What would you call it, then?" Asher demanded. "Convenient timing? A grand entrance? Fa the hero come to save us all!"

"Asher, stop this," Meren begged.

"Meren is right," Fa said, unbothered by Asher's rising temper. "We must not wait any longer, hoping to hide long enough to avoid the Darkness. We must fight."

"Fight with what? We are a peaceful people. We do not wield weapons," Meir pointed out.

Meren's eyes went immediately to the bone blades resting at Asher's hips.

"We were gifted with different weapons," Fa said. "We have simply forgotten about them."

"What weapons?" Athaliah asked.

"I will teach you," Fa said. "If you will accept my assistance," he added, nodding to Jotham.

Jotham nodded back, his countenance deep in thought as he took everything in. "And is this your news?" he asked. "Is this what you came for—to train us?"

"No," Fa said. "I am here to tell you that I plan to journey south. To find the Fount Barakah."

"Fount Barakah?" Meren echoed. "The island in the legends?"

"You know of it?" Fa turned to face her.

"My parents were zealots," she said. "They often told me tales of the fount. That it is the seat of Eloah's magic."

"Yes," Fa said. "But they are not legends. The tales are true."

"Bullshit," Asher spat.

"Asher," Jotham said this time, his tone reprimanding. "Tell us what you know, Fa," Jotham went on.

"The seer told me of a magic called the Summoning. It is rare and ancient and requires a great sacrifice. But if executed properly, it will unite the Light within all of us, summoning us to its power, the power of Eloah."

"So the hero comes to us with folk tales, and all of a sudden we're to drop everything and risk our lives for some cockamamie retelling of færylings' stories? Am I getting this right?" Asher asked.

"Asher, what is wrong with you?" Meren demanded, done with letting him spew his insolence.

"What is wrong with *me*? What is *wrong* with me?" Asher slammed his hands on the table, standing abruptly. "You tell me what you have been through, Meren. Of a so-called friend who somehow magically found you in a raging storm and then *healed* you from a wound you don't remember getting. You don't know him from a twig in the woods, but you've placed your full trust in him. Forgive me if I find your judgment lacking, but it's painfully obvious what he wants, and it has little to do with saving the world."

"Asher, I—"

"And now, because you claim he is our salvation, we are supposed to place our trust in the hero who did not bring you home but hoarded you like a spider in a lair. We are supposed to believe that a male with shreds for wings is going save us all from the blight of the Darkness. Is that right?"

Rage boiled in her own gut as Meren stood, hovering over her chair as her raging wings suspended her in the air. "You know nothing of him. Nothing. I would trust Fa with my life. And if he says that the Summoning is the answer, then I believe him."

"Of course you do," said Asher with disdain.

"And I will go with him to find it," Meren added.

"What?" Athaliah asked. "Mer, you just got back!"

"Meren," Fa said, standing as well.

"I'm going with you, Fa. Don't try to stop me."

"This is a dangerous mission, Meren," said Jotham. "If the Dark Færies learn of what you are doing, your life is forfeit."

"Damn right it's dangerous!" Asher barked. "Not to mention asinine. You will not go."

"I will protect her with my life," Fa said.

"You will stay the Sheol away from her because she is not going," Asher growled.

"I *am* going," Meren said. "I know the risks."

"You know nothing," Asher hissed. "And I will not stand by and watch this ridiculous spectacle anymore."

And with that, Asher flew over the table and out of the room, a fell wind sweeping through the forest.

CHAPTER XX

don't know why he has to be such an ass all the time," Meren growled, pacing.

"Surely he's not an ass *all* the time," Fa quipped.

Meren whirled, facing him fully. When she spotted the smirk threatening the corner of his lips, she snorted a laugh. "I'm sorry he was so rude to you."

"I don't know why *you're* apologizing, Meren," Fa said, and she threw her arms around him again, breathing deeply.

"I missed you. So much. It was as if I could not breathe," she murmured.

Fa pressed a kiss to her brow. "I'm so sorry, Meren."

"It's all right."

"It's not," he argued, his arms tightening around her. "I was wrong. And I hurt you. I never want to hurt you. And I'm sorry."

"You came back. That's all that matters to me," she said. And she meant every word.

Fa merely nodded. "I will never leave you again, Tipharah."

It was in the depths of his obsidian eyes—somewhere in the way the light caught them—that she knew he meant it. Every word. And her soul seemed to sigh in relief, to breathe deeply again after being half-strangled since the moment she'd left him in his faraway home. She reached to touch his cheek, but a knock sounded at her door.

No, not a knock. Someone was *pounding* on her door.

"Meren!" she heard from the other side.

Asher.

Fa caught her chin, his other arm still secure around her waist. "If you're not up for this—"

"It's fine," she said, though her heart had found a new home in her throat.

Fa searched her face for a moment. "You say the word and I will take care of it."

"I know," she said, giving him a weak smile.

He released her, and she crossed her little home to answer the door.

Asher said nothing as he observed the scene: Meren standing before him and Fa not far behind, his thick arms crossed, his face set in stone, his devastated wings hanging with haunting grace from his formidable shoulders.

"I need to speak with you," Asher practically growled. "Alone," he added, scowling at Fa.

Meren turned to Fa, who held her eyes intently. A single nod from her had him crossing the room toward the door.

"Oh, so you need his permission now, is that it?" Asher sneered, also crossing his arms.

To his credit, Fa said nothing as he walked past Asher, his face still set in a mask of stone, his eyes cool and calculating as he held Asher's gaze for a moment. He was out the door before Meren said, "No, in fact he was making sure I am all right with being alone with you. You're not exactly cordial at the moment, Asher."

Fa had closed the door behind him, and Meren wondered how close he would stay, how much he would hear.

Close enough that if she needed him, he would be there in an instant, no doubt.

Asher ignored her comment and stepped up to her instead. "I forbid you to go on this fool's quest, Meren."

"You *forbid* me?" she challenged with a laugh.

"It is too dangerous," Asher countered, his wings like two blades of rigid steel behind him. They did not flutter lazily, did not move at all.

"I am aware of the danger, Asher," she said, moving past him and plopping down on one of her cushions in the middle of the room.

"No, you're not," he said, opting to remain standing. "This is a fool's errand, Meren. You will be killed. You understand that, right? If you are caught, you will die. It will not matter what you are, what you have, it—"

"What do you mean, *what I am* and *what I have?* Asher, what are you talking about?"

"Nothing, Meren. Never mind."

"No, not *never mind*," she said, standing. "Asher, what are you talking about?"

"You will not go," he said, crossing the small space between them and taking hold of her shoulders. But she shrugged out of his grip.

"I will," she said.

"You will not. I forbid it. I am your mate and—"

"Oh yes, of course. I forgot! What with all the hustle and bustle tonight, I was surprised to get all the congratulations!" she sneered. "When is the happy occasion?"

"Meren, don't start."

"No, *you* don't start. Asher, you cannot order me around. I am not your mate! And even if I were—"

"How convenient!" Asher barked. "Your perfect little friend returns, and suddenly you're no longer mated to me!"

"Asher, I was never mated to you!"

He paused—truly paused—and looked at her for a moment. And then he laughed, a wicked, dark sort of chuckle that skittered along her bones.

"I see," he said, nodding. "Your promises mean nothing, then. Of course."

"Asher," she said, reaching out to touch his arm at the sight of the devastation that began to color his hardened features.

But he stepped back, his eyes turning to ice once more as he said, "You are a damned fool. And you will die by your tomfoolery."

"Asher," she tried again.

"I rescind my offer. I will not be mated to a female that is in love with another male."

"Asher," she protested, shocked at his words. "It's not… It's not like that. He's my friend and…"

"You're a damned fool, Meren. You always have been. If you think that male returned here to be your *friend,* if you think he wants to take you off alone into the woods on a quest to find some fable, if you think he has no intentions beyond what is *noble,* you are as blind as you are stupid and you deserve whatever fate befalls you."

And then he whirled, crossing the room in three heavy steps before slamming the door behind him.

"Are you quite done?" Fa asked, standing in the shadows of the chalam branch as Asher emerged, scowling. The moonlight cut through the glittering leaves, casting a silvery glow on the færy's angular face—his features so much like his father's. At the sight of the rage in Asher's eyes, a thousand memories flooded Fa's mind. And when he caught a glimpse of the bone blade at Asher's side, a thousand more followed.

"Oh yes, she's all yours," Asher said with false brightness, gesturing to Meren's door. "I'd hate to stand in your way."

Asher shouldered past Fa, making to fly away. But he froze as still as death, his back to Fa, when he heard him say, "The next time you have something to say, you can say it to me. I don't care what your issue is with her. You will not speak to her in such a manner again."

Asher turned. Slowly. Like ice hardening a shallow puddle. "So you think you own her now." His words were like stones falling into a bottomless lake.

"No," Fa said. "But your problem is that you do."

Asher faced him fully, his eyes narrowing with wicked humor.

"What a dangerous little game you play, Fa. Your father would be proud."

"Damn you," Fa spat.

"I'm already damned. And so are you. But I am curious." He smiled with an oily grin, stepping closer to Fa, almost nose to nose. "I am curious—have you told her, Fa? Does she know who you *really* are? And what will she do when she finds out?"

"Funny," Fa said, willing his face to stillness and his heart to slow down. "I could ask the same of you."

"Rot in Sheol," Asher growled, his lips curling into a snarl.

Fa merely cocked his head to the side. "I'll see you there."

~

"I suppose you heard all of that," Meren said, sitting cross-legged on a cushion in the middle of the room. Her wings hung limply behind her, her opalescent curls particularly glossy in the moonlight spilling into her home. When Fa caught sight of the tear that glistened on her cheek, his pounding heart stopped short.

"I heard enough. And I can see enough in your eyes." He pulled a cushion up and sat down beside her. "Are you all right?" he asked quietly, daring to take hold of her hand again, to play with her fingers. When she had let him hold her hand earlier, when she had let him come in at all… Fa knew she was much more than he ever deserved. He wrapped his hand around hers, and she did not stop him, though her hand was trembling softly.

She kept her eyes down, her words little more than a breath. "I hurt him, Fa. I did not mean to, but I did. And I fear things will never be the same."

He wondered then…wondered what that pain in her eyes meant.

"He asked me to be his mate."

His fingers stilled on hers at her declaration, his heart stopping for a moment again. "Oh," he heard himself say.

"It was something he said," she went on, that lone tear on her cheek finally finding its way to her chin and hanging there, just as he hung on every word she said.

"He asked me if I'd truly rather be alone than to be with someone who cares."

She met his eyes only for a moment before she looked back down. Fa's hand seemed to tremble in time with hers.

"I lied to him, Fa. I lied to him when I said no. And I think that lie has destroyed him."

No.

She had said no.

"Well then, we are both liars," he said, twining his fingers with hers.

She met his eyes again. And this time she held them, her brows narrowing slightly in question.

"I lied to you when I said yes."

That lone tear at her chin was joined by several more when at last she rested her head on his shoulder, silently weeping in the growing darkness.

"I know," she whispered, so softly he almost missed it. He wrapped an arm around her back and pulled her closer to him, letting her tears soak his shoulder.

"It shouldn't have come to this," she said. "It wasn't supposed to be this way."

"He is in love with you, Tipharah," Fa said, the words burning like bile in his throat.

She lifted her head from his shoulder, searching his face for a moment, a question in her eyes that he could not read. "We were friends. For decades. And everything was fine up until he decided he loved me. And then it just felt more and more like I could do nothing to please him. I did not want it to be this way."

"You didn't do anything wrong," Fa tried.

"Didn't I?" she asked, her voice rising in timbre. "I knew what was happening. For years. But I said nothing. Pretended like it wasn't happening. Why couldn't I have loved him? He is a good male and a better friend. He saved my life when I was a færyling, for Eloah's sake!"

"That doesn't mean you owe him something," Fa said, knowing he should not be having this conversation. He had no right to say a damn word...

"Don't I?"

It was indignation, righteous and roiling that welled in his gut. He hated—*hated*—that Asher had made her feel this way. That even for a moment she felt as if she owed him something. "No. You don't," Fa said, his words clipped.

"It's my own selfishness, Fa. That's the problem. But I remember them. I remember my parents. How they were with each other. They could hardly stand to be parted from one another. They were friends, yes. But it was more. So much more. I looked for it. I swear to you that I did. I tried to find something more with Asher. But...it was never there. And I couldn't bring myself to pretend otherwise."

"You don't owe me an explanation, Meren. Love is not for the faint of heart."

"Have you ever been in love?" she asked, earnestness in her eyes.

"There was a time when I thought I was, yes."

"What happened?"

He took a moment to gather his words. To think of what to even say. "All I could think about was the way my mother used to look at her Mate."

"I thought you said your mother and father did not love each other," Meren said.

"They did not. But my mother was Mated to another. By magic. The true Mating magic. I could see it in her, even when I was too young to understand it."

"What happened? To her Mate?"

"I don't think they ever spoke of it to one another," Fa said.

"Why? How could they deny such a thing?"

"Because sometimes, Meren…sometimes the truth is far more damning than a lie."

Meren furrowed her brows, looking at Fa for a long moment. He wondered what she was thinking, what questions were blooming in her eyes.

"And what about you?" she finally asked. "What happened to the one you thought you loved?"

"I could not look at her the way my mother looked at her Mate. I knew I did not love her like that. And so I ended it."

Meren said nothing, only fiddled with her fingers, the pain of what had happened bothering her more than she was letting on.

He tilted her chin so he could see her eyes, losing himself in the amethyst depths. An understanding blossomed there. Understanding and a warmth that nearly undid him. Despite himself, he touched her cheek, basking in the small smile he found on her mouth. Meren slid into his arms. And for the third time that night, Fa wondered what kind of fool he must have been that he let her. And worse, that he reached both arms around her and held her too.

Fa wasn't sure how much time had passed, how long he had been holding her, breathing her in, when she pulled slightly away with a chuckle.

"What?" he asked.

"Why didn't you tell me you were so hungry?"

"What are you talking about?"

"Well, either I have a pet mountain cat I have forgotten about or your stomach is growling like a caracal."

"I'm fine." He laughed, trying to pull her back into his arms.

But she refused, pushing off of him so she could stand. "You need to eat, Fa."

He lifted a brow. "And you are going to cook for me?"

She whirled to face him. "Are you mocking me?"

He bit the inside of his cheek to keep from laughing. "Never, Tipharah."

"I am capable of cooking, you know."

"I've never doubted your capabilities," he said, standing and following her across the room, chuckling softly at the fervor with which she rummaged through her paltry excuse for a kitchen. Cook, indeed.

"Here," she said, plopping a færy cake on a plate and shoving it toward him.

"What's this?" he asked, taking the plate and inspecting it. "Did you make this?"

"No," she said. "Asher brought it to me this morning."

"Did *he* make it?" Fa asked, inspecting the cake a little more closely. Then again, Asher hadn't known Fa would be arriving. Surely he wouldn't have poisoned something intended for Meren…

"I doubt it," she said, hanging a kettle over her hearth fire. "Asher is not exactly a culinary expert."

When Fa narrowed his brows, Meren laughed. "I'm sure Shira made it. She's always making him little cakes and pastries. And he's always ignoring the ogling way she hands them to him."

Fa chuckled, a lightness settling on him that he hadn't known since he had arrived. He took a bite of the cake and wondered why in Sheol Asher hadn't noticed the care with which this Shira person had been trying to spoil him. The cake was delicious.

"Good?" Meren asked.

"Very good."

"Asher is a damned fool," Meren said, turning to stoke the fire.

Indeed.

Fa finished the cake in three bites, downing a cup of water afterward. Meren watched him, a look of casual amusement on her slender face, that curl of hers falling invitingly across her brow.

"We should get some rest. We have a long journey ahead of us," she said wisely.

Fa nodded, standing and looking around the small room she called her home. The bed in the corner was littered with books, and aside from that, there was no real place to sleep. He supposed the cushions in the middle of the room would have to suffice.

Meren had begun stacking books and folding down the blankets on her bed when she said, "It's not as nice as yours, but it's pretty soft."

When he realized what she meant, he said, "Meren, I'm not taking your bed."

"Is that so?" she asked, raising an eyebrow and resting a hand on her hip.

"Yes. It is," he said, turning to push the dandelion cushions together.

"So you can give up your bed for me, but I'm not allowed to give my bed to you, is that right?"

He merely smirked as he continued his work, wondering whether it would be better to let his legs dangle off the end, or leave a gap in between the cushions. Either way, it wasn't a pleasant prospect. Perhaps the floor—

"Fa, you're sleeping in the bed," Meren said. She had marched across the room and taken hold of his hand, attempting to pull him to her bed.

"Meren—"

"It's not up for discussion. If you think I'm letting you sleep on the floor on the last night we'll have among civilization for a good while, you've lost your mind."

"I can sleep on the cushions."

"They're hardly big enough for your backside, much less a bed. You're sleeping here."

"I will not have you sleeping on the floor, Meren."

She huffed a laugh, crawling under the blankets on her bed. "I wasn't planning to."

And as she unfolded the blankets further beside her, Fa was fairly certain the earth itself stopped turning. He reminded himself to breathe. And then to breathe again.

Because Meren wanted him to sleep beside her.

Eloah help him.

"Meren…"

"What?" she asked, her brows furrowed, half-annoyed, half-amused. "Are you afraid?"

"I am not afraid!" he balked, loathing how petulant he sounded.

She said nothing else, only raising those eyebrows a little higher.

He stood there, towering over her, over that skinny bed of hers that was hardly big enough for two people, and contemplated just how damned he was. For Asher hadn't been wrong about that—they were both damned.

But Fa pulled back the covers and climbed into the bed beside her.

And Eloah save him she was warm. So warm.

And when she curled herself up next to him, when she rested that soft, slender little arm of hers across his chest, he knew he was damned straight to Sheol.

Chapter XXI

From the time he was a færyling, Fa could remember wondering what it might be like to live in a færy coven in the heart of a chalam tree. He had been envious of the other young males and their communal lifestyle that was so opposite to what he had known, for his father had never deigned to live like the common færies.

"Your blood, my son, is purer. More powerful. Why would you stoop to live like you are a nobody?"

Perhaps there was a time in his youth when Fa would have agreed with his father. When he would have thought himself above the others. Chosen.

But that time was long since gone, dying with the rest of his legacy. Dying with his mother.

And after just the few hours he had spent with Meren and her coven, Fa wished that he'd had the stones to stand up to his father sooner. To find and make true friends instead of living to constantly drive out the enemy.

And knowing where he was going—what he faced, what Meren now faced—that regret stung all the more. For Asher hadn't been wrong: if they were caught, they would surely die. The Dark færies would not tolerate any attempt against them. Nor would King Asa.

He was surely sending himself to an early grave. And dragging sweet Meren down with him.

Bile stung his throat at the thought.

He stood at the base of the towering golden tree, watching the coven leader attempt to wield the magic within him, watching his calculated patience, his cool focus. Jotham was a king at heart, whether he knew it or not.

The Light færies would surely follow a male like him.

"You're trying too hard," Fa said, pushing off of the trunk on which he leaned. "Find it within, but do not force it."

"Are you certain this will work?" Jotham asked, his first hint of doubt—in Fa or in himself, Fa could not be sure.

"We are each gifted with the Light. It manifests in different ways. Your magic is Wind, Jotham."

"How do you know for certain?" the coven leader asked, his eyes fixed on his hands forming around an invisible sphere.

Fa walked to the leader, resting a hand on Jotham's, capturing his attention. "Because like calls to like. And our magic is the same. I can feel it within you, just as I could feel it within Meren."

"Meren has Wind magic?" Jotham asked, genuine curiosity in his eyes.

That. And Flame. And Water. A marvel, a glorious creation. He wondered if Jotham knew what sort of treasure he had harbored all these years. Fa merely nodded. "Magic is not in the hands, my friend. It is in the heart."

Jotham lowered his hands and waited for Fa to go on.

"Close your eyes, Jotham. And call on the Wind," Fa said, stepping back.

The sunrise began peeking through the forest, shafts pouring through the thick flora in riotous shades of crimson and ochre. He had left Meren sleeping soundly in her bed before the sun had begun her march across the skies, the memory of her soft, deep breaths still warming his shoulder as he watched the leader attempt to find the magic within himself.

And then, like the still moments before a raging storm, the leaves suddenly began to shimmer around them, the blades of grass arching their backs as if bowing to Eloah himself.

Wind.

Strong and true.

The magic was strong within the coven leader.

"You must teach your people, Jotham. You must prepare them to fight with the gifts we have been given. For should Meren and I succeed, war will surely follow."

Jotham nodded solemnly, even as wonder still shone in his eyes over his own magic.

"You are a strong leader, my friend," Fa went on. "It is time to lead your people."

"We will fight, Gibhor. To the end, we will fight."

And then Jotham bowed. And the bile stung Fa's throat once more.

He turned his back and caught the Wind, landing on a branch far above.

"Where did you go?" Meren asked the moment Fa came through her door. The sunrise spilled around him, bathing him in shadow and splendor. When she had woken without him next to her, a little bubble of worry had welled in her belly. A wave of relief washed over her at the sight of his return.

Fa walked into her home, gathering his satchel and few belongings. "I was helping Jotham. He will need to train the other færies while we are gone."

The words were calm enough, but Meren could see that something was bothering Fa.

"Are you all right?" she asked, making her way to him.

"Of course. Why?" Fa asked, still bending over a satchel that was already sufficiently packed.

"Melekfa," she said, teasing him, hoping to lighten the mood. She placed a hand on his arm, and he stilled at her touch, his attention captured by the small flare of light where their skin met.

"Don't call me that," he said flatly.

She removed her hand from his arm, taken aback by the sudden heaviness of his words.

"Fa, what's wrong?"

"Nothing, Meren. We should get going. We'll want to take advantage of as much daylight as possible."

"Fa," she said again, and when he still ignored her, she took his face in both of her hands, forcing him to meet her eyes. "Don't shut me out."

"Never," he said, resting his brow on hers. "Ani ohevet otcha," he breathed. "I'm sorry, Tipharah," he added, his words softening. He wrapped his arms around her, relaxing into her touch as she rested her arms around his shoulders. Light glowed soft and warm around them.

"What's wrong?" she tried again. "Did something upset you?"

He breathed a heavy sigh. "Asher wasn't wrong, Meren. This is a dangerous mission."

"I know," she said. "Are you going to try to talk me out of it, too?"

"No," he answered, and she knew he meant it. "But would you blame me for worrying?"

She touched his cheek, relishing the silver stubble she found there. "I'm worried, too, Fa. Do not think I am unaware of the consequences of what we are doing."

"The Summoning itself requires a great sacrifice," he pointed out, his breath warm on her skin.

"I've been thinking about that."

"Have you?" he asked, lifting his head from hers. Genuine curiosity danced in his eyes.

She pressed a soft kiss to his nose. "Leave it to me, Fa."

~

The morning sun did little to warm them as the færies gathered in the clearing at the base of the chalam tree. Meren looked around at her friends, at their worried faces and solemn expressions. They, too, knew the gravity of the mission she and Fa were about to carry out. But Meren swallowed her fear and walked over to Athaliah, wrapping her friend in her arms.

"Don't do anything stupid, Mer," Athaliah said, her words curling in front of her in wisps of fog as she hugged Meren tightly. "And come back home soon. In one piece, please."

"I love you, Ath," Meren said, huffing a small laugh.

"I love you too, Mer. Please be careful." Athaliah hugged Meren close, as if it would be their last, and a pang of worry followed her friend's embrace.

When Meren pulled away, she spotted Fa coming up from behind, a look she couldn't read on his face. His worry for her this morning had both comforted and terrified her. Just as Athaliah's had. For indeed, she knew they were setting off on an errand that would either make or break them all.

"Are you ready?" Fa asked, coming to her side. He took her hand, his own warm and strong around her fingers, and she knew a kind of calm at his touch.

She nodded, silently fiddling with her mother's ring on her other finger as she sent a wordless prayer to Eloah.

"Derekh tzleha. May Eloah's magic be with you," Jotham said, landing beside them. And that's when Meren realized…

Asher was nowhere to be found.

A heaviness settled on her heart at his gaping absence. Too many things had been left unsaid between them. Too many hurts. Fa squeezed her hand, and when she looked down, she could see a faint blue-and-silver glow between them. She met his eyes and found a sweet smile there.

With one last look at her friends, Meren and Fa set off into the forest beyond.

Chapter XXII

ou must save your strength, Tipharah. We do not have to fly the whole time," Fa said.

"I'm fine, Fa," Meren said, squeezing his hand. But in truth, fatigue was already lapping at her toes like the tide coming in. Flying for long periods of time was one thing. Flying for long periods of time while helping her wingless friend also fly was another. She could feel his magic entwining with hers, their Wind dancing with one another, helping him fly, helping her keep him aloft. But after hours and hours, even the magic could not abate the fatigue, and the soft glow around their joined hands faded ominously as the day wore on.

As always, Fa's keen observation of her needs was spot on.

"Perhaps we should rest for a bit," Fa offered as they rounded a bend, clearing a grove of trees. The day had bloomed glorious and dazzling, the wind crisp and biting as it careened past them.

"We cannot spare any time, Fa. We need to get to Fount Barakah as soon as possible."

"It will not matter how quickly we get there if you are exhausted when we do," he said, squeezing her hand for emphasis.

"Fine," she said, knowing he was right. "We'll find a place to rest here for the night. It will be sunset soon anyway."

Fa did not gloat, did not even smirk at her acquiescence. Which was probably why she agreed so willingly. Asher's smugness alone would have been reason enough to refuse to take a break.

They found a small hole at the base of an oak tree, and Fa immediately set about inspecting it. But he did not go inside. No, Fa called on his remarkable Wind magic, clearing out the nook with a gust that scattered leaves and acorns, twigs and bits of bark. But nothing more, thank Eloah. Meren could only marvel at her traveling companion and his mastery of the magic he had been gifted.

"Where did you learn that?" she asked as she followed him inside, making a small ball of færy light in her palm.

"You'd be surprised what you can do when there are no distractions," Fa said, walking all around the space, looking high and low. When it was clear the hole was empty, he at last faced her, the angles of his face accentuated by the shadows from the færy light. He took the light from her palm, inspecting it for a moment.

"Your magic is beautiful, Meren. Did you know that?"

"Isn't it all the same?" she asked with a breathy laugh.

"Come here," he said, gesturing for her to step closer. And it was only when she really looked at the little blue ball of light that she realized…it was more than just light. It was swirling with an otherworldly luminescence, brushed with whorls of silver and gold, entwining together around a central sphere of cobalt and pearl energy. Light. But so much more.

"I never knew it looked like that," she said, marveling at her own magic.

"I've never seen it look quite like that," Fa said, lifting the little ball of light a little higher so that he could inspect it more closely. "But I would hazard that yours looks different because you are not just a possessor of the Flame, but of the Wind and Water, too."

She eyed the færy light more closely, and sure enough, she could see the effects of each element within the sphere. The fluvial trails of turquoise weaving with the light as if on a phantom wind, eddies of luminescence and energy curling and intermingling. Flame. Wind. Water.

The Light of Eloah.

"It's beautiful," she heard herself say.

And when she looked up at Fa, she saw he was no longer fixated on her little ball of light, but on her, his obsidian eyes spellbound by her own.

"Your magic," he finally said. "It is a rare and beautiful gift. Unlike any other." He released the little ball, and she watched it float to the top of the nook.

His hand on her chin brought her attention back down to him. "You will be a target for the rest of your life, Tipharah. Should King Asa or any of his ilk learn the true nature of your magic, you will never be safe."

Fear struck her heart, pounding wildly in her chest. What if he already knew? What if that was why she was always followed? Always chased?

What if that was why Jotham and Asher had insisted on hiding all these years?

What if they were hiding *her?*

"They know who you are, Meren. But they do not yet know the depths of your magic."

"How do you know that?" she asked. When Fa did not answer immediately, she added, "Does Asher know? Is that why he has kept me in hiding?"

"Yes," was Fa's only answer before turning away from her.

"How do *you* know who I am?" she asked him.

"My mother was in love with a seer."

"A seer?" she asked, before she realized…*oh.* "Nabi? Your mother was in love with Nabi?"

Fa only nodded.

"He told you that you would meet me," she went on.

"He told me that I would meet Malkah Neharah."

"That is not my name."

He turned, facing her fully. "No, it is not. But he believed it would be."

"How? Why?"

Fa hesitated, searching her for a moment, his expression unreadable. "Because of me."

"What does it mean, Fa? What do any of these names you have given me mean?"

Fa took in a breath, hesitation in the lines around his mouth and in his boundless eyes. But the words did not come before a screech sounded outside. Their attention shot to the opening of the nook, the fading light casting the forest beyond in shades of gray. She turned her attention back to Fa, whose eyes were keen on the flora outside.

"Is that what I think it is?" she asked, her words a breath of smoke before her.

Fa looked at her for a moment, his eyes confirming her suspicions.

"Surely she won't be able to get to us in here," Meren said.

"She?" he asked, his interest piqued.

"She's followed me before."

"An eagle," he said flatly.

She merely nodded.

Fa peered out of the nook as far as he dared, scouring the skies. But his search was in vain, for the eagle was not in the skies.

She was on the ground.

Her massive black talon crunched on the ground just in front of them, and Fa jumped back, grabbing Meren and pulling her with him. They landed with a thud at the back of the nook, Fa's arms wrapped tightly around her, his body a fortress around her. She peered over his shoulder, the steady cadence of his heart pounding in time with hers.

He dared not breathe too loudly, lest the bird sense them. Sense them and make them her dinner.

And when her black eye peered into the opening of their nook, it was all Meren could do not to shriek. The eagle looked inside, blinking once, twice, her dark feathers standing on end, her movements sharp and precise, her head tilted to the side as if she were a simple, curious cat. Fa was little more than a statue before Meren, holding her tightly, breathing shallowly, still as death.

A wind picked up, tossing bits of earth and trees toward the eagle. No, not *a* wind. Fa's Wind. Mercifully, the distraction worked enough that the eagle stalked away, out of their line of sight.

It was only when they heard the flap of her wings that Fa let go of Meren and sat down beside her.

"Where have you seen her before?" Fa asked, his breathing still shallow, labored.

"She followed Asher and me. When we came looking for you. She caught me in her talons when…" And she realized then that she had never told Fa about the attack by the Dark færy just before finding him.

"When what?" Fa asked.

"When the Dark færy found me. She would have eaten us had it not been for Asher."

"The Dark færies—they've chased you before," Fa said. She nodded, and he continued, "That's why you always fly low to the ground."

"The attacks always happen in the open air."

Fa nodded silently, taking her hand in his. He rubbed his thumb along her palm, a gentle, soothing touch. "I will keep you safe, Tipharah," he finally said.

"I know," she said, resting her head on his shoulder. "I know."

CHAPTER XXIII

She ignored him. For four whole days, she ignored his glances, his hand squeezes, his silent worrying. They had to get to Fount Barakah as quickly as possible. And the quickest way to get there was to fly. And the only way Fa could fly was if she entwined her magic with his and essentially did what was the magical equivalent of carrying him. For hours a day. Every day. For four days now.

Yes, it was taking its toll.

But she ignored his worrying anyway.

Even when they would stop to eat at midday, to recoup the strength that was waning with every flap of her wings, she ignored him when he tried to ask her to rest. She would just pop a final seed into her mouth, take him by the hand, and leap back into the air.

Because they had to get to Fount Barakah before the Dark færies figured out what they were up to.

By the third day, she could not ignore the ache in her back and wings any longer. Her magic was sputtering, Fa's considerable magic the only thing keeping them aloft at times—floating them on a gust of mighty Wind. But even his magic fussed and worried, wrapping itself around hers, stroking it as if to say, "Please. You must rest."

But she would not.

She *could* not. No matter how taxing.

She had to get to the fabled fount. She had to find a way to perform the Summoning. She had to stop the Dark færies before they destroyed everything she loved. Forever.

But while she knew Fa was worried, she had to at least give him credit for not stopping her. He hadn't insisted that she rest. He had just kept going with her, holding her hand, flying on her Wind magic.

For that, she could have kissed him.

Not that he would welcome such a gesture. He had made that perfectly clear the last time she had attempted.

She stifled a groan as Fa rubbed her shoulders and the space between her wings with expert skill. Having stopped to rest for the night at the base of a fat, low pine branch, she hadn't argued when he began rubbing her sore muscles without a word, even though she knew he was as tired as she was. His body was warm behind her, but the wintry air still blew cool around them, sending shivers up her arms.

"Cold?" he asked, his breath a shock of warmth on her ear and neck. She hadn't realized he was standing so close.

"It's getting colder every day, isn't it?" The thought sent another wave of chills across her skin, for it was indeed cold. Too cold.

The cold of unrelenting Darkness.

She wondered if the mortals had even taken notice. If they had stopped to consider why the weather was so unseasonable. Why the clouds never lifted. Did the humans have any idea what loomed before them?

"Here," Fa said, placing his mouse-fur cloak over her shoulders, still warm from his body.

"Fa," she protested, trying to remove the cloak. He did not let her. "You'll freeze!" She tried to turn and face him, to reprimand him properly.

He allowed her no such liberty, wrapping himself around her, his chest broad and solid against her back.

"*You'll* have to keep me warm," he said. And the way he said it…

She peered over her shoulder, trying to see his face, his expression. The hint of a smirk rested on his lips.

"You want me to build a fire?" she asked, half teasing, half thrilled with her own thoughts.

"Mmm hmm," was all he said.

"I've never been good with flint," she teased, catching sight of the rock Fa had placed before them earlier. Wondering what in the world he had intended for it.

"Oh, you won't need sticks and stones, Tipharah."

She was desperate to see his face, to see what he meant by such a declaration. But still he remained strong and steady behind her, his arms around hers, cupping her hands in his in front of them.

And then she understood.

"Fa," she said. "I can't."

"You can," he said. Calmly. Steadily.

Damn him.

"All right, let me rephrase. I don't want to."

A breathy chuckle skittered along her skin. He was just so damned *close.*

"What is it that you fear?" he asked.

A simple question.

Nothing. Everything.

"I cannot… I don't…"

"Meren, Flame is a part of the Light of Eloah. It is not corrupted. Only those who would wield it for their own gain are corrupt."

"And is not making a fire wielding it for my own gain?"

He laughed again. "Do you plan to take over the world, Tipharah?"

No. But still…

"Why do you think I gave you that name?" he asked, his lips so close…so dangerously close to her pointed ear, sending shivers along her skin that had nothing to do with the cold.

"What name?" she managed, cursing silently at the way her voice sounded so breathless.

"You are brave, Tipharah. Braver than you know."

Brave.

Tipharah.

Yes.

She remembered it now. An old word. The ancient tongue.

Tipharah.

All along, he had been calling her brave. Glorious.

"My glorious, brave one," he said, as if in answer. He formed her hands into a cradle, his magic teasing her own. Coaxing it.

But the Wind could only stoke the flame. The Flame…the Flame had to come from her.

She closed her eyes, cursing the little tremble in her hands.

"Breathe, Tipharah," Fa whispered.

And at the sound of the name he had given her, a tiny fire erupted from her palm.

She sucked in a breath, shaking her hand at the shock. The fire jumped to his hand.

"Sorry!" she exclaimed. "I'm sorry, Fa. Did I burn you?"

"I'm fine, Tipharah," he said, his hands still steady around hers, and he a fortress of warmth, of strength surrounding her. She shut her eyes and focused again, calmed by his patience, his steady magic waiting. Coaxing. Calling to hers.

Flame of cobalt and emerald, of amethyst and pearl erupted from her palm again, and slowly, steadily, she turned her hand, letting it fall onto the rock Fa had selected precisely for this occasion. The rock seemed to sing as the fire danced on its surface. Danced but did not consume. Steady. Unending. The fire would not die until she willed it to.

Magic Flame. The Light of Eloah.

She turned to face Fa, not caring about the elated smile she knew was on her face.

"You did it," he said, and it was more than pride in his voice. It was kissed with wonder. And a hint of something else. Something she couldn't place.

His eyes held hers—a frozen moment, an unmoving star, glittering in the firmament. She cupped her hands between them, building another ball of Light, of Flame. Small and flickering. Fa's eyes glittered with more wonder as his arms came around her, settling steady and heavy on her waist.

They were so close she could taste the spicy sweetness of his breaths. Could see the sheen of the small scars that spread over his neck and collarbone. Scars from his past. From battles fought and won. This warrior of hers—he was beautiful, every scar, every fleck of starlight in his eyes, every shimmer of silver in his glossy hair.

His eyes were fixated on the ball of Flame dancing between them, and when she shifted her attention back to it, she realized…Fa was playing with it. Sending his Wind dancing among her fire. Swirling eddies of Flame. So she added her own Wind. And Water. Until what was between them was something *other*. Something beyond.

A maelstrom encompassed in a miniature vortex.

A hurricane.

Her Wind carried it above them, a storm cloud looming just over their heads, errant drops of miniature rain peppering their faces and the ends of their noses, dampening their hair. The nuisance curl at her brow was soon fat and heavy with rain.

Their eyes were fixed above them, on what their combined magic had made. A tiny bolt of lightning flared from the eye of the storm, and she ducked, surprised.

"That could come in handy in a war," she said.

She looked back to Fa, only to realize his attention had long since left the storm. Wicked delight gleamed in his obsidian eyes as he said, "You, Tipharah, are as ruthless as you are beautiful."

She froze. Breathed. Breathed again. The sound of her swallow seemed to clatter off the conifer in which they were perched. The rain from their personal storm faltered, but the winds did not die.

"You think I'm…" She blinked once. Twice. "Ruthless?" she finally managed, cursing her own cowardice for not asking the question she really wanted to ask.

But Fa knew. She could see it in the way the smile threatened at the corner of his mouth, could feel it in the way he brushed that rain-dampened curl from her brow. "Breathtaking," he finally said.

And the way he looked at her, the way his eyes bored into her… into her very soul…

She might have gotten lost in those eyes, had he not brushed his lips against hers. Soft. Like a feather. A breath of a kiss.

And it shattered her completely.

His magic seemed to dance around hers, and she could feel it— elation, a sweet joy purring from his magic as it wrapped itself around her. Around her soul.

Yes, she heard. *Yes. Home, Malkah.*

She touched his chin, relishing the silver stubble and the golden skin beneath, soft and smooth. "What took you so long?" she heard herself ask.

He lifted a silver eyebrow, the shock of black in his hair rising in tandem. His hands splayed against her back, pulling her closer to him. "After I foiled the first so thoroughly, I wasn't sure if you'd welcome a second attempt."

A mischievous grin curled her mouth. "You did foil it."

"A mistake I do not intend to make twice, B'sheirt." And then he kissed her again. But this time…

The kiss was consuming. Altering. As if he could not taste her enough. She snaked her arms around him and let herself get lost. Found. Shattered. Made whole.

Eloah, this male. This friend who had become so much more. Who had always been more, hadn't he?

He did not relinquish her lips, as if he had been wanting, hoping as much as she had.

This.

This was what she had been holding out for. This *thing* between them, breathing and alive. Formidable and beautiful.

This, she heard. *Yes.*

Fa. Melekfa. Gibhor. Her friend. Her very heart. Soul.

Fa's lips faltered, and when she composed herself enough to figure out why, she realized he was looking up at the glow of silver and blue around them.

Their magic.

Alive.

Merging.

He kept her close but said nothing, his eyes mixed with wonder and something else—something that looked a lot like worry as he observed the dance of Light and Flame around them. His arms were warm around her under the cloak, their miniature storm fizzling to fat gray clouds, misting them with warm droplets, the petrichor pleasant and soothing. Fa's fingers trailed absently down her back, occasionally caressing the very innermost parts of her wings. She might have purred in his arms, might have sighed at his touch. But when she rested her head on his chest and felt that steady heart of his beating in time with hers, she knew she was home indeed.

Chapter XXIV

t was the cold that woke her. Or rather, the absence of heat. Fa's heat, to be precise. An aching cool where his arms had been all night, wrapped securely around her waist, his body pressed to her back.

But now it was just cold. Too cold, even with her fire still dancing heartily on the stones nearby. She sat up abruptly, a tremor of worry settling in her bones when she realized Fa was nowhere to be found.

She called his name once and then again. But he was nowhere within her line of sight. The flames before her seemed to falter with her worry, and the encroaching cold crept along her spine.

"Fa," she tried again, unsure if it was safe to call his name too loudly lest anyone unwanted hear it.

She had begun to fuss with the blanket in which she was tangled when Fa, with the help of his Wind, landed on the branch before her.

"Tipharah?" he asked, a question of concern in his eyes. "Are you all right?"

"Oh, I…" She flushed. She was being foolish, of course. For she realized she could still feel him. Feel his heart in time with hers. She had let her worry ignore it. "Sorry," she finished. "When I didn't see you, I thought—"

"You needn't worry, Tipharah," he said, smiling softly as he crawled beside her, sitting down, a bundle of fruit and seeds in tow. "I won't go far."

"I know, I—" But *was* it foolish? To be so worried? The Dark færies were never far. And the sounds they had heard all night…

It was only because of Fa's wards that they weren't found. And only his steady arms around her reassured her enough to sleep.

He lifted the bundle, a look of playful remorse on his face. "I brought breakfast."

"Food is a language of love for you, isn't it?" she asked, digging into the bounty, hoping for a distraction.

"It's one of them, I suppose. But it's not the main one."

She looked up, chewing a bite of apple. "What is?"

"You," he said, leaning across the space between them and pressing a kiss to her jaw, just below her ear.

But it was not enough. So she took his face in her hands and kissed him properly.

And Eloah save her, the way he kissed her…

She pulled him to her, until he nearly toppled on top of her. He took charge, laying her down with a grace that befitted his easy elegance. He peppered kisses along her jaw, her neck, down her chest. His hands wandered down her back, finding her thighs, lifting them so he could wrap them around him. And Meren… Meren could hardly breathe, hardly think past those hands of his. But then he stopped abruptly, lifting his face to meet her eyes.

"What's wrong?" she asked, breathless. Magic danced around

them, even brighter than when he had kissed her last night.

"Nothing, B'sheirt." He kissed her once, and thoroughly, before he sat back on his heels, pulling her up with him. "But we should keep moving."

Yes. That was true.

Inconvenient at the moment. But true, nonetheless. The worry she had seen last night was back in his eyes, too.

She reluctantly acquiesced, taking his hand when he offered it and downing her breakfast in a few bites before they were off again, flying through the forest with the help of her wings and his Wind. But she couldn't help but wonder why he had stopped himself so abruptly. Why he had ended what was only just getting started.

Was there something Fa wasn't telling her?

~

She wondered for three more days. The cold winds grew saltier and saltier, and she stopped herself from wondering what in the world was going on with Fa only by focusing on what they were supposed to do about the Summoning.

A great sacrifice. That's what Fa had said. The Summoning would require a great sacrifice. But what sacrifice could a nobody offer that would be great enough to summon all of Færydom? And even if she were to summon them, how in the world would she then convince them to join her in her idealistic venture to save the world from the Darkness?

Perhaps Asher had been right. Perhaps this was nothing but a fool's quest.

She toyed with her mother's mating ring as they flew over a bed of ferns, missing her parents. Missing their easy smiles, their infectious laughter, the way their love for each other still lingered in her own heart. The ring on her finger became a branding iron, a reminder of all she had lost.

And all she had yet to lose.

The forest of hazelnuts and conifers thinned with every mile, with every flap of her tired wings. They were getting close to the coast. To the cliffs.

Close to the ocean.

And somewhere out there among the tossing waves was an island—an island that was home to a famed fount. And the seat of Eloah's magic.

Worry roiled in her gut, and it was only when Fa gave her hand a gentle squeeze that she realized she had a death grip on his.

Their magic was now a constant glow around them, and it seemed to get brighter with every passing day.

As if it were merging. And fortifying itself.

She wasn't sure whether to be elated or terrified at the notion that their magic might anticipate something they could not. And worse, as she basked in Fa's steady presence beside her, she wasn't sure whether to be elated or terrified that she had so much more to lose now than ever before. She wished very much that Nabi were here to tell them what to do. What to expect.

Or maybe Shira, with her strange parting words before Meren had left to find Fa—words that sounded a lot like a seer. Something about a sacrifice… Meren wished she had paid more attention to the cryptic words, wished she could remember them, wished she could figure something out. *Anything.*

She wished she could predict the future, if for no other reason than to make sure that at the end of all of this, the male beside her would still be there. That her friends would survive.

That this quest they were on would not be in vain.

"You are lost in thought," Fa said, his first words in a while. The sun was barely past the halfway mark in the sky, and Meren's wings were already aching.

"I was just thinking about something Shira said to me."

"When?" Fa asked.

They dodged a particularly thick tuft of ferns, flying over them but taking care to remain as low as possible. Their magic shone too brightly—they might as well have been a beacon. And if the Dark færies really were like the insects they resembled—moths drawn to the light—she and Fa would be all too easy to find.

A chill shuddered down Meren's spine.

"It was something she said to me before Asher and I left to come and find you." A sound cracked nearby, like the breaking of a twig or the snapping of a branch. Both of them turned to look in the direction from which the sound had come. But even as they flew, neither of them could make out what had made the sound.

Fa turned his attention back to Meren, that worry still limning his eyes. He looked down to their joined hands, to the fire that blazed around them.

"What do we do, Fa?" she asked, heat rising to her cheeks at the sight of their magic—so raw, so exposed, so entwined. Like lovers in the night. She could feel it, the way their magic seemed to bask in each other's presence, saying what neither of them had. She wondered if Fa could feel it too.

"Stay low," he breathed, taking his eyes off of her that he might scour the forest some more.

Another snap, this one louder.

Closer.

Was the eagle following them again?

Or something much worse?

Fa's hand tightened around hers. A breath later, he yanked her to him, wrapping himself and his Wind around her. That's when she realized he was careening them down. Down into the fern, out of sight. She clasped him tightly and held her breath, lest whatever was following them hear.

Fa's heart pounded in his chest, but his eyes stayed keen on their surroundings as his Wind carried them through the thick growth of the forest floor. She was desperate to ask him what he had seen, what they were flying from.

But she dared not make any more sound than necessary.

Fa's arms tightened around her as he used his Wind to practically throw them into a hole in the muddy ground.

"It's the Light, isn't it?" she asked. "The Light between us. They are following it."

Fa said nothing, devastation blooming in his eyes as he nodded.

"What do we do?" she tried.

"It's our magic. It grows stronger the more we use it together."

"And the stronger it grows…"

"…the easier we are to find," he finished.

"But we have to use our magic together. It's…" She couldn't finish the thought.

It was the only way he could fly.

But he knew that. The conflict in his eyes told her so. And with it, she could see a suggestion blooming in his thoughts, practically pouring from him.

"Melekfa, if you think I am going to leave you behind, you are sorely mistaken. I need you. And you promised to keep me safe. You promised with your life." Panic welled in her soul.

"I am not keeping you safe. Not by forcing you to carry me all this way, Meren. You are tired. I can feel it. And you need to—"

"I am *not* leaving you. Do you think you have a chance in Sheol of winning this argument?"

"Tipharah—"

"Don't *Tipharah* me, *Melekfa*. We are in this together or not at all. That was the promise."

"I can help you. I can stay on the ground, fight off any Dark færies that—"

"No," she said, and at her tone, Fa stopped. Looked at her. He took her face in his hands for a moment before pressing his brow to hers. Even such a simple gesture caused their magic to glow brighter, lighting up the hole in which they hid as if it weren't hidden from the sun by a thousand layers of flora.

Lighting up a pair of eyes staring at them from below.

"Shit," Fa breathed, grabbing Meren and pulling her behind him, putting himself between her and the creature with two slits for eyes.

A hiss had them careening out of the hole, plunging back into the ferns like a rock splashing into a placid pond. Fa held her hand tightly as they flew away, the snake pouring himself out of his hiding spot with surprising speed, slithering along behind them, intent to have his meal.

Their magic glowed brightly.

Too brightly.

And another snapping sound had them whirling to face not one but three Dark færies, all with deadly smiles on their faces, black like rotting flesh.

"The king has never liked it when we play with his toys." One of them grinned.

From behind, the snake slithered ever closer. Fa and Meren did not wait, but took off, flying away from the færies, away from the encroaching legless attacker. She could feel the deep well of his magic, Fa using everything in his arsenal to help them tear through the forest at shocking speed.

But the Dark færies were fast, too, keeping up with Fa and Meren with effortless finesse through the labyrinthine forest.

The snake slithered dangerously close below them, snapping his powerful jaw, and Fa cried out in agony. From behind, the Dark færies bellowed wicked laughter.

It was with no small amount of horror that she realized the serpent had bitten off a chunk of Fa's wing as it flapped limply in the wind. And even in their mangled state, it was clear that the bite had been excruciating.

Fa gritted his teeth, the pounding of his heart a war drum in her soul as they flew ever faster through the thick underbrush.

"Come now, Fa, it can't hurt that bad!" said one of the færies, laughing again. Distracted by their gloating, the third Dark færy suddenly cried out. Meren dared to look back and see why, just in time to watch as the snake snapped his deadly fangs around the unsuspecting færy, swallowing him whole.

Enraged by the loss of their companion, the two remaining færies narrowed their eyes with fury, and one of them flung a ball of black flame straight at Meren and Fa.

Meren ducked, taking Fa with her, his eyes watering from the agonizing pain in his wing. The black flame struck a tree in front of them, sending a burst of bark and splinters in all directions. One of the shards of wood lodged itself in Meren's own wing, sending a flash of white-hot pain through her.

Whatever pain Fa had known seemed to have disappeared as he grabbed Meren and pulled her closer, pulling the shard of wood from her wing and careening them up, up, up, until at last they burst through the top of the canopy.

"What are you doing?" Meren breathed, even as her wing screamed in protest.

Fa's Wind blew hot around them, carrying them through the open skies and right towards—

"The eagle!" Meren cried when she caught sight of the winged beast. The great bird, as if she had been waiting, swooped toward them. Meren couldn't help the cry of fear that burst from her.

Fa banked left hard as the bird banked the opposite direction, diving down into the forest like an arrow released from a bow.

And in the span of about two breaths, there was the sound of wicked laughter, a shrill cry, and then nothing—nothing but deadly silence.

"Did she…?"

"Yes," Fa said, still sweeping Meren away from the scene, heading toward the knot of a gnarled hazelnut tree covered in moss and lichens.

She had eaten them. The eagle had eaten the færies alive.

Meren wasn't sure whether to be relieved or horrified.

They landed heavily on the branch, and Fa immediately started warding their hiding place, but Meren could feel the drain on his magic. The ward would not hold long, if at all.

"It will have to do," he said breathlessly, turning to face her.

She had forgotten about her wing and its sharp pain until Fa started fussing over her. But it was obvious he was ignoring his own agony.

"Fa," she said as he tended to her. She tried his name again, but his attention was solely on her wing.

"It will heal. The cut was clean," he said, moving to retrieve the balm he kept in his pouch.

"Fa," she said again, taking hold of his wrist. It was only then that he looked at her. And she could see it—the strain in his eyes, the pain he was ignoring.

"Give me that," she said, taking the balm and practically forcing him to turn for her. She worked it carefully, thoroughly into the end of his wing, biting back a sob at the gruesome sight. His wing. His poor wing. While Fa made no sound to indicate his discomfort, he wasn't fooling anyone. She could see the pain in the tightness of his shoulders, the tension in his back. She finished rubbing in the salve and then began massaging his back.

"You don't have to—"

"I know I don't have to," she interrupted, working hard to smooth out the tension that was as solid as a rock in his back.

"Meren, you are in pain, too."

"I'm fine," she lied.

"Meren," he said, his tone stern, reprimanding. He pried himself from her hands and turned to face her.

She breathed a laugh after a few solid seconds of silence between them. "We're a sight, aren't we?"

But Fa did not laugh. No, there was no humor in his grave eyes. She looked around to see the light of their magic glowing brightly around them.

"Stop worrying all the time," she tried.

"They won't stop hunting us, Meren," he said as he started rubbing the balm on her wing. She nearly moaned at the relief the icy coolness of the herbs brought.

"Then we'll put up wards. We'll fly with them around us."

He didn't say a word as he worked the smooth salve into her aching wing.

"Show me how," she said, knowing her magic was nearly drained from the day's flight, not to mention the attack. But she needed to learn. She needed to know. She tuned to face Fa. "Show me how to make a ward."

Wordlessly, Fa took her hand, turning it palm up and tracing what felt like rivers of fire on her skin.

"What are you doing?" she asked, perplexed as she watched the intricate whorls of light dance on her hand.

"Our magic, it's…merging," he stammered. "I don't… I don't really need to teach you anything. We can just…share."

And sure enough, she could soon feel the strange magic escaping her palms, her fingertips. An unearthly sort of protection. A blanket of something like invisibility.

A ward.

"How…why is it merging?" she asked, as she watched their magic work of its own volition now.

Maybe…maybe it would be enough to hold for the rest of the evening. And all night.

Maybe.

But Fa did not answer her question.

"Rest, Meren. I'm going to find us some food."

"But…your wing, Fa."

"Rest."

And then Fa disappeared.

Chapter XXV

Are you brooding? Is that it?" Meren demanded, stomping towards the puddle not far from the hazelnut tree. The icy wind had settled along her bones, and she had dared to trek from their hiding spot up above to find Fa. But the sun had set, and he had still not returned.

And Meren—well, she was fit to be tied.

"Why are you ignoring me?" she barked, but when Fa turned to face her from the puddle, she realized—

"Eloah, sorry, Fa." Heat. Heat bloomed in her cheeks and neck at the sight of him. His body was obscured by the water, of course, but his clothes lay strewn on the ground at her feet. Fa was bathing. "I'm sorry," she stammered. "I didn't realize…"

"It's all right, Meren," he said, and when she heard the chuckle in his voice, she dared to meet his eyes again.

She furrowed her brows, rubbing her hands on her arms for warmth. "Aren't you freezing in there?"

"It's not exactly warm," he admitted, and she could see the goose-flesh on his taut arms as he sloshed the water over his shoulders. "But

I figured it was better than subjecting you to another night of sleeping next to an unwashed færy."

She huffed a laugh, squatting down to touch the surface of the water. An instant later, Fa was practically moaning.

"Better?" she asked, pleased with herself for how effortlessly she had heated the water with her Flame.

"It's so good it's a pity you're not enjoying it with me."

She slid her eyes to Fa, who suddenly seemed so far away in that black water, the starlight playing on the ripples. Mischief and unadulterated heat danced in his eyes. She found she could scarcely breathe.

But his distractions couldn't work forever. "What is it you're not telling me, Fa?"

His face, actually, his whole countenance shifted. "Meren."

"Do you *want* to leave? Is that why you brought it up today?"

"Of course I don't want to leave you."

"Then why do I get the feeling there is something you're not telling me?"

Fa looked down, playing with the ripples on the water. "I know you can feel it, Meren. What is between us." He spoke the words as if they were his greatest lament. "It will only get stronger."

"Why is that a bad thing?" she asked.

"Meren," he said, his eyes still fixed on the water. She watched droplets as they fell down his smooth skin. "We cannot always be as lucky as we were today."

"You think today was lucky?"

"No, I don't. And it terrifies me to think what would happen if they were to get to us. To you," he added, meeting her eyes again. And there it was—that same agonized worry that had darkened his countenance for the passing days.

"I am a burden, Meren. Without wings…" He trailed off, looking down, playing with the surface of the black water again. It almost seemed to dance beneath his fingers. As if…

As if Water danced with his magic now, too.

As if their magic was truly merging. Becoming one.

His gaze shot to hers when he realized she was before him now.

In the water.

Her clothes left behind on the bank.

The water was nearly to her shoulders, lapping lazily at her breasts. Fa was right. It was gloriously warm against the brisk night air.

"How long have you known, Fa?" she asked, raising her eyes to his after raking them up his lithe body.

He barely breathed, his broad chest rising and falling in quick cadence, the water lapping against him. She dared to step toward him, to shorten the gap between them.

"It's how you found me, isn't it?" she went on. "That night. In the forest."

His eyes were fixed on hers. "No one could see in that storm, Fa. Asher could not find me. Even the Dark færies chasing us could not find us. But you did. You found me. Came right to me, through complete darkness and wild winds."

Fa remained still before her, a statue whose only indication of life was the breath steadily rising and falling in his chest.

Meren pressed on. "It's how I found you in Nabi's lair, too. And it's how you found my coven when you returned. I never told you where it was. But you found it. You found me, not with your eyes.

"You can feel *me*. The same way that I can feel you. The same way our magic speaks to each other. Grows with one another.

"Because we are bonded, you and I.

"We are Mates."

His eyes were alight at the word, but still he said nothing, made no move towards her.

"Why do you fear it?" she asked. "Why do you keep me at arm's length?"

"Meren," he finally breathed, daring a tentative step towards her. The warmth of the water, the warmth of his body seeped into her soul.

Still, he did not touch her.

"You think you're a burden," she went on. "You think you're not good enough, don't you?"

"I know for certain that I am not," he said. "But even I am arrogant enough to ignore that."

"Then what?" she asked. "What is it that keeps you from me? Do you not want this? Do you not want me?"

Incredulous humor limned his worried eyes. "You know damn well that I do, Meren."

"Really," she said flatly, tilting her head to one side. "Because I am standing naked before you and you haven't so much as touched me."

"So you think that I do not want to?"

"I don't know *what* you want anymore, Fa."

She took another step, their bodies nearly touching now. Still, Fa made no move to draw her to him.

"From the moment we met, Meren, I knew what you were. And from the moment you started arguing with me in the forest that day, I knew that I wanted you."

It was her turn to look down, to smile at the memory of her daring to question the legendary Gibhor.

But he lifted her chin so that he could look into her eyes.

"I have been falling in love with you from the moment you came into my life. Even if…even if we were not Mates, I…" He stopped himself, breathing once, twice. Then, "But you must understand, B'sheirt. It is different for us. What is between us is not what most færies call mating. It is…"

"More," she said, finishing his sentence.

"Much more," he agreed. He brushed the curl from her brow as he went on. "When the bond is *accepted…*" he said, heat dancing in his obsidian eyes at the implication of what that involved. "When it is accepted, Meren, it cannot be undone. It is not like most færies and what they call mating. It is not some paltry promise that can be broken at the first sign of inconvenience. It is—"

"I know what it is, Fa. I saw it. Between my own parents. And you've seen it too, haven't you? Between Nabi and your mother."

His nod was nearly imperceptible even as his eyes bored into hers.

Mate.

B'sheirt.

A bond. A covenant. Eternal. Formidable. Unbreakable.

A union that could only be forged by the magic of Eloah.

A gift, rare and pure. Priceless.

"I want you to be sure," he went on, trailing a trembling finger down her cheek, her neck, along her bare shoulder. "That's all I'm saying, Meren. I want you to take all the time you need to decide what you want."

"You act as if I have a choice." She laughed, skeptical.

"You do, Meren," he said, and there was no jest in his emphatic words. "Beyond the need, beyond the…compulsion," he stammered and paused, as if he were stifling his own compulsions with every ounce of brute strength within. He peeled his eyes from her bare shoulder before he went on. "It is still a choice. The magic of Eloah is always a choice. It is never forced upon us."

"What if I don't want a choice?" she asked, running her hands along Fa's solid arms, relishing the cording of solid muscle below his golden skin.

He shuddered at her touch, her words, and she could feel the fight within him—the war between his words and his thoughts.

"Just…" He shut his eyes, pressing his brow to hers. "Just promise me you will consider it carefully, Meren."

"And is that what you need? To consider it carefully?"

"I made my choice the day you learned to catch the Wind—when I saw the hunger, the determination in your eyes. I knew right then that if you'd let me, I'd follow you to the ends of the earth."

"So why is it that you can have your mind made up, but I cannot?"

"You do understand what the word *eternal* means, right?"

"Ken, hev," she said. *I do, love.* He pulled back slightly, meeting her eyes at her use of the old language. She could see the questions blooming, the words brimming at the surface. But she did not allow him to speak.

"I am not afraid, Fa. I know the Light grows brighter between us. That's the point, isn't it? Darkness can only be driven out by one thing. We're meant for more, Fa. Maybe you and I are supposed to lead the way. Maybe that's why we found each other."

He wanted to protest; she could see it in his incredulous eyes. But she didn't allow it, snaking her arms around his neck, pressing her body to his—her whole body. Every last inch.

Fa's eyes glazed over, his breaths short and hot on her neck as he slowly gave in to her, leaning to press a kiss to her throat.

"Tipharah." He breathed onto her skin as his hands found her waist, resting heavy on her hips under the steamy water. "Oh, my Tipharah."

"I am yours, Fa. I have always been yours. And that is how I want it to remain."

His lips found their way to her jaw, working across her cheek toward her lips. But she pulled away before he could kiss her, instead taking his face in her hands.

"N'shl hevv vah shlurn," she recited, remembering the words her mother had taught her all those years ago.

The Mating covenant.

"Vivenadd 'l ed hivr shl al-ovohm. Nitzchi," she added. Magic flared hot and bright around them.

Light. Hers and his. Mingling. Dancing.

Merging.

A tear fell down Fa's cheek, its coolness caressing her skin as Fa kissed her softly. His eyes sparkled in the starlight, his smile sweet and unfaltering as he repeated the vow in the common tongue. "I am my beloved's and she is mine. Bound by the light of Eloah. Evermore."

His eyes held hers in wonder, and he brushed a knuckle down her cheek. "Meren, I love you."

"I know, you stubborn bastard," she said. "I love you, too."

She could feel it—their magic entwining, weaving in and through the other's. An eternal tapestry of Light. Beckoning, practically begging to finish what they had started.

She could feel the grin on his mouth when Fa kissed her again. There was power in his kiss. Hunger. It was a lover's kiss, heady and uninhibited. He ran his strong hands along her back, her wings, pressing her to him with a fevered need that echoed her own.

His hands wandered down to her thighs, hooking them around him, the water sloshing around them with their frenzied movements. The Light—their Light—flared brightly, a wild flame roaring to life.

"Fa," Meren breathed, breaking their kiss. His lips, however, simply found other places to explore. "Fa, not here," she protested, worry nagging at her. If they were found…

He at last took his lips from her skin, meeting her eyes. A smirk—cool and satisfied, mixed with a hint of heady delight—colored his features. He didn't really give a damn if they were caught right now. No, Fa had only one ambition at the moment. But he complied nonetheless, leaping into the air, her body still wrapped around his as his Wind took them to the knothole in the tree above them. She hardly had to fly, their entwined Wind was so strong, formidable.

He kissed her neck as they soared through the icy air, and a delighted laugh bubbled from her belly. She caught sight of their clothing on the Wind, too, landing like bits of dandelion fluff inside their nook.

He landed with an easy grace on the mossy branch near the knot, still holding her to him as he walked the last few steps to their hiding space. She could feel the bite of their magic on her skin as they passed through the ward they had made earlier, and even felt a little more magic escape Fa as he fortified it for good measure.

He laid her down on his Wind, floating above their blankets like a cloud lingering above a valley, his hands languidly exploring every inch of her as if he could not get enough, could not savor enough.

"Tell me something," Meren dared say, running her hands along the edge of his tattered wings. "Can you move them at all?"

Fa furrowed his brows in curiosity. "Why do you ask?"

"I just…I want to see them."

Gently, so gently, Fa laid her down on the blankets beneath them. A moment later, she understood why. Yes, he could extend his wings. It took a great deal of effort and magic to do so. But for her…for her he would.

She propped herself up on her elbows, reaching out in awe at the sight of them. Their sheer breadth. Their haunting tatters, floating on a phantom wind. The shimmering iridescence—like a blanket of ice and pearl, quicksilver and stardust. The rips were jagged, gnarled, as if something horrid had taken his wings from him. Something wicked. Dark.

A tear escaped despite herself, and Fa sighed deeply as she ran the tips of her fingers down the shreds. At last he relaxed them again, sitting back on his feet. Meren sat up too, touching his cheek. He held her hand to his face and looked at her—looked deeply into her eyes.

"It is you who are the brave one, Fa," she finally managed. "I've never known anyone more remarkable."

Fa, who had overcome too many obstacles, who had not let the loss of his wings stop him. He was truly the most beautiful creature she had ever known.

Fa pulled her to him, settling her on his lap, running his fingers between her wings as he kissed her lips, her chin, her neck.

"My Tipharah," he breathed.

And then he laid her down, the bond between them lighting up the nook—and her soul—in silvery-blue splendor.

~

She laid spent and sated beside him, her breath having found a regular cadence again. His body was a summer day stretched out beside her—golden and warm and glorious. She turned onto her side, exploring the skin of his broad chest, running her finger along each silvery scar. This creature—this magnificent creature beside her was hers. He had made her his own, too.

Bound by magic. Bound by their love.

She kissed his chest and smiled.

Eyes closed, Fa's arm curled up around her, tucking her closer to his side. He kissed the top of her head, his breath a caress of warmth in her hair as he said, "I love you, Malkah B'sheirt."

"So many names," she teased. "Are you ever going to tell me what they mean?" She propped herself up on her elbow, resting her head in one hand as she let her other continue exploring him. She found his wings and pulled them through her fingers, savoring the silken softness of the tatters.

"You know what they mean," he purred, his eyes still closed at her ministrations. She delighted in the sight of him, laid bare and serene before her, her eyes devouring every inch of him as she wondered why in the world someone as beautiful as he would want anyone as unre-markable as she.

"Some, yes. Not all, though."

His eyes opened, and something in his countenance faltered. She wasn't sure she liked the shift. "What is it, Fa?"

"Meren, there is something I need to tell you."

She propped herself up more, tilting her head to one side, wondering why her heart had started pounding.

Because Fa's face was grave, that's why.

Whatever he was about to tell her—

"Dear me, is this a bad time?" she heard a new voice say, and she whirled to face the creature of Darkness casting a shadow over them.

Chapter XXVI

hope I'm not interrupting," the Dark færy purred, raking his eyes over their exposed bodies.

Fa yanked a blanket over Meren, caring nothing for his own modesty. "Get out," he growled, his voice low and dangerous as he curled up to his feet. A chill shuddered down Meren's spine at the promise of violence in his growl.

"I knew you'd eventually take your revenge, Fa," the færy went on. "But I must admit, I never thought it would be something as base as finding you between the legs of my brother's mate. It's pretty low. Even for you."

His brother's mate?

His brother's *mate?*

Meren's eyes darted to the tattered wings that hung from Fa's back, the jagged cuts that could only have been made by something gruesome, something grotesque.

Something like a bone blade.

"Asher?" she heard herself breathe. "Your brother is…is Asher?" she asked, frozen under the weight of that realization.

Asher's brother was a…Dark færy. If the blades at this one's side—twins to Asher's—weren't telling enough, then his build, his demeanor surely was. He was the dark mirror image of Asher.

And bone blades—bone blades that could shred wings to nothing but tatters…

Bile stung the back of Meren's throat as she willed herself not to retch on the ground, shock holding her, freezing her in place.

Fa stood resolute before her, his magic stirring, gathering—an axe ready to strike.

The Dark færy cocked his head to the side, a wicked smile curling his coal-black lips. "I cannot say it surprises me that he didn't tell you. He's always been a self-righteous prick. But I admit, neither did he tell me what a pretty little thing you are. No wonder he couldn't seem to leave your side." The færy raked his eyes over her, and even under the thick blanket, she felt exposed before him. "I wonder what he will think of you now. If he will still want you after your brazen whoring."

She felt Fa's magic seethe, steadily building as he moved silently between them. He glowed, a subtle light gathering around him. A wild blue flame roaring to life.

The Dark færy seemed oblivious to it. "Then again," the færy went on, flipping a bone blade and catching it with lithe ease, "it never really mattered whether it was Asher's seed or my father's, so long as it was royal blood in your belly. I can only imagine what my father will do to your pathetic, wingless lover here when he finds out about your cuckoldry."

She was going to retort, to argue that she did not belong to Asher. That she never would. But Fa's magic had already struck, a whip of Flame and Wind and Water lashing out and wrapping its deadly ire around the Dark færy's throat, pouring down his mouth. Searing his skin.

"I'd be careful of your words, Ahaz. They may be your last," snarled Fa, his magic—*their* magic glowing bright around him.

"Fa," she cried out in fear at the sight of her Mate's fury, watching the Dark færy falter. Fa's magic was a force unto itself. It was as if he had been preparing for this moment his whole life.

A helpless, guttural sound grumbled from the Dark færy's throat. Fa relented only just enough for Ahaz to breathe. But it was enough.

Ahaz retaliated, flinging his Darkness at Fa, a tentacle of wicked, magic fangs poised to devour. The Dark magic ripped along Fa's skin, tearing boiling gashes along his arms. But he made no sound, not even so much as a breath as he unleashed himself upon the Dark færy again.

Meren could hardly breathe as she watched Fa strike blow after blow using his magic. No, *their* magic, as if he were exploring his new abilities gained thanks to their Mating. And he liked it. She could see it in his eyes—Fa liked the power he possessed. The power in his veins glowed terrible and beautiful around him, his own nakedness obscured by the sheer magnitude of his magic. A king of Light and Terror.

But one moment, one breath for Fa to catch himself was all Ahaz needed.

The Dark færy growled, his skin covered in burns and boils, throwing his magic out like a net of black smoke, blinding and suffocating them both. But when that net retreated…

Meren screamed, the pain too much as the Darkness shredded her, scratching over her like a caracal's claws. Every inch burned like a living flame along her skin, and hot tears poured down her burning cheeks. She gritted her teeth, not knowing what part of her hurt worse—her wings, her back, her hands. Her body writhed with the heat and the screaming agony of Ahaz's Darkness as it devoured her.

But it did not last, that Darkness. It ceased almost as violently as it had come as Fa erupted—Wind and Water and Flame, a mirror to the miniature storm they had made only a few days ago. But this time, it was Fa alone who made the storm. He no longer needed Meren to access that Water, those Flames. His storm swirled and devoured, pouring down the Dark færy's throat, fire scouring his dark skin, drowning and burning and suffocating him within a matter of seconds. Meren felt the sheer power of the storm as the winds stirred over her aching skin. She felt the cool sting of the rains Fa summoned as they misted her in the nook of the tree. Ahaz collapsed, and Fa wasted no time setting his prone body alight with Flame before kicking him out of the nook. Obsidian smoke followed in his wake as the dead færy fell out of sight, the sickening smell of burning flesh filling their nook.

And then Meren breathed. In and out, carefully, as the lingering pain seared her body. She collapsed onto their blankets. It seemed a lifetime ago that she had lain here this morning, wrapped in Fa's embrace, his body singing in time with hers as he worshipped her with reckless abandon.

"Meren," Fa whispered, dropping to her side. His hands that had only moments ago wielded terror and fury now searched her delicately, carefully, his skin returning to its usual golden glow. Her tender Mate. Her terrible warrior.

"Tipharah," he said again, brushing her sweat-dampened curl from her brow.

Agony, pure and undiluted, covered his face. Agony and unending remorse.

"My sweet Tipharah," he said, his hands trembling.

"Fa, we must keep going," she said, trying to sit up again. "They won't stop coming. We have to get to Fount Barakah." But the pain—it surged and drowned her, and she fell back onto the blankets, gasping for every breath.

"Shhh," Fa said, and she saw tears falling fast and freely down his face. He stroked her cheek gently, over and over again. "Shhh, my love. You must rest. We must get you to safety."

She felt the soft breath of his magic as it poured around them. Another ward. One that likely wouldn't hold long against the Darkness. Not now that their magic shone so brightly.

"We have to go now, Fa," she insisted, trying to move again. But her body betrayed her; she could not sit up. Screaming pain like fire burned down her back, her arms, her wings…

His hands trembling, Fa picked up one of the blankets, tearing it into strips. The harsh sound grated on the headache she hadn't realized she was nursing.

"Fa. Now," she ground the words out against the pain. Whatever that Darkness had done to her, it had been thorough. It felt as if she'd never be without pain again.

"Tipharah," he said softly. Too softly.

She stilled, looking at him. But he kept his eyes on the blanket he was tearing into strips.

"Fa, if we don't leave now—"

"Tipharah," he said again, at last looking up, agony still in his eyes. "Your wings."

That was all he could bring himself to say. She stopped breathing, understanding suddenly the tears that wet his cheeks, that look of utter devastation on his face as her wings screamed in agony.

Her *shredded* wings.

CHAPTER XXVII

ipharah, we must get you to safety at once. You will need a healer. I can bind your wings for the journey, but if we do not do something soon…"

He couldn't finish the sentence. Then again, she couldn't finish the thought. So she shut it out. She pushed up on her hands, shaking violently with the agony. But she kept at it until she was sitting up again, nearly vomiting at the pain.

"No, Fa. We have to keep going."

"Meren, you…you cannot fly," he said. "Not like this. And if we don't see to your wings now…"

She didn't care. "I will crawl if I have to."

"Meren, it's an island. Across the *ocean*."

"Then I will swim." Desperation clawed, gnawed at her until she was nearly drowning in it. She cut him off before he could protest further. "Don't, Fa. Please don't. You promised to help me. Now help me. I saw your magic. You don't need me anymore. You—"

The horror in his face at her words soon shifted to devastation. "I don't know if I can fly us over such a distance, Meren."

"You have to try. You promised me, Fa. You *promised* me."

He took her face in his hands, holding her eyes for a moment, searching. Searching for what, she could not say. Then she felt it—an icy cold wind coming over her wings. Soothing. Freezing away the pain.

"If you won't let me get you help to heal them, at least I can numb them."

She huffed a sardonic laugh, but there was no smile on Fa's darkened face.

"Why didn't you tell me it was Asher who took your wings?" she asked in the silence between them.

"I didn't want you to hate him," he said, gathering her clothes. He went to painstaking measures to move her carefully as he dressed her.

"It's too late for that," she said, wincing as she lifted her legs so that he could slide her stockings over her feet. "I will hate him forever."

Fa stopped dressing her, taking her chin roughly. "You're better than that, Meren. I wasted my life hating him. I won't let you do the same."

"Is that what that was earlier? Your hatred coming out of your magic?"

Fa looked down, disgust hardening his features as he worked to lace her supple boots up her legs. "That was a shadow of the male I never want to be."

"And what male is that?"

He gingerly worked her petal tunic over her head and around her wings. His icy Wind did wonders to numb the searing pain. He was lacing her tunic up her back when she heard him say, "My father's son."

Fa crawled back around to face her. "Do you think you can stand?"

She nodded, bracing herself for the pain she knew was about to assault her. But then, "Fa," she said.

He was busy gathering their blankets into his pack, his shoulders tight with worry.

"Fa," she said again. He finally turned to face her.

"What is it?"

She looked him up and down, and when his eyes followed hers, they both burst into a much-needed laugh. Fa was still naked.

"Not exactly the post-mating celebration I had in mind," he said, helping her to her feet. He set about deftly dressing himself in quick, precise movements.

"What exactly *did* you have in mind?" she asked curiously. She was so weak. The distraction was welcome.

He was dressed in a matter of moments, picking her up and wrapping her around him as he jumped from the branch. He landed beside the pool at the foot of the tree before he finally said, "A lot less Darkness. And a lot less clothes."

Fa gathered their Wind and leapt into the air.

He couldn't fly. Not without her wings. The farther they went, the more evident it became: they would never make it across the ocean. Even if the island were only a mile away, it would be too far. Even with their magic combined, fortified, growing, it would not be enough to fly them that distance.

Because her wings were gone, never to return.

Fa's icy Wind remained a constant at her back, and while it bit painfully into her skin, she ignored it for the sake of the greater pain she would know if that numbing let up.

She wondered if Fa had known the same kind of shocking emptiness when he had lost his wings. Did it take him a long time to believe it was true, too?

Devastation bloomed in the pit of her stomach every time he had to descend to the ground and leap again. She had no idea how they would get to the fount now. No idea how they would ever have a chance to perform the Summoning. And the more devastated she became, the more she hated the Dark færies. Hated their lust for *more*. More power. More Darkness. More færies to steal. To corrupt. The lust that had rotted their souls like their bodies—from the inside out, turning their skin as dark as a moonless night, cracked and withered. Turning their wings to onyx flecked with gray, like mold and lichens on a crumbling facade.

The more she thought about it, the more she seethed with it. Burned with it.

And Asher.

Asher had lied to her. Nearly fifty summers together, and he had not once bothered to tell her who he was. Who his father was.

Asa, the corrupt king of the færies. Murderer. Slave driver. Liar. Asher was the son of a black-hearted villain. And he himself wasn't much better. A liar. A thief. Asher had taken Fa's wings by his own hands, with his blades.

And for what?

Maybe Fa hated his own father. But he couldn't possibly hate him as much as Meren hated it all. Her eyes burned with it, her throat closing up. Fa's steady arms around her, the feel of his heart beating in time with hers—things that had become precious, priceless in so short a time were no comfort to her now.

"We'll find a way," Fa said. His first words since they had departed. She wanted to believe him, but she knew his words were empty. "We'll find a way, my Tipharah," he said again, and she wondered if he was saying it just to convince himself.

Within the span of an hour, they made it to the shore. The Great Sea roared like a mighty beast before them. Opening and closing, opening and closing like a gaping maw with every crest of the waves. It would surely devour them whole if they tried to cross it. She thought of the massive ships the humans built to sail it. Monstrosities of wood and canvas and craft—meant to conquer those mighty waves. She thought of how many times those brave vessels succumbed to these waters.

Yet here she and Fa stood before the ocean, two tiny, wingless færies with the audacity to think they could brave the pounding, merciless waters.

Defeat sang a mocking song, set to the rhythm of the pounding waves in her soul.

Fa set her down gingerly, taking a moment to fortify his numbing Wind on her wings. She didn't care. Let the pain come. Let it be a reminder of her failure. The ocean mocked her. So did her wings.

Fa took her face in his hands, forcing her to meet his eyes. "Don't you dare give up now, Tipharah."

She couldn't help the tear that slipped down her cheek, falling over his thumb. Fa pressed a gentle kiss to her lips, in stark contrast to the fierce determination she saw in his eyes.

"You are the one who taught me to stop living in fear, Meren. You. We've come this far."

"To go no farther," she said, a sob threatening to escape.

"No. We will stop this Darkness. Once and for all. Let's go home. Let's get you healed. We will try again come the spring and—"

"No, Fa. There will be no second chance. You heard Ahaz. They are coming for us. For me. They want me, and I don't even know why. I—"

"You don't know why?" Fa interrupted. "You don't *know* why? Meren, for all your observation, you are certainly blind to your own merits. Not only are you brave—braver than anyone I've ever known—not only are you kind and beautiful, Meren, you are strong. So strong. And your magic is a fortress of that strength. You are the daughter of a pure, rare kind of magic. It was a gift given to you, Meren. Because your parents were true Mates. And they gifted their magic to you when they conceived you in that love.

"Do you know how rare that is? How precious? Those Dark færies—they have known about you from the moment you were conceived. Because your parents were strong, too. They fought. They fought alongside my father in the færy wars."

"You knew them?" she asked, meeting his eyes.

"No, my beloved. I never met them. But I knew of them. Everyone did. They were the most revered and the most wanted færies in existence. Because they never stopped fighting. Even long after the war was over, your parents never stopped believing in a better world. And whether they knew it or not, they gifted that faith to you.

"I knew who you were the instant you came into my life. I knew because I knew that Asher had saved their daughter. It's the only reason I never killed him for what he did. Because I had heard the story: Asher defying his own father to save you. I don't know why. I never knew why. Maybe he believed in a better world, too. But for all the killing, for all the bloodshed, somehow when it came to you, Asher gave it up. He abandoned his father to protect you.

"Maybe it was for selfish reasons. Or maybe it was because he truly loved you. And that's why now, Meren—now is not the time to hate him. He had his reasons for what he did to me. And they were not unjustified. I've spent enough time hating him for the both of us. I hated him until the day he showed up with you by his side. You, my Mate.

"Had I known, had I ever even imagined that my Mate would be someone like you, someone so pure and beautiful, I would have run from it. I would have run as far and as fast as I could. Nabi told me you would come. He told me I would find you someday. But had I known it was going to be you, I would never have even considered asking you to deal with all of this. Not for me, not for anything, Meren.

"But you came into my life. And I'm selfish enough that I couldn't leave you alone. I couldn't walk away from you. I tried. Eloah knows I tried.

"But your Light is too bright. Your heart is too pure. And I loved you from the moment that Light touched me.

"So I will finish this with you. I will fight with you. To my very last breath, I will walk this path with you. Because I think you're right—I think we were meant to do this. Together.

"Together, B'sheirt. Together, Malkah Neharah. For that's what you are, isn't it? You are the Queen of the Light. In every sense. And I don't fear it anymore. So I'll be damned if I let you."

Malkah.

Malkah. Neharah.

Queen. Of the Light.

Nabi had called her a queen. So had Fa. She looked into Fa's eyes again. Into the beautiful depths of that endless obsidian. She looked, and she understood. About Fa's father. And the færy wars. And all the running, all the hiding Fa had done. Because he was running from who he was. He was running from his fate, his destiny. His inheritance.

Except maybe he wasn't running anymore. Maybe he was—

Fa crashed her to the sand, covering her whole body with his. He looked up, his keen warrior's eyes searching the skies. She looked above, to see what he had spotted, her heart lodging in her throat at the sight.

The eagle circled above them. A graceful predator, assessing its meal. A huntress prowling, those mighty wings of hers gliding on the wind without effort. Bile burned Meren's throat, her eyes stinging with sudden tears at the sight of those glorious wings.

But the eagle made no move to descend, and when Meren looked closer, the bird's languid swoops through the air were not those of a bird on the hunt but… The eagle was…she was…

"Fa," Meren whispered, pushing him off of her. He sat up with her, slowly, carefully, as if any sudden movements might make the eagle change her mind.

But she didn't. And when she landed before them, cocking her mighty head to one side, Fa seemed to understand too, for he made no move to run or hide. The winged beast squawked once, blinking fast.

She was so much bigger this close, and despite her newfound gumption, instinct had Meren longing to run for cover. But she didn't, because she knew. She knew Fa did too.

The eagle…

The eagle wanted to help them.

She met Fa's eyes, finding the same wonder there that she knew was in hers. The eagle squawked again, gesturing with her head a few times as if encouraging them to climb on her back. And at the absurdity of it, Meren laughed out loud. Fa glanced quickly at her, as if he were afraid her outburst would be their death.

"You're not serious, Meren," he said when he realized she meant to let the eagle fly them to the fount.

"Whyever not?" she asked, shrugging off the arguments she could see building in her Mate's eyes as she strutted over to the eagle and started climbing her wing.

"Meren, this is a wild animal."

"So? I think she wants to help us."

"Meren," Fa ground out. "They don't think. They eat. And then they look for their next meal. This has to be a trap."

"You can't have it both ways, my love," she said, grinning wickedly as she settled on the great bird's neck.

Fa only raised his eyebrows and crossed his arms, making no move to follow her.

"She cannot be so incapable of thought that she can't help us, and yet cognizant enough that she can think of some sort of lure that would convince us to climb on the back of our own impending demise."

"Is this supposed to convince me?" he drawled.

"It looks like I'm going to the Fount, after all. With or without you. Though I would prefer it if you joined us. You could consider it a Mating gift."

He eyed her warily but strode to the eagle's great wing, still extended for his use. Fa reluctantly climbed the beast, mounting behind Meren and wrapping his arms securely around her middle. She could feel his magic gathering, just daring the eagle to try anything.

She chuckled as she turned to plant a great kiss on Fa's cheek, a bubble of absurd laughter threatening to escape. The eagle took off with surprising speed, and Meren let out a little yelp that started off as shock and turned into something like wonder. Fa's arms tightened around her.

Within seconds, the ocean was a blanket of silver and sapphires below them, the wind a welcome, beautiful caress on her cheeks and through her hair. She breathed a deep sigh at the crisp bite of the air on which the eagle glided with little effort. The great wings flapped only now and again.

Within a few moments, the island was visible before them. Fa had been right—she never could have swum to it, for it was miles from the shore, surrounded in great breakers, foaming white upon impact.

However, it wasn't the island that held her attention but the glow that came from it. Golden and splendid.

Fount Barakah.

The seat of Eloah's magic.

She could feel it, that magic, calling to her deep within. A question and answer. A song and a riddle. A storm and the calm.

The closer they flew, the more she knew she had been right—the Summoning was the only way. The magic of Eloah the only answer.

The ocean beneath them shimmered under the blazing sunlight, churning around the island as if in perpetual worship. But the closer they flew, Meren realized that the glow—the Light from the Fount—was a river. A river of Light, of magic, pouring down the mountainsides, churning in great, golden waves into the ocean. It snaked through the waters in all directions.

The Fount. The seat. The magic of Eloah. Pouring into the world.

She wondered why this place was only legend. Why all creatures, mortal and immortal alike, did not speak of it, sing of it all the time.

How could creation have so easily forgotten about such marvelous things?

The air grew richer, somehow, the closer they flew. Purer. The skies bluer. The clouds whiter. The sun brighter. And the island before them greener than any flora on the mainland. Untouched. Untainted.

It was not long before the graceful bird arrived at the shores of the lush island, swooping on the wind through the thick trees that climbed up the mountainous terrain. A jungle of flora and fauna, giant singing birds, endless slithering snakes, great lithe cats. The island was teeming with life—as if the magic fortified it. Made it stronger. Bigger. Purer.

It was clear no human had graced this place in centuries, maybe more. A forgotten garden of glorious, impossible splendor. An island that held every answer to every question ever posed and more. And magic. Ripe and thick. Practically dripping from every glossy leaf, every billowing cloud.

Fount Barakah. Legend, indeed.

The eagle landed at the foot of the thickest tree Meren had ever seen, its branches reaching up into the heavens, thick with moss and lichens, fat leaves and glowing toadstools. The trunk alone seemed as wide as a mountain, rich with growing vines and the brightest birds. All the life that clung to its branches seemed wilder than normal. Agitated, even. Chirping, stirring with a frenzy that mimicked the river of light that billowed from the towering boughs. It was a waterfall of sorts—golden light pounding down with a thunderous roar, careening into a pool beneath. Not Water. Not Flame. Not Wind. Something of all three.

Magic. Eloah's magic. Her soul practically sang in its presence, and Fa's eyes danced with the same wonder she knew kissed her own.

The Fount was something out of a dream. A wild, raging dream that could devour and make whole all at once.

The pool of Light magic seemed to churn of its own accord, leaping over itself, wave upon wave. Great birds of impossible color glided around the fat tree, singing piercing tunes as they worked their way up and down, up and down the towering heights. Thick snakes slithered along its branches, dipping their heads low, not to devour prey, but to dance. Mice and hares and foxes and toads leapt wildly at the base, their songs a raucous chorus.

The animals definitely seemed agitated. Stirred up. She wondered what it meant.

From the corner of her eye, she spotted something brighter than the brightest light. It glowed with a preternatural radiance that warmed the air around them. She turned, and Fa turned with her.

A white wolf.

With fur perfect and gleaming in the golden light of the Fount, he stared at her, still as a gravestone. Not even his mighty chest moved with his breaths. His eyes were gold and piercing, and something *other* gleamed in them.

"Messengers," she heard Fa say. She did not turn to face him, too consumed by the haunting beauty of the wolf. Fa went on anyway. "These are the ancient ones," he said. "Existing since before the creation of the world. They are his legions. His messengers. His warriors."

Providence had an army? An army of wolves?

Fa breathed a soft laugh. "They are not wolves. They just take on that form when they're in the mortal realms."

The wolf tilted its head ever so slightly, as if to agree with Fa. But he kept his fiery eyes fixed on Meren. As if to hold her. Remind her. Assure her.

She was here for a reason.

It was only after a long moment that Meren realized the other animals were not bothered by the wolf's intimidating presence. The mice and squirrels and small creatures—all an easy snack for the snowy beast—did not falter in their frenzied dance around the tree. As if they did not fear him. And he, in his pure, radiant splendor, paid no heed to them either. Only to Meren.

Messengers.

Without a single word, she knew what the wolf had come to tell her.

It was time.

She looked again at the lush island around her. There was nothing serene or calm about Fount Barakah. It was a mighty force, feeding the whole world with its unfathomable power. Even the air itself buzzed with its energy.

"So what was that plan of yours?" Fa asked over the din. She took hold of his hand, squeezing it for her own reassurance.

"Just keep watch for me," she said, kissing his cheek before striding towards the churning golden pool.

She fussed with her mother's mating ring, twirling it around her finger as she had absently so many times before. A lump formed in her throat, an ache at the thought of letting go of the only piece of her parents she had left.

But it would work. It *had* to work. The Summoning required a great sacrifice. She could think of nothing greater than letting go of the only piece of her parents, of her past, that she had left.

Gingerly, carefully, she slipped the ring from her finger, setting it on her palm, tracing it with her finger one last time.

"This is for you, Mama," she whispered.

"Tipharah," she heard Fa breathe beside her.

But she did not look at him, did not let herself see the worry she could hear in his voice.

"Surely there is something else," he said.

"It has to matter, Fa. It has to mean something to the bearer."

"Tipharah," he tried again.

"Please, Fa. Don't talk me out of this."

Fa did not. In fact, he covered her hand with his own, wrapping their fingers around the ring. He brought their joined hands to his mouth and kissed them once. Twice.

"Bring forth the Light, B'sheirt," he finally managed.

In an instant, the light around them vanished, like the snuffing of a great candle. A single still moment had Meren and Fa frozen in wordless stupor. And then it came—a blinding wave of Darkness rippling towards them, slamming Fa into her, the weight of his solid form toppling her to the ground.

Fa's eyes were as wide as harvest moons as he panted above her, breathing a foul word.

"What is it?" she asked.

Fa could barely speak for the fear she could see trying to swallow him whole. "The king."

Chapter XXVIII

Another wave of blackness rippled towards them, and Fa used every ounce of magic he could muster to cover his beloved, to shield her from the brunt of it. Fear welled in her eyes, but he would not let it win. Not when they had come this far.

So he stood. And he helped her stand with him. He sent a new wave of ice-kissed Wind to her wings for good measure and said, "Go, Meren. I will keep you safe."

With wide eyes, she nodded and turned towards the Fount, her mother's ring clasped in her delicate hand. Fa sent a ward around her and turned to face the source of that Dark magic—the King of the Færies descending on a black cloud, surrounded by an army of his own fell ilk, sons and slaves alike, blackened by the poison of their own making.

Dark Færies. At least fifty of them. Their teeth were worn down to spikes, their wings black and menacing—an army of black moths. Slaves. Whether son or acolyte, they were all slaves to the Dark master who pulled their puppet strings. Who leashed them with his fell power.

King Asa's black face was as familiar as if Fa had only seen him yesterday, instead of nearly a century ago, his gaze as serpentine as Fa remembered.

Fa gathered the magic within himself, sizing up his enemies.

The king merely smiled.

"When my sons told me of your destination, I hardly believed it," King Asa purred, his billowing cloud tumbling before him, setting him on the ground with dark grace. "You were always the sensible one of your father's sons, Fa. I never took you for a fool."

"I see only one fool here," Fa hissed, the magic within him practically singing, readying itself to fight. The Flame, the Water he had inherited from his Mate only hours ago, and the Wind he had spent the better part of the last century honing. Perfecting. Waiting for this very moment.

Even if Nabi hadn't warned him, Fa had known this day would come. He had been running from it, hiding from it for too long.

Heir Apparent versus the Fraudulent King. The king who had stolen his throne and kept it through bloodshed and slavery.

Fa had never wanted his father's throne. Nor had he ever cared about the Darkness that King Asa had spread like a virus across the land.

Not until he had met Meren and seen the hope in her eyes. The determination.

His Mate had reignited the fire that had once burned brightly in his soul. The fire that had been snuffed out with his father's savagery. With his mother's death. With his own failures that mounted with every passing year.

But one look at his Mate, and that fire had rekindled. And with it, the growing knowledge that he would face Asa again someday.

Well, that day had come.

He would not fail his Mate. He would not fail his people.

This dark army—they could be easily bested. They were little more than foot-soldiers. Puppets. Their numbers did not intimidate him—he had killed as many before with only his Wind.

But the king…

The king's magic roiled around him, a lion pacing before its prey. Black smoke that could choke out life, Dark magic that would gnaw at Fa's very soul if it got close enough. With barely a flicker of his pinkie, the king could send every soul here to their death. Fa had seen it himself when this king had killed his own father—when this fraud had taken down the true King of the Færies. Fa wasn't sure his newfound magic could stand against such staggering power. The power Asa had gained off of the souls he had enslaved over the last century.

His father had not been wrong to fight against such a male. He had only been wrong to take that fight too far—to kill the innocent along with the guilty in the name of peace. His father had been wrong to forsake his mother for his harem of willing whores—looking for what Fa had found in Meren. Searching for a Mate who would gift him with her power. A rare, pure gift. Fa wished his father were alive this moment if only so he could tell him, show him that Mating was a gift. He had known it the moment he had met her. It was not a lucky chance. It was a gift given by Eloah himself. And Meren…Meren was the sweetest gift Fa had ever known.

"What did you think, Fa?" King Asa mocked, gesturing to the Fount. "That you would come here and somehow find a way to wield the magic that no one has unlocked in a millennium?"

"Magic is not meant to be wielded, Asa. Or didn't you know that?"

A wicked chuckle. "That is your problem, Melekfa. You're too noble for your own good."

Melekfa. His true name. Meant to mock. To jeer at the male he had never become. The position he had never lived up to.

"There is nothing noble about me," Fa said. *Distract him.* He needed to keep the king distracted as long as possible while his Mate gave up her beloved ring to perform the Summoning.

It would work. It *had* to work. Everything they had done had led them to this moment.

"No?" Asa sneered, cocking his black head to one side. His great wings spread wide behind him, black and gray with not an ounce of color or light. His horde slowly gathered around him, encircling them in black Darkness as they hovered on wing. "I could have sworn all of you færies were the same. You always thought yourselves better than the rest. Pure. Untainted. Above. It's nauseating, really, all that nobility."

"I am not my father's son."

"Clearly not, Melekfa. But you're just as much of a bastard, aren't you? You kill without remorse and call it your duty."

"I kill only when threatened. Unlike you."

"Is that what you tell yourself in order to sleep at night? Tell me, Melekfa, do you fuck only when threatened, too, or was taking my son's mate just for sport?"

"I am not Asher's mate," Meren growled, coming to Fa's side and gripping his hand in hers.

He shot a quick glance at her, asking a question with only his eyes.

Is it done?

She nodded once and turned her attention back to the Dark king.

Fa did not dare glance back at the Fount, did not dare let the king know that his Mate—this brave, beautiful, impossible færy—had made the sacrifice right under the Dark king's nose. Nor did he dare indulge his curiosity in wondering what would happen next. He couldn't afford to let his attention waver from Asa.

Was anything happening? How long would it take? The island had already been in such a frenzy when they arrived. Fa had expected to find a serene haven. Instead, he had found an island churning and roiling with magic.

But why?

"You belong to him," said King Asa. "He saved your life, did he not?"

"That does not mean he owns me," Meren said, her shoulders back, resolute. Eloah save him, she was glorious. A queen of Light and valor.

"You're all the same, aren't you? Duty bound so long as it suits you. But I confess that you, Meren, are indeed clever. For you have aligned yourself in such a way that no matter what, you'll be the Queen of the Færies, won't you?"

Her brows furrowed, and she stole a quick glance at Fa before returning her attention to King Asa. "What?"

He chuckled, a dark sound. "Don't act like you didn't know, Meren. It's disappointing."

Something was wrong. Why wasn't the king making a move? Why wasn't he unleashing his Darkness upon them? And why wasn't the

Summoning working? Fa had expected the Fount to be doing…*something* by now. What, he couldn't say, but…

"Don't hold back, Asa. Do tell what it is you think I should know about my Mate," Meren sneered.

"My, my, Melekfa," the king said, turning to Fa. "Don't tell me you truly haven't told her."

"There is nothing he hasn't told me," Meren snapped.

"Oh really," the king drawled.

"Meren, I tried to tell you," Fa started to say, his nerves fraying. "I wanted to, I just… I didn't know how."

"I know, Fa," Meren whispered. And it wasn't disgust in her eyes. It was…it was…knowledge.

"Your *mate* here, Meren, is the heir to the throne of the færies," said King Asa. Meren whirled to face the Dark king as he went on. "Or *was*, I should clarify, before I killed his father and the rest of his pathetic family. The slippery little bastard has escaped me for decades, hiding like a coward behind his own magic. Thanks to you, he's been quite a bit less discreet lately."

Meren turned her steady eyes to Fa, waiting…

"I don't want it, Meren. I don't want the throne. I never have," he pleaded, desperately trying to get her to understand. To make her see that he never would become the male his father had been. The power-hungry bastard that burned anything in his way.

But he was already, wasn't he? King Asa hadn't been wrong. He had killed Dark færies without thought, without remorse. After his mother had been murdered, he spent the better part of a decade retaliating against anyone who associated with Asa and his sons. And when he had killed too many of them to count, it was Asher who had found him. Asher who had shredded his wings in revenge for the Dark færies Fa had slaughtered. So he had hidden himself away, thinking he was doing the world a favor. But he had never been able to escape who he was. His failures. His father had been right. King Asa had also been right—he was a mockery to the throne. A wingless, murdering mockery.

"You don't want it?" Meren asked, and he could see disappointment welling in her eyes.

He had to help her understand. Had to make her see he meant it. He would not become his father. Or the monster before them. The one who still made no move to attack, not even a flicker of Darkness from his fingertips.

"Meren, I didn't tell you because I have no intention of taking back the throne. I never did. I swear it."

"Why?" she asked. "Why not?"

"You saw me, Meren. You saw what I am capable of."

"Yes, I do see you. Better than you do," she said. "You would run from the throne and leave us with a monster."

"I *am* the monster, Meren. I cannot escape it. I am my father's son whether I like it or not. And now, with your magic…"

He shouldn't have said it. The moment the words escaped his lips, he regretted them. The look in Asa's eyes only made it worse.

"Interesting," drawled the king, steepling his black fingers in front of his chest, drumming them against one another. Phantom wisps of smoke curled from his fingertips. "How terribly interesting. Why, I've not heard of the true bond since…well, since her poor parents. And what a pity, for what powerful færylings you two would have borne."

In the span of a single heartbeat, the King of the Færies unleashed himself upon them—so fast that Fa did not have time to think, to even react. The blackness of Asa's magic was absolute, so dark that Fa was blinded by it, fumbling around in the created midnight, crying out Meren's name.

"It's no use, Melekfa. I have no need for both of you, not if your magic is shared. Might as well eliminate the more powerful of the two."

Asa's words hung in the air, but Fa did not let them register as he fumbled around on his hands and knees, calling his Mate's name over and over again.

But she did not answer.

The Darkness slowly began to clear, like fog on the banks of a river. Fa still called Meren's name over and over again. But she gave no reply, made no sound.

Had she been hurt? Or was she hiding?

And why was the king so calm?

"You've grown tiresome, Melekfa," said the king. "Let's see just what you're really capable of."

Something like a bolt of lightning struck Fa's chest, and he cried out at the agony of it. But it stopped almost as soon as it started, and Fa did not waste the breath.

Instead, he let out every ounce of the magic he had been gathering within himself.

The king's army hissed as some of them fell like flies. They rushed for him, but he was ready, flinging a wave of Flame-kissed Wind towards them. More fell even as their bastard of a king watched, his own formidable wards protecting him from the burning waves. Fa reached out his hands, crying out in fury as a great wave of water poured out, flooding the surrounding forest. Dark færies flung their fires at him, grazing his arms and legs like fiery darts. Fa cried out through ground teeth, catching the Wind and hovering over the Dark king. He gathered the rogue balls of dark Flame, swirling them into eddies of fire around himself. The king watched with eyes hungry for the magic he was certain he would soon absorb into himself, enslaving the Light once more for dark purposes.

But Fa would allow him no such thing. With fury pounding in his veins, he gathered the floodwaters he had released only moments ago, their might bending at his every touch, as if eager to devour. He hovered above the maelstrom of his own making, dodging rogue darts of fire as they came his way.

And then he unleashed himself.

Casting a quick ward toward Meren, knowing his magic would find her wherever she was, Fa let loose the fury within as the waves pounded outward, a tsunami of Water and Wind and Flame that devoured every last one of the Dark færies that remained.

Except one.

When the waters settled, Fa landed on his feet before the king, prowling towards him, ready for whatever attack Asa had planned.

"I've no plans to kill you, Melekfa. You're much too useful to me alive now," Asa said. "But I cannot have you getting any ideas now, can I?"

An oily Darkness crept along his skin, and he knew—he knew what it meant. What was happening. Fa could feel Dark shackles curling around his hands, his feet, even his neck.

The king would take him alive. Make him his slave. A mindless puppet of unfathomable magic. Meren's magic.

Fa fought against the shackles that bound tighter and tighter around him. But he was no match for them. He could not stop the king from taking him alive.

He called out Meren's name once more, secretly hoping she had found a good hiding place, that she would escape the madman before him. But still, she made no answer. His heart pounded in the silence that ensued, thundering with the knowledge that his mind would soon no longer be his own. That the king would control him like a puppet on strings.

"Meren!" he called out again.

But it was not Meren who answered.

A voice kissed with darkness. Male. Powerful. And angry. It growled as the færie approached. "You have taken your last slave. It ends today."

And Asher, son of Asa, King of the Færies, let out a cry that made every leaf in the jungle tremble as he flew with shocking speed, flinging a blade of bone with all his might.

The blade landed with a sickening thud between the king's eyes. A breath later, Fa realized his shackles were loose. And there could only be one reason for that.

Asher had killed his father.

King Asa was dead.

Chapter XXIX

Fa met Asher's eyes, which blazed with fury and rage.

"Why?" Fa heard himself ask.

"For her," was Asher's answer, the rage quieting to cool wrath and then to sobered awareness. "For you," he added, bending his knee. Asher bowed his head, tears falling down his face as he added, "Melekfa."

My king.

Fa did not allow himself to take it in. Did not allow himself to even think on what had happened. He stole one glance of the remains of the Dark king behind him before turning his attention to the clearing beneath the Fount. As the Darkness slowly dissipated, he finally caught sight of the one thing he sought.

Her.

Meren.

Sprawled at sickening angles at the base of the now tranquil pool, her limbs twisted and limp, her body still.

"Tipharah," he breathed. "Tipharah."

He ran to her. What was only a few steps felt more like a thousand miles as horror gripped him. He collapsed on his knees beside her, cradling her head in his hands. The animals that had once moved raucously around the fount had calmed, still and quiet, a peace over them that was as preternatural as their frenzy.

"Meren," he said, bending over her, pulling her to him. She was grotesquely limp in his arms, her skin pallid, her face serene. "Talk to me, B'sheirt. Tell me you can hear me."

But she did not speak, did not move. Nor did her chest rise with any sign of breath in her lungs.

"Meren," he croaked around the lump forming in his throat. "Beloved. Please. Answer me."

She did not.

Minutes passed, and she still did not.

Fa heard a sob escape his throat as he buried his face in her curls, still shimmering in impossible shades of cerulean and amber and amethyst.

Meren. His true Mate. Beautiful and brave and selfless.

He rocked her against his body as he wept, crying her name over and over again as if she would somehow answer. As if his grief could bring her back.

But it would not. The longer the moments ticked by, the more he knew it to be true. And the more he was swallowed by the hollow absence where once the fire of her soul had burned brightly within his own.

She was gone. And she had left behind nothing but ash.

He felt a hand, warm and familiar on his shoulder. Tears fell hot and thick down his face, pooling at his lips as he looked up to see who stood beside him.

"Nabi," Fa sobbed. "Please. You must help her. You must bring her back."

Tears fell from his friend's eyes, too, as he crouched beside them and touched Fa's face with fatherly affection. "My son," Nabi said. "I am so sorry."

"You have to help. You have to bring her back," Fa pleaded, holding her limp body close to his own as if he could give her his warmth. Give her his magic. His very breath.

"It does not work that way," Nabi said, his ancient face riddled with sorrow. With a grief Nabi himself knew all too well: the keening ache of losing a Mate. "Life is Eloah's to give and to take."

"I cannot…I cannot live without her. I cannot do this without her, Nabi," Fa cried, burying his face in her neck again, rocking her in his trembling arms.

"You can," Nabi said, his warm hand returning to Fa's shoulder. "And you will."

Fa only shook his head, breathing in her lingering scent, hating the coolness that was stealing over her skin.

"You must, Melekfa. Do not let her death be in vain."

"I cannot do this. I won't do this," Fa pleaded.

But Nabi squeezed his shoulder hard enough that Fa looked up at his friend once more. "You must, Fa. She believed in you. She did all of this because she believed in a better world. She sacrificed herself for all of us. Don't you dare let that be for nothing. Look around you, Fa. Look what your Mate did. For you. For all of us."

And so Fa did.

Light færies. Hundreds of them. Maybe thousands. Gathering, converging around them. Rueful smiles on some of their faces, hope in others.

Meren had performed the Summoning. It was why Nabi was here. Even Asher.

He looked down at her again, and that's when he saw it—her mother's ring lay beside her. Rejected from the Fount because…

"Her life," he breathed. "Her life was the sacrifice."

"No," said the ancient seer. "It was her wings."

Fa furrowed his brows, tears still falling fast and free down his face. "She lost her wings before we ever got here. That's impossible. I—"

"You forget, Melekfa, that Eloah sees all. She did not need to be here to perform the Summoning. She made the sacrifice when she chose to go on without them. I saw it. And I felt it. We all felt it. The moment she lost her wings, the Summoning had taken place."

"Then we did not have to come here. She did not have to die," Fa said, bewildered.

"*You* did have to come here. Because you had to face Asa. You knew that. You've always known that."

"I told you," Fa cried. "I told you she was too good for all this. That I did not want her to face this."

"But she did, Fa. She chose this. All of this. She chose *you*. Because she loved you. Not because she was your Mate, but because she loved you. Just as you love her."

It was Nabi's speaking of her as if she were a thing of the past that did him in, bringing a wave of deep sorrow over Fa as he looked down at the limp angel in his arms. The female who had given everything for the Light she so deeply believed in. He tasted the salt of his own tears as he bent and pressed a lingering kiss to her lips, already cold and blue in death.

"B'sheirt," he breathed. "My beloved B'sheirt."

When at last he looked up again, he saw Asher standing nearby, tears streaming from his eyes. He bowed his head once more, his shoulders slumped, his wings limp behind him.

Fa could not bear it—the thought of standing up. Of moving on. Of living in a world without Meren.

But Nabi was right. The færies who gathered around them needed him. Needed a king to lead them. He knew that what Meren had done today was only the first step in a much larger plan.

The humans needed the Light færies. The Dark færies still plagued them and would continue to do so even though their king was dead. Another Dark færy would rise to continue their dark quest. And war would come. It was already coming.

Fa needed to stop hiding. He needed to be the king Meren believed in.

He looked at the færies gathered around him, the solemn hope in their faces. Jotham stood just across the clearing, his small coven gathered closely around him. He bowed his head and said, "I sent her to find you, Melekfa. It was a seer who told me you were alive. That you would lead us once again."

Fa looked at Nabi, who shook his head, nodding to the færy standing beside Asher. A færy with iridescent wings and hair of golden sun. Shira. She smiled ruefully, bowing her head to Fa.

He looked down, choking back tears at the sight of his Mate, limp and lifeless. He was about to gather her in his arms so that he could stand when he spotted her mother's ring again. An ache tore anew at his heart as he realized he hadn't even had a chance to give her a Mating gift. Hadn't even had a chance to properly celebrate.

He picked up the ring, a lingering fleck of golden light from the Fount still clinging to it. He slid it onto her finger, kissing her lips once more as he breathed between sobs, "I love you, B'sheirt. In this life and the life to come, I will always love you."

He stood, his knees weak from grief, carrying his Mate in his arms as he looked around at the eager faces, the sea of Light færies waiting patiently for their king to address them.

"She was your queen," he said. "We will honor her. And then we will fight in her name."

The eyes of the færies around him grew bright with hope as he spoke. Nabi placed a hand on his shoulder, nodding his head.

And so Fa took a step. A single step towards the future that awaited him. The future without his Mate.

His future as the rightful King of the Færies.

And then Asher surprised him, coming to stand in front of Fa, his face ashen with grief and remorse. He bowed deeply to Fa before he stood again and said, "Melekfa. Let me. Let me carry her for you. Please."

And for reasons Fa could not explain, he handed his beloved Mate to the male before him, his gaze clinging to the lingering glow on her finger where the Light from the Fount lined her ring.

Asher nodded his head, gratitude like Fa had never seen on the male's face. He took Meren in his arms, and for a moment Fa imagined what it must have been like all those years ago when Asher had found her hiding in her dead parents' home. When he had carried her to safety, hidden her from the monster that was his father.

A fierce sort of gratitude washed over Fa. If it had not been for Asher, he never would have met his Mate. Never known her sweetness, the sheer rapture of her arms. Even if he only had her for a brief moment of his life, he would be forever grateful to Asher for it.

But the moment Meren's body pressed against Asher's, the male winced, crying out as if he had been branded. He nearly dropped Meren, but Fa stooped to catch her, only to find a burning circle of flame where her hand had pressed against Asher's chest.

Fa knelt to the ground, cradling Meren against him, grabbing her hand. He shot a stricken look at Asher, who was just as bewildered as he. A searing light pierced their vision as Fa pulled Meren's hand towards him, the ring he had given her blinding them with Light and Flame.

And Fa could have sworn Meren smiled.

CHAPTER XXX

olor.

Too many colors to explain.

Colors she knew well, and others she had never noticed before.

A world without end. An unfathomable expanse. Mountains so tall and valleys so deep, views so splendid the entire world was visible from every vantage point. Great, billowing clouds racing through violent cerulean skies. Thunderstorms gathering in the distance, lightning careening across distant valleys. Close enough to touch. Far, far away.

A mighty gate separated her from the expanse beyond. Towering and shimmering in the splendid light. But it was not a warning. It was not a threat. No, this gate was open. Open for her. She stood on the end of a branch of a chalam tree at the gate, with branches like arms reaching for the world beyond.

She breathed in. The air was so thick and pure it filled her lungs, her very soul with magic.

With the magic of Eloah.

Home.

This was home.

What she had known before was merely a shadow, a portrait of the truth.

And every fiber of her being ached, longed to be here, consumed with a gratefulness for the intense beauty around her.

A warmth consumed her, and she turned to see a stag. Tall and proud, he stood beside her, glowing radiantly from his pure white hair and towering, flaming antlers. He held her eyes for a moment—eyes that told her of the mysteries of Creation. A glimmer that reminded her of every promise from every legend.

Eloah.

Creator.

Mighty One.

Providence.

Wordlessly, he bowed his head to her. She bowed in return, standing on the branch of the chalam tree and marveling at the magic that poured like Flame from every tip of his antlers. He turned his mighty head, looking out along the boundless horizon of this world of his, pride and wonder coloring his otherworldly features.

He had plans, this one. And he was carrying them out. A promise for the whole world to see. One thread of the tapestry at a time. She could feel it to the very marrow of her tiny bones.

She understood it so easily here, beside him. Like the spilling of dawn light across a valley of wheat. She could see it so clearly. All the worries she had held before were gone, and in their wake, nothing but peace, knowing that it was all in hand. It was all a part of a plan. And she had played her role well.

One moment—a flash of a memory. Of a love borne of truth

and Light. A light that caught her eye. She looked down at her free hand—a ring.

A ring she hadn't put there. Glowing gloriously, even against the boundless light of this place.

He must have felt it, that flash in her soul, for the stag turned to face her. She asked the burning question without uttering a word.

He merely tilted his head to one side. He did not need to speak, this stag of the purest white. But she could hear his words all the same. And she knew she had her answer.

Chapter XXXI

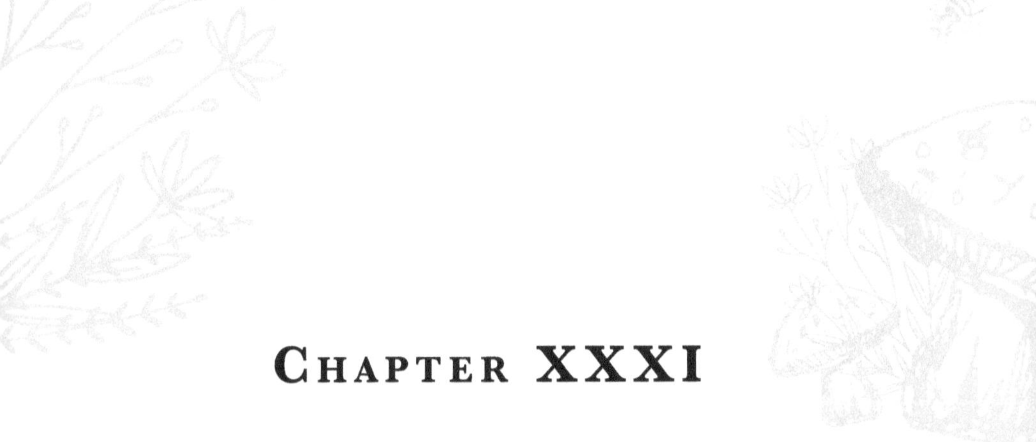

lame. Fire. Heat. Drawing, beckoning, guiding.

She followed it.

Followed it home.

Home, yes, Malkah. For now.

Yes. For now.

But not forever. Forever was somewhere else.

Somewhere *other.*

A familiar cadence, a rhythm. A heartbeat.

She felt herself smile.

Meren, she heard.

A name.

Her name.

Given to her by her mother and father. The Mates who had given birth to her nearly a century ago.

She heard that name again, and at the familiarity of the voice, at the truth in it, she opened her eyes.

And smiled again.

"Melekfa, why do you cry?" she asked.

The king before her froze, disbelief in his obsidian eyes. The shock of black in his hair was thicker now, darker. She reached up and touched that hair, distracted by the Flame, the Light coming from her finger. From her mother's ring.

"Meren," she heard him breathe again. As if he dared not say it out loud for fear that it wasn't real. That *she* wasn't real.

"I'm here, Melekfa. I've come back to you."

His breath caught in his throat, his lips trembling, his eyes welling with silver tears. She reached up to catch one of those tears. She heard audible gasps as she sat up, but did not bother to see where they had come from. She just took his face in her hands. Her beloved Mate.

Home.

She was home when she was with him.

"I don't understand," he said, his voice rough, stricken. "What happened?"

"He let me come back," she said. "He let me come home."

"Eloah," Fa breathed, his chest rising and falling in a quickened pace.

"Eloah, yes. He has many names."

It was obvious Fa didn't really care. He pulled her to him so tightly she could scarcely breathe. She laughed and gave herself to him, pouring herself into his arms with abandon.

She was home in the arms of her Mate.

Fa's breath was warm on her neck as he held her. She dared to open her eyes and take it in, the scene unfolding around her. Thousands of eyes around her stared at them, enraptured with the moment.

Light færies.

The Summoning…it had worked.

She laughed through a wave of tears as she hugged Fa closer and watched the færies smile.

It was a youngling who had her pulling away from Fa, but only just. Fa kept an arm around her as he, too, looked to see what had captured Meren's attention.

The youngling carried two wreaths of flowers in her hands—dandelion crowns. She lifted them to Meren and Fa, her young eyes full of hope as she said, "Melekfa Neharah" and placed the crown on Fa's head. Then, "Malkah Neharah" as she placed the other on Meren's.

King and Queen of the Light.

Fa bowed his head to the young one, who blushed at the king's acknowledgement before backing away, returning to her mother's arms.

Fa returned his attention to Meren, taking her face in his gentle hands, his loving eyes full of tears and joy, hope and Light. He kissed her softly before he said, "My queen."

"You were the king I was waiting for," she said. "The one we were all waiting for."

Fa breathed a laugh through his tears, pressing his brow to hers, Light flaring around them.

And when he kissed her, it was thorough and glorious, and she smiled as she kissed him back.

~

The wind whipped that nuisance curl of hers into her eyes without remorse as she soared on the back of the eagle, her Mate's arms wrapped securely around her middle. The countryside was a blur of flora beneath them as they made their way north.

North to the realm of the humans.

North to the destiny that awaited them.

It would only take a few days to get there, but it would be perilous nonetheless, what with the host of færies in tow, their magic shining brightly against the skies, a beacon to any predator—færy or beast—who lurked in these skies.

But it was a risk they had to take. To stop the Darkness. To finish what they had started.

King and Queen of the Færies. Meren laughed at the thought.

"What is it, B'sheirt?" Fa asked from behind her. The eagle swooped low on a pocket of wind, and Meren's stomach launched into her throat at the sensation.

"In all my days, I don't think I'll ever forget the looks on everyone's faces when our friend here decided to land right in the middle of them."

Soon after they had announced their intention to fly north to the human realm, the eagle had flown in on a silent wind and perched herself right in the middle of the færies, who began screaming in fear. And when Meren and Fa had mounted her? Well, it was as if Sheol itself had frozen over, for not a sound could be heard, and one could have seen the whites of the færies' eyes from a hundred miles off at the sight of the færy king and queen atop a predator.

"We should give her a name," Fa said, and she could feel his smile against her skin where his chin rested at her shoulder.

"Any ideas?" Meren asked her Mate.

"Hmmm… How about Terror in the Skies?"

Meren laughed, and Fa squeezed her middle for emphasis. "Doesn't quite roll off the tongue."

"Færy-Eater?" he tried again, and Meren barked a laugh.

"You're terrible, B'sheirt."

Fa pressed a kiss to her cheek, the wind whipping his silver locks against her ear and neck. "That's the first time you've called me that."

"Shouldn't I?" she asked. "You are my Mate, after all."

"And what a lucky færy I am to have such a glorious Mate."

Meren stroked the eagle's neck, the feathers soft and silky against her fingers. She leaned back against Fa, letting him wrap himself around her.

"What about Kanaph?" she mused as the eagle soared gracefully over a small lake.

"Wings," Fa said, his words rumbling from his chest against her back. He kissed her cheek again. "It's perfect. But I thought you said you didn't know the old language."

"I don't speak it, Melekfa. But you forget my parents were zealots. They taught me the old ways, some words of the old language in particular."

"That's how you knew the Mating vow."

She nodded, smiling as the wind whipped her face.

Fa pressed a soft kiss to her neck. "And did you know what all your names meant then, Malkah Neharah?"

"I do now, Færy King."

"I'm sorry I didn't tell you sooner."

"I know why you didn't," she said.

"Nabi told me my Mate and queen would come. That someday you would rule by my side. I didn't believe him. And then when I met you, when I realized what a gift you are, I wanted to run from it. I tried to. To protect you. To keep you away from all this."

She knew that already. She had understood it the moment she understood who he was. Fa hadn't let her leave his home without him because he *didn't* want her; he had done it because he *did*. And he loved her too much to subject her to the fate that he knew awaited him.

"I think that's why he let me come back," she mused.

"Eloah—he let you?"

"He gave me the choice. You were right, Fa. His magic is always a choice; it is never forced on us."

"What was he like?"

"He was a stag. A great white, fallow deer but... Fa, I don't even know how to explain it. He was so much more. He was everything at once. He was the sun, and he was the stars. He was winter, and he was summer. The war and the petrichor. The peace and the storm. Thunder and lightning. Beginning and end. The humans call him Providence, and when I saw him, when I saw his Light and his splendor, I knew why.

"He has a story he wants to tell, Fa. And he wants to tell it through us—not just the færies but all of his created things. We are a part of it. Paving the way for the Promised One. The redemption he has promised. And you and I, we are a part of that story. The humans, too.

"There was this gate before me. It was glorious and towering, an intricate sculpting of the finest metals and stones. And beyond it...a world like I've never seen. A world of color and stars and cloud and light. Forests and raging rivers and valleys and mountain ranges. I could see too far, too much. And I longed for it. One glimpse, and it consumed me, the wanting to be there. To be with him. And he would let me. I knew he would let me in to the paradise that awaited me. But I knew—just by looking at him—I knew he would let me come back, too. I knew that I wasn't meant to die. Not yet, not this day. That's not how he intended it.

"We're the Perdurables, Fa. We are meant live, to fade from one life to the next together. But it is not we who are immortal. And I understood it. One word from Eloah, and I understood it. It's love that is immortal, Fa. He tells his story in love. He tells the world who he is in love. And our story—yours and mine—it's really his story. And it has only just begun."

Fa hugged her closer to him, pressing his lips to her cheek. She felt his tears, cool and wet against her skin.

"What was it?" Fa asked, his words a caress on her cheek. "What was the word he said to you?"

She smiled, warming at the memory of it. "He spoke to me, Fa. In my heart. He called me Tipharah."

She could hear the laugh that lodged itself in Fa's throat, cut off by the tears that fell freely. It seemed he could not hold her close enough.

"That's when I noticed my mother's ring. Somehow, it was on my finger again even though I had given it to the Fount. And it was glowing—shining with impossible Light. I don't even know how it got there, but I knew what it meant."

"I put it there," he said, his words clipped with emotion. "When you…when I lost you, I couldn't bear the thought that you would not have a piece of us to take with you, that I hadn't given you a Mating gift. I saw your mother's ring lying next to you, so I put it on your finger and said my goodbyes. I—" Fa's words caught, and he took a moment to breathe again before he continued. "I will get you a proper Mating gift. I don't even know if it's tradition or not, but I know that Nabi gave my mother one. I hadn't even realized it until she died. But when I saw Nabi wearing the ear cuffs that my mother had worn for as long as I had known her, I knew somehow that he had given them to her. And that they had most likely been a token of their bond. For some reason, I couldn't bear the thought of you not having a token of our love."

"I don't want a different gift, Fa. Don't you see?" She lifted her finger, observing her mother's ring, still glowing faintly with the Light from the Fount. Fa took her hand in his, observing with her.

"It was love, Fa. It was your love that brought me back to you. When I saw the ring, I saw you, and I knew I wanted to come back to you. To finish what we started. And I knew he would let me.

"In the span of a heartbeat, it was as if I opened my eyes—another set of eyes—and you were there before me. And you were crying."

"You came back to me," he breathed, his words raw, laced with disbelief. "You were offered the heavens, and you came back to *me*."

"We'll go back, Fa. You and I, we will go there someday. But we will go there together. Our bond—the love we share, Fa—it is perdurable. In this life and the next, we will be together."

Chapter XXXII

ore are coming, milord. From the north," said the færy. Fa cursed himself for not knowing his name as he said his thanks. He did not know many of the names of the line of færies who had visited them since they landed for the night. And Fa cursed himself again for the years he had spent in hiding, not being the king these færies had been praying for.

"It's Thalen, my king," the færy said, his head bowed low.

"Thalen," Fa repeated. "Thank you for your report. Please let General Asher know to expect more færies by first light."

Thalen looked up, shock in his young features. Meren, too, looked up, her eyes alight with a similar brand of disbelief. But there was something else in her eyes. Pride.

"Asher, milord?" Thalen tried. "Forgive my impertinence, but do you know that Asher is the son of—"

"I know who he is. And he is my general. You will report any more arrivals to him."

"Yes, Melekfa," said Thalen, bowing low before flying out of the nook at the base of the oak branch.

Meren cocked her head to one side but said nothing.

"What?" Fa asked in mock annoyance.

"Your general?"

"He is the most highly trained færy I know. And to top it off, he is skilled with weapons, which will certainly help when we face the remaining Dark færies."

Meren took a step toward him. And then another. Her broken wings fell with unfair beauty from her slender shoulders. Færy light glimmered off of the strands of cerulean and amethyst in her curls, and her lips quirked to one side. "Does Asher know of the honor you have given him?"

"I'm sure he will soon enough. I have no doubt he is in that line of visitors tonight, since I am sure there is much he would like to say. Particularly to you."

Her lips slowly curled into a proud smirk, but she said nothing as she made her way to him, deliberate step by step. And the look in her eyes…Fa's heart thundered in his chest.

"He is a færy of the Light, is he not?" Fa went on as his Mate slipped her slender arms around his neck. "He was summoned same as everyone else. I would be a fool not to appoint him to my armies in some capacity."

"Indeed, Melekfa," purred Meren before she kissed him soundly.

"What?" Fa asked, slipping his arms around her. The love of his life. The queen who would rule by his side. The Mate who returned to him. He kissed her again.

"It's just that I cannot resist such a male," Meren said when at last he relinquished her lips.

"And what sort of male is it that you cannot resist?"

"A noble male. A male who would forgive. A male who would lay aside his pride for the sake of peace. Such a male is second to none in my eyes."

"Well, it's a good thing you're stuck with me for all of eternity, then, isn't it?"

"Indeed, my king. Indeed."

She kissed him again. Hungrier. Deeper.

"If you keep kissing me like that, I shall have to put up a ward and keep any remaining færies from bothering us for a while," said the king of the færies.

She huffed a laugh, her body warm where she pressed it against his. He kept his hands securely around her. "There will be time enough for that later, Fa. We have a line of eager subjects waiting to speak with us, to offer us their fealty. It would be impertinent to brush them off."

"Such a dutiful queen." He hummed, his lips hovering over hers. He kissed her once again, but he could feel a question blooming.

"What is it?" he asked.

"Why? Why would you do this for him?"

"Because he is your friend, Meren. And if he is your friend, then he is mine as well."

She tilted her head, knowing there was more. Knowing he wasn't saying everything. He huffed a laugh and pressed his brow to hers.

"Because he offered to carry you. When you—" He couldn't say it, couldn't bring himself to utter the word. To remember that she had *died*. "He offered to carry you for me."

And Fa had known. He had understood that Asher was sorry— deeply sorry for what had happened. That he had made a choice. To offer to carry the king's burden was an ancient gesture, one of unfailing loyalty. There were few who even remembered such traditions. But

Fa did. And he knew Asher did, too. And so he had let the male who should have been his enemy carry the love of his life for him. He had let the rest of the færies see the peace and loyalty between them.

A solemn silver tear fell down Meren's cheek, but instead of wiping it away, Fa bent and kissed it, kissing away another as it fell down her other cheek. Then he heard someone clear their throat.

It was Asher, standing in the opening to their nook for the night. His eyes were alight with so many things. So many words yet unsaid. So many regrets.

Fa held Asher's stare for a moment before looking back at his Mate in his arms. She was looking at Asher, but she showed nothing on her face. She was waiting to hear what her friend had to say.

So Fa kissed her cheek and walked out, letting Asher speak to the female he had rescued from certain death nearly fifty summers ago. Asher bowed low as Fa passed him. Fa nodded his head, clasping Asher's shoulder before leaping from the branch and catching the Wind.

He stood before her. Serene. A sadness in his eyes that she'd never seen before. And then he bowed. And he brought her hand to his mouth and kissed it softly.

"Malkah Neharah," Asher said, his head still bowed low.

When he stood upright again, she smiled softly and said, "I'm still just Meren."

"You are my queen," Asher said. "It suits you."

She could see the silver lining his eyes, the tear threatening to fall. She wasn't sure what to say, where to even start.

"I came to apologize," he said. She folded her hands before her, took a breath, and listened to her friend.

"I suppose he's told you everything," Asher went on.

About Fa's wings, he meant. About why Asher shredded them with the bone blades that still hung at his sides.

"He didn't, you know," Meren said. "I figured it out. I was angry with him that he hadn't told me. But do you know what he said? He told me that he hadn't wanted me to hate you. That it wasn't worth it."

Asher looked down, toeing an invisible stone. And Meren realized it was the first time she had ever seen him look so disappointed. Disgusted. With himself.

"I was so angry, Meren. I wanted to kill him for killing so many of my father's men. But I couldn't do it. I couldn't best him. And I hated him even more for that."

"War brings out the worst in us all," she offered, wondering what the coming days and weeks would have in store for them. What this war—not just between the færies but between all of creation—would do. What rifts it would cause. What great divides it would forge.

Asher met her eyes then, searching, his gaze full of so many things he wanted to say. "I put you in an impossible position, Mer," Asher said. He shut his eyes, swallowed once, and continued. "From the moment I found you, you became the most important thing in the world to me. I took one look at you, small and shivering, and I knew that I had to help you. I had to get you out of your home before my father found you and turned you into the example that he had made of your parents. I looked at you, and I knew that the world could be better—that what my father offered was not how it should be.

"So I got you out of there. I brought you with me, hid you away, keeping you safe the only way I knew how. You became a symbol to me, Meren. You became the anthem in my heart—you taught me what Light was, and you showed me that the world could be a better place, a purer place.

"Somewhere along the way, I decided you were mine because of it. And not only that, but that you could not belong to anyone else. I watched you grow from a headstrong youngling into a smart, daring female. And I loved you for it. I still love you for it. And somewhere along the way, I decided I wanted you to love me, too. I thought I could make you.

"So when you came back and he followed you…when I saw the way he looked at you, I wanted to claw his eyes out for it. But worse, when I saw the way you looked at him, I knew I had been wrong. You weren't mine. You had never been mine. And I hated you for it. I thought you owed it to me.

"It wasn't until you left—until I knew I had lost you—that I stopped to realize how wrong I'd been. That you didn't owe me any-thing. And when I stopped for a moment to consider it all, I realized you had never once looked at me the way you looked at Fa. And that I had never looked at you the way he did, either.

"And I understood. For the first time, I understood. I had always loved you. I will always love you. But maybe…maybe you were right. Maybe I really was the brother you never had. Or never wanted," he added with a breathy laugh.

Meren laughed too, placing her hand on Asher's arm. "I always wanted your presence, Ash. I always will. You've been my friend through thick and thin. You saved my life, gave me a chance. I will never forget it. Nor will I ever be able to repay it."

"You don't have to repay it," Asher interjected. "The point is, Meren… I'm sorry. I have regretted many things in my life, but hurting you has been the greatest regret I've ever known. I don't deserve you. I never have."

She put her hand on Asher's arm, squeezing gently. "Love is not about what we deserve, Ash. It's a gift, plain and simple. And I love you, too. I always have. And I always will."

That tear finally fell down his cheek, and Meren flung her arms around him, holding close her friend, her rescuer, her brother.

Chapter XXXIII

t was difficult to take the leap off of that branch. Difficult to ignore the instincts that reared their ugly heads. But Fa knew he needed to give Meren a moment with Asher. And he knew Asher needed to speak his piece to Meren.

So Fa had stepped away. Against his better judgment, against every fiber of his being that screamed at the idea of leaving her with the son of his greatest enemy, Fa had stepped away.

Maybe Asher had once been the enemy. But Fa didn't think he really was anymore.

"Something troubling you, my son?"

Fa turned toward the sound of the seer's old voice, smiling at the sight of him.

"No, Nabi. Not troubling," Fa said.

"It is difficult to have even a short distance between you, is it not?" Nabi asked, a knowing smile in his eyes.

"How did you do it?" Fa asked, falling into step beside the seer as they walked at a languid pace near the base of the tree. All around them, færies bustled, settling in, preparing for another long journey tomorrow.

"You learn to breathe again, but you never fully take a breath," said Nabi distantly.

Fa observed his friend, the male who had loved his mother, been her Mate. His spindly hands were clasped behind his back, his skin as thin as a dragonfly wing, his hair as light and frail as the fluff from a spring dandelion.

"How old are you, Nabi?" It was a question he had never dared ask. Not until Meren brought it up. He had always assumed Nabi was ancient. But why would his mother have fallen in love with an ancient færy?

Nabi puffed a breathy chuckle. "That is a question I've often wondered why you never asked."

"I think I've always assumed you were ancient," Fa admitted with an embarrassed smile.

"And now?" Nabi asked, facing him as they walked through the tall grass.

"I do not believe you are as old as you look."

"How did you figure it out?"

"I didn't. It was Meren. She realized…" Fa stopped walking. Nabi took a few steps before he stopped too, turning to face Fa fully.

"She realized it is not we who are immortal. But love."

"And a life is only half-lived without it," Nabi added. Fa could see the deep sorrow, the endless longing behind his wise smile.

Nabi turned, strolling deeper into the lush grasses. "She is quite right, you know. I've only got about eighty summers on you, Melekfa. But in the years since I lost your mother…"

Fa understood. Even in the brief time that Meren had been gone from him, he had felt it. The heaviness. The emptiness. The ache that had settled along his bones. All those years before he'd met Meren, when he thought he'd been lonely—they were the palest shadow of what true loneliness was, what he'd felt after his Mate.

Sorrow washed over him. For his friend. For his mother. For the tragedy of their story. "Why, Nabi? Why was Meren allowed to come back to me and not my mother to you?"

Nabi turned again, that look in his eyes—the one he held only when he had something of deep importance to share. "Because, Melekfa, I was not hers to come back to."

"You were *Mates,*" Fa said. The first time he had ever said it aloud to Nabi.

"Yes, we were," he admitted. "But she belonged to your father. They were bound in covenant."

Fa scoffed. "My father did not honor it. Not for a moment. He had a harem of whores waiting for him. All of my brothers were born of other females!"

"Even so, Melekfa, your mother was his queen. They were bound to one another."

"That's completely unfair!" Fa fumed. "My mother never knew love from my father."

"It is not a matter of fairness, my son," Nabi said. "Not in the eyes of Eloah. A covenant is eternal. Love—love is the gift. You are not bound to Meren because you are Mates. You are bound because you chose to be. I've always told you that true magic, the magic of the Light, is a choice. It is never forced upon us. You chose her, and she chose you. The magic between you is a gift. A blessing. But it is not what binds you. It is what makes you stronger. And it certainly makes the bond much deeper. But it is love that makes you immortal.

"That's the whole point, I think. Love. Eloah writes his story on the hearts of his creation through love. I think perhaps it's the truest magic there is. Because love is always a choice. And that choice is the gift."

"Why would my mother ever choose my father over you?"

"We had not met before they were bound, before she took the oath as his queen."

"How did you do it?" Fa asked. "How did you taste such a love and walk away from it?"

"That's just it—I never tasted it. I never knew your mother, not in that way. I knew what she was to me the moment we met—a sentiment I would hazard you can understand. She knew, too. But we never spoke of it. We never once had a conversation about it. I loved her from afar, watching her as she ruled this færydom in dignity and grace alongside her impetuous king. But I had a moment of weakness. One moment. And I sent her a gift with no note. A token of my love for her. She never spoke to me of it. But I knew she knew what it was. And from whom it had come. She wore it every day of her life."

"The ear cuffs," Fa said. "The ones you wear now."

"How did you know that?" Nabi asked.

"I don't know. But I do know that it matters when a gift is given in love. And it can have eternal implications." His own Mate would not have come back to him—come back from heaven itself—if not for such a gift.

Nabi's eyes were solemn and sincere. "Indeed, my son. Indeed."

"I am glad you loved my mother. And I am glad she knew it."

"Do not think our story a tragedy, Melekfa. We basked in the joy of you together. You were the one thing we could share. Our love for you. Our joy in watching you grow up. You became the son to me that I knew I would never have. You are all the more precious to me that you are borne of my Mate, the female I loved."

"You are my true father, Nabi. You always have been."

Nabi teared up, his words clipped with emotion. "Now those, my son, are the sweetest words I will ever hear."

~

"What are you doing out here?" Fa asked, crawling to his Mate's side. She sat perched on the end of the long branch, the view of the night sky unhindered by the rest of the tree, their nook for the night a long walk down the branch behind her.

"Couldn't sleep," Meren said, taking his hand when he sat beside her.

"Surely you are tired."

"Funny enough, no. I suppose coming back from the dead gives one a new sense of life and energy."

Fa did not think it was that funny, and it must have shone on his face, for she said, "Sorry."

She settled herself into his arms, resting her head on his shoulder, breathing deeply, contentedly.

"I thought I would come out here and enjoy the peace while I can. The stars are beautiful tonight." She looked up, and he joined her, observing the twinkling firmament in silent awe. The blanket of glittering stars, the swath of cloud only visible on the clearest nights—greens and blues and ochres and crimsons streaking across the sky in a mighty river of color. Just above them, a rustle caught their attention. They looked up to see their eagle companion settling in above them like a guard for the night. Meren breathed a chuckle.

"Well, if that won't scare the shit out of every Dark færy from here to the mountains, I don't know what will."

Fa laughed too, kissing her head where it rested on him. "Did you have a good conversation with Asher?" he asked.

"I told him you made him general," she said, and though he couldn't see her face, he could hear the smile in her voice.

"What did he say?"

"He said you and I were both insane and too damned noble for our own good."

"I think he might be right on both accounts," Fa offered. "But did he accept?"

"Yes, he did. With tears in his eyes."

Fa squeezed her, pressing her closer to him. "I am glad," he said. And he meant it.

"I know," she said, looking up at him. "And I'm even more in love with you for it."

"Good thing, because you're stuck with me now."

She kissed him. And Eloah help him, her kiss… Fa gathered the magic within himself, putting his wards around them.

"You won't make us invisible, you know," she said against his lips.

He looked at the light shining vividly from them, from every place they touched. "At this point, I hardly think it matters."

She laughed. "Shall the whole of færydom know our business, then?"

He kissed her again. "I think there's enough magic between us they'd be blinded from any true detail."

She gave him a look, raising an eyebrow. "Take me to the nook, Melekfa. I want to make love to my Mate without an audience, thank you very much."

"I don't know how much good it will do. We glow any time we're close these days." Fa swept her into his arms, catching the Wind and gliding her down the length of the branch.

"That won't do us much good going into battle, will it?" she said, a hint of worry in her words. Fa set her down in their nook, kissing her once, twice, before moving his fingers to the laces that ran down the back of her tunic. She smiled and snaked her arms around his neck, pressing her body against his.

Mate. Love. Queen. And perhaps his favorite of all—*his*. She was his. Evermore.

So he smiled broadly and without restraint as he said, "We've been in the shadows long enough, Malkah Neharah. It is time to bring forth the Light."

299

THE PERDURABLES (THE CHALAM FÆRYTALES, BOOK IV)

SNEAK PEEK: BOOK V

My friends, this is just for you. Because so many of you keep asking me. I love that you're asking. You have no idea how much I love it.

So here's a sneak peek of what's going on with the humans of the Chalam world we're living in. Please bear in mind: this is completely unedited. Literally, I pasted it directly from my writing software (I use Scrivener, in case you're curious). So if you find typos, congratulations. Three years on this same manuscript and I still didn't see them. If you wonder what the heck is happening, don't worry. So do I. But I wanted you to get a sneak peek of the next book, and rest your weary souls at ease. It's already written. It's going to be edited this summer (2020), and will be in your eager hands soon.

Read on... and be prepared to be pissed off at me again.

Morgan

302

Book V: Chapter I

ot for the first time today—not for the first time in weeks, she tried. Again. She tried to feel him, to tell him she was all right. Despite the fact that it went against her plan, that it went against every careful calculation she had mulled over with the former Navarian commander, Adelaide of Haravelle, Queen of Har-Navah tried desperately to just *feel* her husband across their bond—across that miraculous connection they had always shared. The connection that had come alive when they married in Haravelle what seemed like a lifetime ago.

But like every other time since she had parted Benalle Palace, she felt nothing but cobwebs in the breeze. She felt nothing across that bond but cold, endless darkness. And not for the first time, she wondered what that nothingness meant. For her husband. For their marriage.

For her kingdom.

Adelaide breathed a shuddering sigh, willed herself to calm, and squared her shoulders.

Insane. She was insane. Haplessly, pathetically insane. There could be no other explanation for why she was trudging up the cobblestone pathway, chained at the wrists and ankles to a woman behind her, and another before. And countless more before that.

Servants. Slaves. Women, every one of them. Captured for their duty to Crown and country. Except Adelaide hadn't been captured. She had found the band of traveling prisoners exactly where Commander Titus had told her they would be—the only information she could pry from him before he insisted she hide herself away. Let the world think her dead. On a ship headed for the western continent of Medinah—that's where Titus thought she was. But instead it was on silent feet that she had infiltrated the rudimentary camp of prisoners and woven herself among them in the night. A willing captive. The next morning, tied up among the countless other women, the guards didn't so much a bat an eye in her direction as she took up with them and headed for Goleath.

Headed for her destiny.

A woman far in front of her, with hair too gray and skin too wrinkled, had been rejected from her *first duty*, as the soldier had put it, and shoved into a growing crowd of dejected women. All of them trudged with stooped shoulders, the burden of this war King Derrick was waging already taking its toll. And it hadn't officially begun. Yet. But its darkness loomed over the kingdom—over the world—like an impending storm.

Another woman walked to the mistress at the head of the line. Acceptable. Wordlessly, she was shoved behind a wall in the darkness of the castle, out of Adelaide's view.

The next woman in line stepped up for her appraisal. "Barren," a gruff man said from nearby. Adelaide turned her attention to him, to see the ring that rested on his finger and the scowl that lingered on his face. Wife. She was his *wife*. And he was giving her over to a life of Providence only knew what, for the sole reason that she was barren.

Nausea roiled in Adelaide's gut, and she covered the small swell of her belly with her hands.

Stupid. This had been a stupid idea. She was sending herself—and the life of the child that might still live in her womb—straight to the slaughter like two hapless, meager lambs. She pulled—yanked again—on her bond with Ferryl.

And felt nothing. Just as she still felt nothing in her womb. Not a flicker of movement. Not a sign of life. She told herself again, for what felt like the millionth time, that it was too soon to feel anything. That it was too soon to know for certain if the blade she had taken at the coronation ball was a mortal wound to her unborn child.

"Get her out of my way," said the mistress, whom Adelaide could now see clearly. The barren woman was shoved aside, her chains rubbing raw on her wrists, blood dripping slowly. She kept her eyes forward, not stopping to glance even once at the husband who had betrayed her. And it struck Adelaide how young she was. No more than twenty-five at the most. Her long, auburn locks fell in a haphazard mess down her back, but she was beautiful, with pure skin and haunted eyes.

Worthless to her husband.

Bile. It burned in Adelaide's throat like a wildfire rising to consume, body and soul.

The mistress called, and Adelaide stepped forward, wondering if she'd survive this fool's mission she had concocted for herself. Wondering if she'd survive this chasm between her and everything that mattered. Wondering if this cockamamie idea would work. If for no other reason than the barren woman trudging away from her, she would risk this. She would end this dark blight of the reign of King Derrick once and for all. This—the only way she could.

Adelaide was thankful that, if nothing else, the shackles were spread far enough apart on the chains that the other women couldn't feel just how violently she was shaking.

Acknowledgments

I keep having to write these and I keep acknowledging the same people over and over again. If nothing else, it has taught me what a wonderful tribe of weird, loyal, honest, and entusiastic people I surround myself with. I love you all.

So instead of going into details again, I will sum it up with this: you know who you are. You know I'm writing this to you. Thank you. You give me motivation to keep going. Writing novels is a perilous, introspective form of psychosis, I'm fully convinced. You're the padding on my walls.

Morgan

About the Chalam Færytales

Want to know more?
Visit http://ChalamFaerytales.com

~

The Chalam Færytales Series:
Book I - The Promised One
Book II - The Purloined Prophecy
Book III - The Parallax
Book IV - The Perdurables
Book V - Coming Fall 2020

Writer. Musician. Artist.

In case you're unaware, Morgan is much more than an author. You can find exclusive art, original music, and so much more at her website:
MorganGFarris.com

@ Morgan G Farris

ABOUT THE AUTHOR

So let's just be real here... My name is Morgan and I'm a chronic over-achiever and avid binger of *The Office.* When I watch *Lord of the Rings,* I watch the extended versions, and they're still not long enough. I won arguments in elementary school by out-quoting everyone with my vast knowledge of *The Princess Bride.* So yeah, I'm kind of a big deal.* I used to have a mohawk‡. And once I had purple bangs‡. But I try not to let that dictate my current fashion choices, which are just as confused, I confess. Bless.

In my spare time, I write. A lot. Songs, stories, articles, novels... It's just this thing in me that I have to get out. The book you're reading, part of *The Chalam Færytales,* is sort of a magnum opus of all the things that have been stirring in me from the time I was a kid—musing about the existence of humanity, pondering the wonder of God and the ongoing work of redemption... you know, kid stuff. I'm real proud of it (that's my Texanese coming out. Fight me.) I'd be honored if you left a review of it somewhere on the interwebs. (Consequently, I'm convinced that novel writing is just an acceptable form of psychosis, but it's definitely a beast within me that roars to be freed. So I pet it and feed it and let it dictate my fingers on the keyboard without regrets.)

But even if you don't ever read another one of my novels or listen to one of my songs, I can't thank you enough for reading this one. I hope I can bring a little magic to your world in some way.

The art in me manifests in various forms—from my books, to my music, to my digital art and even the occasional article. I get confused about what I should call myself: author or musician or songwriter or graphic designer or armchair theologian. I think it's probably safe to say I'm just an artist at heart exploring the magic around us. Thanks for exploring with me!

*This is sarcasm.

‡This is not sarcasm.

Other places to find Morgan:

Facebook.com/MorganGFarris

Instagram // @MorganGFarris

Twitter // @MorganGFarris

YouTube // MorganGFarris

MorganGFarris.com